Love Again

by

Sophia C. Simmons

PUBLISHED IN THE UNITED STATES
by
Aaron Book Publishing
Bristol, Tennessee
November 2008
Sales Orders (423) 212-1208
First Edition, First Printing

Cover Design: Kellie Warren-Underwood

D i s c l a i m e r

This document is an original work of fiction. Any resemblance to persons living or dead is purely coincidental. It may include reference to information commonly known or freely available to the general public. Any resemblance to other published information is purely coincidental. The author has in no way attempted to use material not of his own origination. Aaron Book Publishing disclaims any association with or responsibility for the ideas, opinions or facts as expressed by the author of this book.

Scriptures are taken from the New International Version (NIV)

Printed in the United States of America
Cataloging-in-Publication

ISBN: 978-0-9819195-2-2

Copyright by Sophia C. Simmons

ALL RIGHTS RESERVED

Love Again

by

Sophia C. Simmons

Dedication and Acknowledgments:

Most of all I'm thankful to God who has healed me, comforted me, inspired me to move on from the pain and blessed me with so many wonderful people to thank. I am grateful to my beloved family, Shelly Dennis, Jon Simmons, & Dawn Jackson for being supportive through life's ups and downs. Especially my sisters, Kelly Simmons, Mollie Simmons, and Clara Long, who graciously offered their support and didn't think I was crazy when I said I was going to write a book. To Kysha Bias, thank you for so eagerly reading and re-re-re-reading all my drafts. To Eric who pre-paid for the first copy. Thank you Degriot Space, a Yahoo group of writers who offered their time and criticism of many rough drafts. Thank you Kingman, Arizona and my friends at the bank, although this is not the kind of city I'm used to living in, God has brought me here, and I have met some of the kindest people of my life living here. To my new friend Kevin Ward, thank you for your ear, support, honesty and kindness, you're a brilliant writer. Thank you Tim Rouse, my publisher who found me online and spurred me on to completion. Thank you Mom, you're a caring & beautiful woman. Thank you Dad, for being a hard worker, loving father, and faithful husband. Lastly, I can't go without saying I guess, a thank you of sorts to the men who have broken my heart, without those painful lessons I may never have written my books. May God bless you and I pray you find what it is you seek in life.

For my beautiful, intelligent, vibrant children, Tony, Terrence & Shahdae. My love for you and yours for me has inspired me more than words can say. I love you with all of my heart.

Foreword

There's an axiom that says the best stories are those which touch all of us. Those in which we see a little bit of ourselves. In this story of love, redemption, and triumph Sophia Simmons speaks to all women, of our struggles to love, be loved and to most of all love ourselves. This story speaks to the strength we all have, whether we know it or not.

Cynthia, the sensitive but strong main character, will leave you with mixed emotions in hopes that she finds what she is looking for…true love. You'll laugh; you'll cry and pray for her strength. With the love of her children, her family and her strong spiritual back ground, she finds that regardless of life's struggles, the light that shines through that perpetual shadow can be seen. You'll find that the old saying "you can't keep a good woman down" reigns true in this reality love story. Will Cynthia make it? Can she make it?

Kelly D. Simmons

"Love Again"

by
Sophia C. Simmons

Prologue

Cynthia went over near the window of her bedroom and peered out for a few moments. It was fall, and the large oak tree in the yard was losing its colorful leaves as a mild wind breezed through it. Partly cloudy, a storm was on the horizon and the rumbles of thunder broke through the silence. Her mind began to unfold memories, one by one. She pondered her years in Kingstown, her marriage, family, and children. Her mind drifted back into the time she'd spent with DL and she realized she could finally remember him without feeling sadness.

She grasped the handles at the bottom of the old window and pulled it up. Feeling the fresh air gently blow through the screen was like a whisper from a muse. She grabbed a note pad, pen, and a picnic blanket that was laying folded in the corner, then stepped outside making herself comfortable under the tree. She clipped the picture she'd found of DL to the top of the paper, and she began to write of the only love story she had ever known . . .

Chapter One

Early evening in Las Vegas, Nevada, and it was still hot. Unseasonably awkward even for the desert this time of year, it was about ninety degrees in the shade. The sun was not as high in the sky as midday, but you wouldn't know that judging by the relentless heat that scorched the ground. Thin traces of white clouds laced the periwinkle blue sky and there was no relief of a breeze as the sun's swelter boldly lingered into nighttime.

DL grabbed his things from the passenger seat and scurried across the parking lot. He stood at the large glass front doors of the building and punched his code into the security pad. He made his way down the hall into the drab computer room where he worked for a small software company in technical support. Sluggishly, he forced his tall and wearied body to his desk. Too many days of little sleep left him drained. "I hate this job," he thought as he had so many nights. He hadn't worked there for quite a year yet, so he stayed.

He pulled his keys from his pocket and tossed his jacket over the chair. He didn't usually take much time getting dressed for work and had thrown on a nice, but wrinkled royal blue button down dress shirt and a pair of baggy blue jeans. Though stylish, the whole outfit was pulled from the bottom of his closet, he felt it could stand one more wear before washing.

The office he worked in had no windows, tan and gray cubicles lined the walls, very basic and plain, with a few dying plants here and there. If he didn't stop for fast food on the way to work, he usually got his dinner from the old vending machine that decorated the corner. He dropped a few coins in and got a soda.

"What's up, Aaron? Anything interesting going on tonight?"

"Nope. Samo shit, different night."

Only he and one or two other employees were there overnight and it was generally slow, so there was a lot of time in between calls to do what he wanted. Usually that involved goofing around on the Internet. Playing games, looking up stupid trivia, and meeting women. That's where he met Cynthia.

As he emptied the contents of his arms on the desk, his mind began to drift back to the night he first chatted with her online. He was on MySpace uploading new pictures he had taken from a recent trip to San Francisco. He considered himself an amateur photographer and wanted to add them to his page. After logging in, he saw he had a new note in his inbox. He still had it saved. "I think your photography is very nice." He looked at the picture on her page. She was sitting sideways with her head tilted and immediately he was attracted to the radiance of her big beautiful smile and her lovely black hair. He had the feeling she was someone special. He quickly typed a note back: "Thank you. You are very pretty. Do you have Yahoo? Maybe we can chat."

Before the night ended they were chatting. They chatted about the things people chat about when they're trying to get to know one another: Where you live? What you do? Do you have children? Are you single? Do you live alone? All the staple questions you have to get out the way before getting to the point.
He typed: "Your online name is interesting freeofcare. Why do you call yourself that?"

She typed: "Jus been through a lot....Trying not to concern myself with the troubles of life 2 much anymore."

"What troubles?"

She typed: "Relationship troubles mostly....Going through a divorce right now."

"Oh ok . . . Hopefully I'm not being 2 nosy."

She typed: "No it's ok....You ever been married?"

He typed: "Yea . . . 2 times."

"Wow! Ok now I won't be 2 nosy . . . lol"

"Just haven't met the right girl I guess . . . So . . . freeofcare what is your real name? If that's ok 2 ask?"

"It's ok . . . If we're chatting it's nice to put a name with the photo . . . SinCityVirgo, lol . . . My name is Cynthia . . .Yours?"

He typed: "Darren"

"Are you kidding me? HA!"

He typed: "Huh? Why?"

"That's my son's and my soon to be ex husbands name lol"

"Oh wow really?"

"Yes really! Maybe that's a bad sign . . . Maybe I should move on... lol"

He typed: "Or maybe it was in the cards that you should be with a Darren but you got hooked up with the wrong one :)

"Ha! We'll see I guess."

"We will? :)"

She typed: "lol maybe . . . Do you always go by Darren? . . . I mean do people call you anything else?"

He typed: "I've been called a lot of things . . . lmao . . . But some people call me DL . . . My name is Darren Lewis."

They chatted for over an hour during which DL asked for her phone number several times, but Cynthia would quickly decline. She had never met a man this way before and it made her nervous.

She typed: "You could be a psychopath, lol."

"I promise. I'm not."

"Are you from Las Vegas?"

He typed: "No. Georgia. After I got divorced . . . Didn't want to go back there . . . and my brother has lived here for like ten years. . . So I thought I'd start over here."

"Oh . . . u like?"

"Yea so far it's cool. Been here about a year."

"Were did you live before Vegas?"

"Texas . . . Lived in Dallas for bout 3 years."

"Move around a lot, huh?"

He typed: "Yea...I spent six years in the Air Force . . . Can I call u?"

She typed: "No."

"Why?"

"Cause . . . I said . . . u could be crazy :)"

"I promise . . . I'm not."

"You promise?"

Eventually, after a few days, Cynthia finally gave in and gave DL her phone number. They had talked almost every day since. He thought, "This is the perfect beginning to my new year." That was January, it was now March, and so far, Cynthia was a dream come true.

He settled into his rickety old office chair, obviously in need of some belt tightening, and scooted up to his desk. He signed in to his work email and reached for the phone. His inbox was full of work tickets left incomplete by the day shift employee so he couldn't call her right away. Disturbed by the interruption of having to work at work, he blurted, "Dammit."

The work took longer to complete than expected and he was frustrated. When he was done it was about nine o'clock, and in Arizona, where Cynthia lived, it was ten. He was afraid she would be asleep and he'd miss talking to her that night. So he checked first to see if she was online and signed into Yahoo. She was. He typed: "Hey there"

She typed: "Hi"

"How was your day?"

She typed: "Ok . . . Yours?"

"Just slept mostly. Is it 2 late 2 call u?"

"No. Call me. :)"

"k"

Cynthia answered, "Hello?"

DL felt a rush when he heard her voice and his heart skipped a beat. He answered, "Hi baby. You sound sleepy?"

"I am."

"Awe, I don't want to keep you. I wanted to call earlier but I've been really busy."

She replied, "That's okay. I understand you're working."
They talked for nearly three hours, then Cynthia looked at the clock. "You know what? I better go to sleep I have a meeting before work at six forty five in the morning."

He replied, "Alright. I'll call you tomorrow. I miss you."

"I miss you too."

They hung up and DL called her back within a few moments.

Cynthia looked at the caller id and smiled. She answered, "Hello?"

"I just wanted to tell you, Cynthia, I'm so glad that I met you."

Her eyes teared up a little. "Awe, thank you. Me too, goodnight."

Chapter Two

Six in the morning, DL headed home from his ten hour night shift, "Damn it's hot already." He climbed into his truck with his arms full, threw his work bag, a few cd's, and an ice cold bottle of Snapple Apple onto the passenger seat. As he started the engine he flipped down the sun visor and picked away the sleep in his eyes. He looked confidently at his face—dark, rugged, handsome—and gave a wink, then turned his head side to side. "I need a shave." He popped on his baseball cap and set out on his thirty minute drive home that would only take ten minutes if it weren't for the traffic.

His big, clean, midnight blue Escalade gave him the illusion that he owned the road, and he usually weaved in and out of lanes as if he were running late. After loosing his temper to road rage a couple of times, and flipping off an old man for driving too slow, he arrived in front of his apartment. Since he loved his truck more than life, he parked diagonally taking up two spots to ensure no one parked too close.

He unlocked his mailbox, retrieved the pile of envelopes inside and began sifting though them. "I know there's nothin but bills. Maybe I'll be lucky and some long lost relative died, and I have a check. Junk, bill, bill, junk, junk, bill." He stood near the trash can tossing in what he considered to be unimportant, but came to a stop staring at one of the envelopes. "Hmm, what's this? Doesn't look like a bill, but it's not a check either." He flipped it over examining it for a return address and his eyes zeroed in on the red lipstick print sealing the envelope. The scent of a sweet strawberry perfume was evident.

He sniffed then read:

Cynthia Wilson
2200 Harbison St.
Kingstown, Az

Surprised and pleased, his joy was that of a child who had just received Halloween candy. "Awe she wrote me" He kind of skipped toward his front door but quickly regained his composure and looked around making sure no one saw. He went inside, got comfortable on the couch, and anxiously opened the envelope. The letter was written on specialty stationary, soft pink with airbrushed roses, and her script was very elegant. He read :

"*Dear DL,*

I took the time to write you an old-fashioned letter in my own handwriting, because I wanted you to know how special I think you are and how much I have treasured these last couple of months getting to know you. You have been so wonderful, compassionate, and kind. You're such a good friend and I really needed that right now.

Our conversations have been so meaningful and genuine. I enjoy talking to you and I loved finally meeting you. That night will always remain frozen in my memory. You held me in your arms until I fell asleep, no sex, no nakedness, no kissing. Just two people who needed realness. After being neglected by my husband for so many years, I don't think that I could find words that would truly express how much that meant to me. I don't know what the future holds for us but I do know today, I'm so glad we found each other. Always, Cynthia"

Although he resisted it, her words pierced him right in the heart, and he fought the tear that came to his eye. "Wow." He leaned his head back on the sofa and recalled the day he first laid eyes on Cynthia. It will forever be frozen in his memory too.

In eager curiosity he waited for her in the lobby of Arizona Charlie's Casino. His breath taken by her beauty as she approached, he still managed to push out what he hoped to be at least one coherent word, "Hello." Trying his best to appear calm and cool, he wondered if she could see him sweating.

Her skin was tanned and smooth, somewhere between cream and caramel. He reached for her hand, it was as soft as the petal of a flower and her nails were manicured and pink. Her face was lightly made up but really not necessary; her beauty was so natural.

"Hi," she shyly replied, then smiled with dimples small but deep. Her round nose perked up, and a little cleft appeared in her chin. Her brown eyes twinkled like fireflies in the evening and her innocent appearance was like an angel's. She wore her hair curled in spirals and it touched her shoulders, full and long. She had the perfect physique: not too thin, not too big, but with just a little thickness in all the right places just the way he liked. And he would never forget those jeans she was wearing.

As the bells and alarms rang from busy jackpots, and streams of people stammered back and forth by them, they were lost in each other in an instant. For them, it seemed dead silent. He leaned in for a friendly hug. Her scent reminded him of a beach summer breeze, maybe coconut. She embraced him in return. "It's so nice to finally meet you," she said. On the phone her low and almost boyish voice didn't match the sweet face in the pictures, but now seeing her and hearing her, it seemed a perfect fit.

They went to lunch and Cynthia stepped away to the restroom. She found the waitress and told her it was his birthday. (It wasn't.) To DL's surprise, they brought him a free chocolate fudge cake a la mode. In embarrassment, he accepted it, and Cynthia sat and giggled while a staff of six eighteen-year-old servers sang happy birthday to him, loudly in the middle of the full restaurant. He was pleased that she had such a silly sense of humor.

They went to the movies and saw a very good action-packed film, but it had a really stupid ending. They both looked at each other in confusion and said, "What the Hell?" At the same time and laughed. Afterwards, they went back to his apartment and talked while sitting on the couch. DL could almost smell her alluring fragrance just thinking about it. He wanted her that night, but didn't want to risk violating what a perfect evening it had been. He held her while they watched one of her favorite shows, Forensic Files, and as they spooned, they fell asleep.

Day and night now he thought of her. Her sweet face had remained a faithful image in his mind ever since. He lifted the letter to his nose and with his eyes closed, he breathed in slowly as if it were oxygen, then fell asleep.

Chapter Three

Cynthia woke up that morning high on feelings, she couldn't sleep very much. She climbed out of bed, took a look in the mirror and started in on a self talk. "Are you really ready to feel like this? You told yourself, 'no men right now.'" She had only been separated from her husband of eleven years for a little more than four months. But she knew with all of her heart that relationship was done. It had been a horrible marriage, from start to finish, and she was afraid to begin again. When she got married, she was dead set against divorce, but due to circumstances that were out of her control, it had come to just that.

She shook her head in uncertainty and sighed. "It's way too soon." After taking care of one man for so long, seeing other men and dating had become a little awkward and foreign to her. She was living a life that didn't feel like her own. She brushed her teeth and continued talking to the mirror. "After all," she told herself, "You have plans to restore your life, strengthen the kids, and get physically and mentally healthy again."

Pulling on sweat pants and a sweat shirt, she was pleased because she had dropped over twenty pounds in the last few months and felt quite attractive. She admired her 135-pound frame in the mirror while hearing the taunts of her ex-husband in her mind, because over the years he had repeatedly told her she was fat. Those dark memories sometimes weakened her, but this morning she felt strength.

The battle inside continued: "I don't really know him, even though we talk all the time I've only met him once. How can I feel this way?" She continued the debate between logic, reason, and the heart all the way across the street to the park where she often walked and prayed in the mornings.

Still very early, the sun had just risen, it was brilliant and proud as if God hung it there as a portrait. One beautiful thing about the desert is no matter how piercing cold or extremely hot the weather is, there is always a clear, radiant blue sky. This morning was no exception. It was still quiet with only the songs of a few early birds chirping in the trees. The air was crisp, cold, and a bit windy. One or two dedicated runners breezed around the damp dirt track. Cynthia bent down touching her toes for a stretch then, as she walked, she began to pray about her upcoming divorce and her children, desiring the strength and wisdom to help them through this.

She prayed a lot about her new friend. She thought about all the things they talked about. All the nights they had spent hours on the phone talking and laughing about anything and everything; they had so much in common. As for the things they didn't agree on, they listened to each other's opinions respectfully, like how he used to get frustrated when his wife would wash his pants without checking the pockets, and once destroyed his passport.

Cynthia laughed aloud and said, "My ex used to get upset with me for the same thing."

"Why do women do that?" he asked with annoyance.

"Hello! We carry purses. We don't use our pockets, so it doesn't dawn on us to check them any more than it dawns on you to put the toilet seat down. It takes time to adjust."

"Oh. Okay. That actually makes sense."

They both laughed, she loved that they laughed so much when they talked.

During one of their conversations, Cynthia had explained to him that she had made a decision to be celibate after leaving her husband and asked how he felt about that.

DL replied, "I can respect that babe."

She could tell that it took him by surprise. "I think it gives people more time to become better friends."

In her heart she knew she was losing her religion. After meeting him and feeling that physical pull on her body, it would be very hard to keep that commitment if she continued to see him. She sat down on the green grass under a pine tree and laid back with her knees up in the position to do a few sit ups. With her hands behind her neck she looked up into the deep blue sky and her mind drifted.

When she first saw DL's picture online she thought, "He looks okay." But after actually seeing him in person, she felt he was far better looking than the picture gave him credit. She remembered meeting him at the casino. She stood across from the front door near the wall, tucked behind an ATM machine so she could watch him walk in and catch a glimpse of him before he could see her. She thought, "If he's ugly I'll just duck out."

But he wasn't and she didn't. She watched him come through the glass doors and enter near the front desk. As he removed his shades and slid them into his left chest pocket, she became feverish. He made his way down the aisle through the rows of slot machines.

He walked with a smooth swagger and held his head up with confidence, not arrogance. She approached him smiling, and he said, "Hello."
His voice was soft and mellow, and she thought, "I'm gonna melt right here in the middle of the casino." His six foot frame was the perfect fit to her five foot two; she loved tall men.

His skin was a perfect shade of chestnut, and his face was boyish and kind-looking. If he robbed a bank no jury would ever convict. His eyes were big and deep, and dark underneath as if he wore liner, but he didn't. There was something in them that drew her. They glowed like embers. His lashes were naturally long and curled, a woman would pay for those. His nose was perfect, like the one Michael Jackson wanted before he went too far. His face was clean and shaved, except for an artsy groomed goatee, and his lips were full and sexy. He wore two tiny gold-looped earrings, one in each ear.

When he reached for her hand, she took his and it felt strong, but somehow he held hers with tenderness. "I like him," she thought. "He actually knows how to dress." She looked him over and complimented him, "Nice jacket." She touched the edge of it rubbing the fabric between her index finger and thumb. She thought, "Armani, black, maybe even purple label, about forty two long."

Cynthia thought about how much fun they had that day, and how she fell asleep in his arms. Somehow the way he held her that night seemed to erase everything wrong in her world. Darren hadn't held her in years. He worked the third shift most of their marriage, and when he was off work he would generally go out until all hours of the night. When he was home to sleep, he slept on the couch. He often told her he hated sleeping with her. The rare times he did, it was out of guilt from some fight they had, or from her "nagging"—in his words.

Sometimes, he would come in from work and Cynthia would make a conscious effort to be very loving. When she reached out to him, he would take a deep breath in bother and stand there with his arms to his side while she hugged him. "Ugh! You finished?" He would say. Finally, unable to bear the pain of being rejected day after day just for trying to display affection, she just stopped, and he rarely initiated.

Just then, a burst of energy surged through her body and she pushed out thirty sit ups then popped up from the grass dusting herself off. She continued thinking her choices through while jogging around the track. The reality that she and Darren had not slept together for at least five months before she left, and now it had been four more, started to flutter through her body as she thought about DL. She sprinted a lap around the track in minutes.

Cynthia had become a young mother in high school and the challenges in her life during that time prompted her to seek God. When she was about eighteen, she began to spend her life very involved in church. Over the years she had developed doctrinal values and beliefs, but right now, she was being pulled in all kinds of different directions inside.

As she walked back home, her mind was in motion like a spinning top. "It was pretty easy deciding to abstain when I had been through so much trauma. Being intimate was the furthest thing from my mind. I couldn't imagine feeling this way again." She paused trying to shake it off. "What am I doing?" She thought as she arrived at her front door. "I can't do this, not now."

She went in and headed down the hallway to her bedroom to get ready for work. Her apartment was warmly decorated with earth tones, dark chocolate-colored woods, and splashes of colorful reddish accents. There was a complete entertainment center in the living area, which included a 42" flat screen TV, dvd/cd player, surround sound and all the oldies she could stand. The couch was a cinnamon color, large and plush with lots of pillows. The entire place was beautifully detailed with lovely vases and scented candles, different sizes and styles. There were flourishing potted green plants, and a few personal photos of her and the kids gave it a homey feeling.

In the corner was a fudge brown wooden ladder book shelf next to her PC. The shelves were lined with all kinds of magazines, books, and novels, some she'd read and some she planned to read. On the walls hung a collection of rare photographs with artistic custom-made frames, and uniquely designed hand-crafted mirrors.

The rest of the apartment was no exception. Her distinct decorative talent spilled into the kitchen and dining area as well. The bedrooms and bathroom looked as if they belonged in the pages of a home design magazine, yet she had a way of making the whole place feel cozy, comfortable, and lived in.

Her ex had never allowed her to decorate when they were together, he thought it was a waste of money. So this was one of the first things she did when she moved into her own place. She loved what she had done, and it was apparent that she had a talent for it. Although in leaving her husband, she struggled financially, she took pride in the fact the she could find such beautiful items in discount stores and consignment shops. No one ever guessed it. Everyone that visited would compliment her saying how warm and inviting the apartment was.

She made a cup of coffee and plopped down on the sofa. Pulling a fluffy red throw pillow behind her, she leaned back and sipped. She propped her feet on top of the coffee table and breathed in the silence. She was still trying to get used to the change of not being with her children every day. They were at Darren's house this week so it was a calm and quiet morning.

Summer, her daughter, eight, and Little Darren, her son, eleven, usually argued with each other all morning while getting ready for school. Although it drove her crazy, she was used to it and missed it when they weren't with her. Her oldest son, Anthony was seventeen. He had just received a basketball scholarship and was on his own in California. "Finally after all these years, I have peace in my home. No arguing, no worries about his temper, who he's with, where he is. I can just sit here and enjoy my life. This is truly nice." She smiled and went off to work.

Chapter Four

Seven thirty that morning, Cynthia hopped into her Mustang and drove off. She had saved for years to buy her car and it was pretty much the only thing she owned since the divorce. It was a Wimbledon white 1966 coupe with a V-8 and dual exhaust. She'd just had the tan leather on the bench seat re-upholstered and it was nice.

Cynthia enjoyed blasting her music with her favorite songs to wake her up in the mornings, and she loved oldies. She pushed the dial, and listened as the DJ introduced the next song. ". . . And here's a song for all you ladies who have finally had enough. Mary Jane Blige." It had a catchy rhythm and the lyrics caught her attention. She couldn't turn away: "Why'd I play the fool, go through up and downs? Knowing all the time you wouldn't be around. Maybe I liked the stress, cause I was young and restless but that was long ago. I don't wanna cry no more."

Cynthia found herself totally in sync with Mary, she felt as though this was her life's theme song. Dancing as she drove along, she tried to prepare her mind for the day. She worked as a bank manager in the unknown Arizona town she lived in. Residing there only about two years now, Kingstown was a bit lonely at first. However, her parents had moved out from Pasadena, California, to retire and they now lived in the apartment just a few doors down from hers.

Shortly after that, her younger sister, Mona, and her little boy, Simon, had come to live there as well. Kingstown was not the most attractive city. Very small, dry, dusty, and not very green, but it was cheap.

She started out at the bank as a teller and had worked her way up quickly. Coming from a metropolis like Los Angeles, this sparse little town was a piece of cake. She was quite confident in her skills as she had worked in banking off and on for over ten years, only stopping to have her children. For a few years she had her own Internet business; she sold clothes, shoes, and accessories in her own online retail store. It was moderately successful for a little more than three years until she made the move to Kingstown with Darren to buy their first home, and in his words "start over."

Darren promised her then that everything he had done in the past would be over, and his persuasive words convinced her to trust him again. She could still remember him holding her closely with his arms wrapped around her so tightly she almost couldn't breathe. Kissing her romantically, he looked directly into her eyes and said, "I swear honey, I'll be a loving faithful husband to you from now on."

She believed him, and with hopes that this last attempt to save their marriage could possibly work, she agreed to move to Arizona. When that plan failed miserably she was forced to give up her business because of financial hardship and went back to banking. It wasn't the career she desired, but she seemed to be good at it and this opportunity fell into her lap at just the right time.

Cynthia entered the office about an hour before opening everyday. "Good Morning." She said loudly for everyone to hear, then poured some coffee and headed for her desk. Her assistant, Pauline, approached her desk. She was a hard worker but sometimes panicked about small details. "Huh! I'm so glad you're here. Amber called in sick, so we'll be short on the line again today. Were you planning to pull out your cash drawer?"

"Pauline, you know if I need to I will, but I have to finish the monthly reports today. It'll be alright. We'll make it just like always. Stop letting these crazy customers stress you out."

Pauline cutting her eyes over at a teller said, "It's not the customers that stress me out usually."

Cynthia lowered her voice to a whisper. "Don't let your crazy co-workers stress you out either."

Pauline started to walk away and muttered, "Crazy? Dumb is more like it."

Sometimes Cynthia felt like she did when she was rearing Lil Darren and Summer. "Pauline! Watch it."

"Alright. Alright."

Cynthia appreciated her job, but what she really wanted was to go back to school and become a Christian therapist and self-help book author. She worked in a church for a little while in college and loved helping others with life's struggles and the feeling of fulfillment it brought to them and to her. That was where she met Darren, in church. He presented himself to be a God-fearing, loving, and hardworking man.

They started out as friends and within a year they had fallen in love. He wasn't the most handsome man in the world, but he was funny and very kind to her. He would always tell her how much he loved her and how beautiful he thought she was. At the time she was young and gullible and trusted him way too easily. He possessed such a magnificent singing voice that the first time she heard him sing she was completely awe stricken and could hardly believe her ears. It was the voice of an angel. He proposed to her sooner than she'd expected him to, but still she accepted. She was certain at the time that what they had was real and she felt she loved him.

It was about six months into the marriage when he put his hands on her for the first time and Cynthia was forever changed. The relationship, though not from lack of her trying, continued to spiral downward from there. Inside of two years, the abuse had continued and he became unfaithful as well. For years she prayed, toiled, and fought for their family, but nothing worked. There wasn't a day that went by now that she didn't wish that she had left him sooner. But a fire inside pushed her beyond those regrets.

Though being in a relationship again scared her, she told herself, "Not all men could be the way he is." Her mind shifted to her new friend and how gentle and sweet he was. With DL in her thoughts, she felt calmed, and continued on with her work day.

At six thirty, as they were leaving, Pauline asked, "So are you going to the gym?"

"Huh? After ten hours of paper pushing, fixing bank errors, and counting hundreds of thousands of dollars, I just want to go home. I'll get up early and go in the morning."

Pauline added, "And don't forget, selling the checking accounts, and credit cards and loans to people who probably shouldn't have them." They laughed as they walked toward their cars.

"Oh and we mustn't forget being cursed out by three different customers for overdraft fees."

Pauline continued, "Oh and crazy old Mr. Rogers. He made a withdrawal again today, then forgot and came back thirty minutes later saying there was a fraudulent withdrawal from his account."

"No, he didn't do that again?"

"Yep. He did."

They hopped in their cars and waved. "And tomorrow it starts all over again. See ya."

"Bye."

When Cynthia arrived home, she dropped her bag by the front door and kicked her shoes into the corner. She grabbed the phone from the charger and started thumbing through the caller id. "Nobody important." She went into the kitchen where she poured a cold glass of water and threw a chicken breast on the George Foreman and said, "Thank God for this thing." She hated to cook meals when the kids weren't there—too much food was wasted. She sipped her glass then, brain dead from the day, pulled herself back to her bedroom.

She stood in front of the large mirror that hung over her dresser and brushed her hair. She disrobed, leaving her clothes on the floor, and went into the bathroom and hopped in the shower. The steamy warm water felt good running down her weary body. With her head hanging down and eyes closed, she turned and let it soothe her back. She lathered up the wash cloth with a vanilla-scented body wash and inhaled the pleasant aroma.

Then she remembered, "Oh, let me hurry before DL calls." Just as she was drying off she heard the phone ring. She wrapped the towel around her semi-wet body and answered it without looking at the caller id.

"Hello?"

"Hey hun."

"Hun?" she thought, "This isn't DL." She asked, "Darren?" It was her ex. She felt bothered. "What?"

"Dang!" He retorted, "Don't sound so happy."

"What Darren? I'm a little busy. Are the kids okay?"

"Yea, I just wanted to see if I could come by and pick up some of Lil D's pants."

Cynthia knew he was just trying to come over and hopefully catch her vulnerable like he had in the past. Most of the kids' things were at his house because when she moved she didn't take much with her. She felt upset, but thought, "I'm not going to get into a stupid argument." She just answered, "No, don't come by. I'll drop some off in the morning before I go to work."

"Oh . . . okay. What are you doing?"

"I'm trying to wash up and eat dinner."

"Oh, okay, I'll let you go then . . ." He paused as though he wanted her to reject that offer.

"Alright, bye."

Cynthia hung up, not giving him time to say much else. She grumbled, "All those years that man couldn't care less about anything I was doing. Now all of the sudden he wants to talk on the phone." She was relieved that her emotion toward him had faded. After all, for over ten years she had loved him with all of her heart and did everything she could to be the best wife she knew how to be. But no matter what, he continued with his destructive lifestyle. When she decided enough was enough, she left. She made the commitment to herself then, that she would push through all the pain and sorrow no matter how long it took. Through months of crying and dealing with the soreness a broken marriage brings, she was finally able move on.

She put the phone down near the sink and hung her towel on the hook over the door. She picked up a jar of body butter, sat on her vanity chair, and starting with her legs, massaged it onto her body. She brushed her wet hair back into a sleek pony tail, then rolled it into a bun. Looking closely into the mirror, she put night cream on her face and delicately tried to treat the blemishes. She slid into her comfortable pink cotton Hanes t-shirt and panties, tied on a long black satin robe and slid on her little black footies. Then she went back into the kitchen to prepare a grilled chicken salad. When she finished, she sat down in front of the TV and clicked it on with the remote. "Oooh, The Brady Bunch. I love TV Land."

The phone rang and she jogged back to the bathroom to grab it, mumbling, "Man this better not be him again!" This time she looked at the caller id. It was DL. Her face lit up and her voice switched from rough to sweet, "Hello."

He said, "Hi pumpkin."

"Hi D."

He asked, "How was your day?"

"It was a typical bank day. I think I counted a million dollars today."

"Wow! Did you get me some?" They chuckled. He asked, "What are you doing?"

"Eating dinner."

"Oh okay, I won't keep you."

She quickly declined, "No, it's okay. I can talk."

And they went on to have one of their typical night long conversations. She learned more about his two divorces. DL had one son from his first marriage who was now eight years old. He never got to see him because he lived in Washington with his mom, and he and his ex-wife didn't really get along. She had remarried and he thought it was better to let them be a family.

Cynthia couldn't help but give him her opinion. "Even if they are a family, you're still important. If that's okay for me to say."

"It's okay, but she makes that very difficult. The last time I tried to send for him she said he could only come if she could."

"Wow, I'm sorry. I bet you miss him."

"Yea. I do."

They talked about their parents. Cynthia was glad hers had moved closer. DL had lost his mother ten years prior to cancer. He explained, "I was in the Air Force when she got sick and couldn't even get approved for a leave. I always feel so bad that I wasn't with her when she passed."

Cynthia asked, "And your father? He passed on too?"

"Yea, just about five years ago."

They talked about their age difference. Cynthia was three years older than him and she would jokingly dismiss his opinions saying he was still young, just a baby. He would quickly refute that with "Uh huh, I'll show you a baby."

They talked about their childhoods and the differences in where they both grew up. She was born and raised in Southern California. He was from a small town in Georgia she had never heard of and the name she could never say correctly.

"What's the name of that city again?"

He answered, “Hephzibah.”

She asked, “Hek-zi-bah?”

“Nooo, HePPP-zi-bah.

“Where’s that near? Atlanta?”

“No. It’s closer to Augusta.”

“You know you’re country, right?”

Together with her witty sense of humor and their differences in upbringing, that became a constant joke in their conversations. If he would mention other states in ridicule, like Alabama or Arkansas, she would correct him.

“Babe, you’re from Georgia. That’s the same thing as Alabama.”

He answered, “No it’s not.”

“I’m from California; everything south of here is country, and Georgia, Arkansas, and Alabama are extremely country.”

He hated when she said that but it was so funny that he let her get away with it.

“Damn Cali people, you’re all arrogant and uppity.” They laughed.

He asked, “So do you have the kids this weekend?”

“I do, they’ll be back on Wednesday. Why?”

“I was wondering when I would see you again?”

He knew, because she had mentioned it before, that although she was willing to date again, she wasn't comfortable bringing a new man around her children unless the relationship had enough time to be serious.

"Um, I'm not sure." She was hesitant; her emotions were mixed because although she liked him, she was afraid of that as well. "What the heck." she thought, "Fear gets you nowhere."

She shyly suggested, "Maybe next weekend?"

"YAY!" He cheered as if he were at a ball game.

"See? You're making me nervous."

"Why? Wasn't I a good boy when you came up here last time?"

"Yea, that's what scares me. I'm sure that's one of your tricks."

They laughed, but she was serious. He asked, "You want me to come down there?"

For some reason, Cynthia was not quite comfortable with that. Kingstown was so small and there was literally nothing to do. There was a Wal-Mart, a K-Mart and a hand full of two-star restaurants. There was only one three-screen, run-down movie theater, and the name posted outside on the marquis was: THE MOVIES. Everyone's feet stuck to the floor and generally the film would break about half way through. It was so decomposed that it was sure to be closing down any day. The bar/club scene was not even worth mentioning.

She answered him, "Uh … No. I don't think so."

"Why? What's the name of that city again? King- what?

"Kingstown."

"I've never heard of that."

"I know. There's only about three kinds of people who have."

He chuckled, "Who?"

"Travelers know it from stopping here to get gas while on their way some where else. Bikers, because old Route 66 runs right through here, and the third kind we'll just call desert people."

He asked, "Desert people?"

"Yea. I really can't explain it. They're something like a cross between cowboys and trailer park types. This whole town reminds me of an old, boring western movie that nobody wants to watch."

"Damn." he said, "Why are you staying there?"

She laughed. "I really do want to move, but I'm in the middle of this divorce. Plus my ex and I have already moved four times and I'm not sure if I should uproot the kids again. I have a decent job, and I've managed to meet some nice people here."

She looked out of her window and watched as a tumbleweed blew through the dirt field next to her apartment and sighed. "I think I'd rather come up there. It'll get me away from this dusty, Godforsaken place for a little bit, but you have to promise to be a gentleman."

"I promise."

Chapter Five

The week flew by with the kids, as it always did. Cynthia tried to keep her time on the phone short when they were home with her, so she and DL hadn't talked as much. This was their last night with her before going back to Darren's so she wanted to make their favorite dinner: hamburgers and fries. She always made a garden salad along with it to balance out the meal.

She played her favorite Lionel Richie cd and while she was preparing dinner, she wondered if DL talked with other women when she wasn't available. Then she snapped out of it. She thought, "He's not my husband, he can talk to whoever he wants." Unlike Darren, who spent his time on the Internet meeting women while he was still married to her. As she cooked, her mind and emotions slipped back into the pain of when she first discovered that.

One night when she was eight months pregnant with Summer she couldn't sleep. Number one, because of all the marital issues they had, and number two, because she was just uncomfortable from the pregnancy. She remembered she had just dozed off when she heard this BUZZ BUZZ. Darren had left his pager at home. It was on vibrate, sitting on top of the television. She didn't see it there and when it started to buzz in the middle of the night in her half sleep haze, she imagined there was a big bug in the room and it startled her.

Cynthia sat up in bed and clicked on the lamp. Afraid to step onto the floor she just looked around. Realizing it was his pager, she laid back down. It stopped, then started again. Then again.

The third time it dawned on her, "Who's trying to reach my husband at one in the morning?"

She called the number and a woman answered, "Hello."

Cynthia fought the instinct to hang up, "Hello? I'm answering a call to my husband's pager."

"Oh, I'm sorry. I was trying to reach Darren."

"Yes, Darren is my husband."

"Wow. I'm so sorry. He never said he was married."

Cynthia questioned, "This is a long distance area code. Where do you live?"

"Philadelphia."

"Philadelphia? How did you meet my husband?"

"We met online. But had he told me he was married, I swear I never would have been calling. I'm so sorry."

"No. It's not your fault. Goodnight."

Cynthia felt as though she could literally feel her heart shatter like glass in her chest. She started to call other numbers in the pager and spoke to four different women that late night. All of them had met Darren either on a party line or the Internet. When she got off the phone she felt her pregnant belly cramping and wrapped her palms wide around the sides of her stomach, hoping to ease the pain of the contractions.

She grabbed her pillow and began to cry uncontrollably into it, so Anthony and Lil Darren couldn't hear her in the next room. In tears, she prayed for relief. "This explains all these nights off work, at work." At the time, they didn't have a computer at home so he was at work using the company's computer. Darren came home about three that morning and when Cynthia confronted him with what she found. His response was, "What are you doing looking in my pager?"

As Cynthia was deep in thought, Summer dashed into the kitchen, shouting and pulled on her shirt, "Mommy! Make him leave me alone!"

Carrying the emotion she was still feeling from being lost in a bad memory, Cynthia quickly turned around from the stove in frustration and burned her hand on the pan. "Ouch! What is it baby?"

"Darren keeps bothering me!"

Lil Darren shot in, yelling an interjection, "She keeps taking my crayons!"

Summer yelled, "Na ahh. Those are my crayons!"

Cynthia shook her hand and ran it under cool water in the sink. "Okay! Okay! Now you both just stop it. Leave each other alone or you're both going to your rooms for the night."

She paused to gather herself and took a deep breath. "Summer, come help Mommy in the kitchen." She winked an eye at Lil Darren as if to let him know she was on his side. He walked away pleased and went back to his room. She took Summer into the kitchen and allowed her to help, this comforted her as well. Cynthia kissed her cheek, "You okay, sweetpea?"

"Yea. He gets on my nerves!"

"Settle down, sweetpea. Settle down."

"Your hand okay, Mommy?"

"Yes. It's fine."

All was calm for at least ten minutes until the next war broke out. They worked together to finish dinner. While Summer set the table, the phone rang. Both of the children dashed to answer it. Cynthia wailed out, "Wait a minute!" Thinking it may be DL, she wasn't really ready for the kids to know she had a male friend. But she was too late, Lil Darren had already answered.

"Hello?" He gestured to Cynthia in excitement. "It's Daddy!" Then got back on, "Hi Daddy. You coming to get us tomorrow? Okay . . . Okay . . . I love you too. Hold on." He reached out to hand the phone to Cynthia, who said, "Let your sister talk."
He handed the phone to Summer who talked for just a few moments. She said goodbye and tried to hand the phone to Cynthia. "Daddy wants to talk to you." With no exit this time and both kids staring up at her, she took the phone.

"Hello?"

He asked, "What's up?"

"Just busy cooking dinner. What's up?"

"I'll pick up the kids about seven tomorrow. Is that okay?"

"That's fine, bye."

Cynthia hung up without giving the opportunity for any conversation. She thought, "Now he knows he could have told them that." The phone rang again. She saw on the display it was Darren. "Huh!" She answered while walking back to the bedroom so the kids couldn't witness her attitude.

She was annoyed. "Hello."

"Why did you hang up so fast? Dang."

"What Darren?"

He asked with subtlety, "Can we talk?"

"About what? If it has to do with the kids, then yes. If not, no."

"Come on, Cynthia."

"I'm not going to start this with you tonight Darren. Goodnight." She hung up the phone and shut off the ringer for the night.

Chapter Six

Six thirty Friday morning in Las Vegas. Like most 24-hour cities, in idle observation you couldn't really tell if people were coming or going. DL was headed home from his shift, stuck in traffic, and irritated. But instead of getting upset as usual, he was relieved because he had the next three days off. The music from his car stereo thumped loudly and he thought about Cynthia. "I get to see her on Saturday."

As he bobbed his head and rapped along with Tupac it dawned on him, "That's tomorrow!" He felt a surge of energy and pushed the large truck through the traffic like an ambulance on its way to an accident scene. He parked outside his apartment thinking, "I need to clean up." As he got out of his truck, he saw from a distance that there was a female guest waiting outside his front door. He approached cautiously, not recognizing who she was at first. "Surprise!" she said with a welcoming smile and motioned toward him for a hug.

A little caught off guard and disturbed, DL pulled away. "What are you doing here, Leslie?"

She asked, "Aren't you glad to see me? I couldn't get a hold of you for the last few days so I just stopped by."

"Well, you probably shouldn't have done that. I'm really tired." He didn't motion to open the door, hoping she would just go.

Her face saddened and she pulled a cigarette out of the pack to take a smoke, then turned to leave.

He grabbed her arm, "Look, I'm sorry."

He pulled her closer and wrapped his arm around her lower back then kissed her cheek. He waved one hand through the smoke, and with all the sincerity he could fake said, "It's just not a good time baby. I had a rough night. I just worked twelve hours and I'm really tired."

He had met Leslie online last November. Her picture was lovely, but when he met her in person he thought, "Either she had an excellent photographer or she's just very photogenic." She was a chain smoker, painfully skinny, her skin was bad, and what little hair she had was always gelled back or hidden under a hippie-style hat. He found out later that the picture she had online was taken when she was twenty five, now she was near forty and life's struggles were physically evident. For some reason, he kept her around. He'd convinced himself that he shouldn't cut any ties just yet. "After all, who knows?" he thought.

He was in the habit of keeping extra women around like some people save packets of ketchup from a fast food restaurant. You may never need them but if you run out of the good stuff, it's nice to have them handy. DL pecked her on the lips, "I promise I'll call you later."

Leslie took a last hit of her cigarette, dropped it to the ground and stepped on it. She puffed out a cloud of smoke, and smiled sweetly with all teeth showing. She looked up into his eyes with disappointment, and moved in closer for another kiss, "Okay . . . Bye . . . Call me later."

Her teeth distracted him, they looked like little yellow pieces of Chicklettes gum lined across her mouth, and her breath smelled of early morning, smoke, and coffee. His face soured. But he forced himself and pecked her lips again.

"I will baby, I promise." She left.

On a normal day, he would have brought her inside, ate some cereal and fell right into bed with her, but not today. All he really could think about was Cynthia—how drop dead gorgeous she was, and those jeans she was wearing last time. He rushed inside, locked the door behind him, and peeked out of the window to make sure Leslie drove away. Starting with his kitchen he cleaned every room in the small one bedroom apartment he called home. He fell asleep around three o'clock only to wake up at six to a ringing phone. He checked the caller id: It was his brother, Roger.

He answered bothered, "Hello?"

"What's up bro? It's me."

"I know! What? I'm asleep!"

"I need a ride to my gig tonight."

"Tonight? What time?"

Roger hesitated to say, "Uh, now. I missed my ride."

"Alright man, I'll be there in a minute. Damn!"

Although his brother irritated him most of the time, it was clear he cared about his well being. He would drop whatever he was involved in and do anything for him. Roger was ten years older than DL, but much less responsible, if that were possible. A musician, living in a small bachelor place in Vegas. He floated from band to band, gig to gig, and whatever lines he used on the ladies worked, because he always had one.

He was a small man, about five foot eight and handsome. Almond skin and clean shaved. He kept his fade low and his hair was more salt than pepper now. His suits, although trapped in an 80's time warp, were always sharp, pressed to perfection and everything matched perfectly right down to his shoes. Often the top three or four buttons of his dress shirt were left open and he wore a white gold link chain with a sizable scorpion medallion, revealing his zodiac sign in case anyone was interested.

Roger possessed a larger than life personality. Sober or drunk his energy level was always the same as a six-year-old at Disneyland. He knew how to play the game like most musicians do and for years he played it well. But now in his mid forties, it was obvious that the game along with excessive drinking and gambling was taking its toll. He had lost his driver's license a year prior for DUI, and quite often he called on his brother for rides.

DL didn't hesitate. He sat on the edge of his bed, head in hand, rubbing across his forehead in a failing attempt to wake up. "Maybe if I hop in the shower?" He got up, grabbed a towel from the closet, went into the bathroom and reached behind the shower curtain to turn on the water as he took a wiz.

He heard his cell phone ring in the bedroom, shook off and jogged in to try and catch the caller. "Shit." The display read, "missed call." Before he could check who it was, it rang again. He looked and saw that it was Leslie. Un-fazed he tossed the phone back on the bed and got in the shower. In the fifteen or so minutes it took for him to get ready she had called three more times. His cell rang again.

He looked in annoyance, "Damn!" This time it was Roger.

"What's up?"

"Dude, where are you?"

Not letting on that he hadn't left yet, he said, "I'm almost there, peace."

He hung up before he asked anymore questions. As he shot through the city streets figuring them to be moving quicker than Vegas Friday night traffic on the freeway, he reached for his cell to call Cynthia and confirm their plans for the next day. Just as he picked up to dial he heard a piece of a ring and it was too late—he had to answer not knowing who the caller was.

"This is D."

"Hi. What's up?"

Not catching who the female voice belonged to, he replied, "Uh, on my way to take my brother to his gig. You?"

"Nut-ting much."

The voice was light and soft, with an accent. Familiar, but he just couldn't place it, so he asked another question, "Uh . . . How was work today?"

The sweet voice answered, "Remember I do no work on Friday."

Then it clicked, it was Haney, a nice Asian girl he met last year. He would mess around with her every now and then. She was cute, but a little uncoordinated. Her accent usually got on his nerves, but he liked to have an assortment.

She asked, "Are we still go out tomorrow?"

He muttered to himself, "What the fuck?" He had forgotten all about planning a date with her weeks prior. "Uh, tomorrow?"

She responded, "You forget?"

"I meant to call you . . . I have to drive my brother up to his gig in Primm tomorrow and he just told me, uh, earlier today." He paused rather proud of how quick he came up with that. "I'm sorry baby. Can we reschedule?"

She was clearly discouraged. "Oh, that okay. It will have to be next mont, cause I go home for tree week on Monday. Or what about tonight?"

Something about that accent made him feel horrible. His eyes rolled up in confusion he mumbled, "Tree week? Oh . . . three weeks." In guilt, he answered, "Tonight? That's cool."

Tired, hungry, and irritable from sleep deprivation, he didn't feel like being around anybody, but he still suggested "We could go check out my brother's gig over at Caesar's at eight."

She perked up. "That sound good."

"Alright, I'll pick you up in about an hour."

"Okay, I be ready one hour. Bye."

"Bye."

DL hung up and tossed the phone down on the passenger seat. "Dammit! How do I get myself into this shit? I have got to start turning this damn phone off!"

He arrived in front of his brother's apartment. Roger was standing out front, all of his musical equipment surrounding him. "Now I gotta get out and do manual labor, damn!" He popped the hatch to his truck, and got out with a rash look on his face. He grabbed a big black speaker and almost threw it into the back.

Roger quickly motioned to stop him. "Man, what the hell is wrong with you? You know how much that cost?"

DL snapped back, “Man, fuck you! Maybe about as much as you owe me?”

He threw it into the back of the truck. Then reached for the bass. Roger grabbed it with urgency, “No! I got this. Just get your ass back in the truck!” Roger finished the loading and climbed into the passenger seat.

DL sat there with his elbow leaning on the window holding the side of his head, breathing deeply in frustration. He found himself often doing things for other people he didn’t want to do. To his own detriment, he had a hard time saying no and he would bottle it all up inside.

Roger looked over at him as they pulled out and sensed his frustration. “Man, I’m sorry about asking you for the ride so late. I appreciate it though.”

Roger reached up and yanked on the sun visor to use the mirror and one side of it broke off. DL slammed on his breaks in the middle of the road, “Man, what the fuck!”

The screeching sound of breaks in his rear pierced the sound barrier. In a panic, he pulled over into a parking lot, and stared at his brother. He shook his head in anger and disillusionment as the visor hung on one side. He often felt like he was babysitting a young child when they were together.

“Man do you see what you just did?” He reached over and tried to pop the broken latch back into place but it didn’t work. “Damn!” Roger felt guilty, “Sorry man, damn. I’ll pay for it.”

DL took a deep breath, rolled his eyes, and tried to calm down. He pulled back out into the street. “Forget it, it’s cool.”

Roger tried his hand at fixing it and the whole thing fell off and onto his lap. In shock he paused, lifted his hands up and said, "OOPS!" He picked it up and tried again to somehow maneuver it back into place. DL didn't even bother looking at him. Holding back his anger he said, "Just leave it alone man, PLEASE! Before you tear a hole through the roof!"

As they rode along, Roger tried to cheer his little brother up. He reached over and tickled at his armpit and chin, making baby noises. DL could be like a bear at times and then turn into a puppy. Roger kept tickling him. Then made up a tune singing, "Man, I'll fix it, I'll fix it, I promise, I will fix it."

DL slapped his hand away as he drove, trying to stay angry but couldn't. Finally he cracked a grin, then laughed. "It's not just that . . . I'm really sleepy. I forgot I told Haney I would take her out tomorrow and I had to change it to tonight, last minute. I'm tired. Man, I was going to drop you off and go back to bed, now I gotta take this chick out. I had to lie . . ." He stopped mid-sentence, "Oh, by the way, if she asks you, I'll be with you all day tomorrow in Primm."

Roger sat there listening but not understanding. He asked, "If you're tired, why didn't you just keep it for tomorrow? Why did you change it to tonight?"

A look of delight came over DL's face, "Dude, cause Cynthia will be up here tomorrow."

Roger hadn't met Cynthia yet, but he had heard a lot about her. He knew his little brother really liked her. He was kind of jealous but he was happy for him. "Don't worry bro, I got your back. But you seriously need to tighten up your game."

"My game is tight."

"Shit. My game is tight."

"What? Man, your game ain't been tight in years."

"Whatever. I never needed your help lying to nobody. You get too caught up."

"Yea, I do. I love women. That's my only problem."

Roger clapped his hands, rubbed his palms together and licked his lips, as if about to eat a tasty meal. He said, "So you get some Asian booty tonight and some new booty tomorrow. I wish I had your problems."

DL quickly replied, "Man, I'm not messing around with that girl tonight. I'm tired! I'm taking her to your show, then I'm dropping her off at home and going to my apartment by myself and going to sleep!"

They pulled into the parking lot and parked. Roger leaned over raising his eyebrows repeatedly like Groucho Marx. "So, then you get the new booty tomorrow?"

DL just looked away and got out. He lifted the hatch and started emptying the equipment, obviously ignoring his comment. Roger punched his arm and asked again. He danced around like Sugar Ray Leonard and took jabs at him. DL stopped, paused and took a deep breath. In a low voice, he said, "I don't think so, man. She says she's celibate."

Roger froze, stunned in silence with his mouth hanging open as if he had just seen a ghost. With a loud booming reply, his voice could be heard throughout the parking lot: "What the fuck! What? . . . Celi- what? Man, I can't even say that word. That's a bad word."

DL put his finger to his mouth, "Man, shhsh! She says she's celibate. I told her I'd respect it."

They started walking toward the back entrance of the stage with their arms full. Roger was bewildered. "You will? That's cool, respect it. What time is she supposed to be up here tomorrow?"

DL answered, "About three."

Roger replied, "That's cool, be celibate all day. Then send her ass back to Arizona at about eight and go pick up the Asian at eight thirty, and get de-celibatized." They laughed.

DL turned and looked at Roger, "Man, you always talkin shit!" He put the instruments on the stage, then walked back out the door.

Roger followed with a slight jog, trying to catch up and shaking his head. "Man, I don't think that woman is driving all the way up here to watch TV with you again. She's gonna give you the booty." They paused by the truck and Roger looked DL in the eye, pointing his index finger into his own chest, he said confidently, "Man, trust me I know women. You want me to get her started for you?"

DL looked at him as if he were crossing a forbidden line. "See? There you go again, constantly talkin shit."

Chapter Seven

Saturday, Cynthia woke up to a crisp bright sun beaming though her bedroom window. She looked over at the clock and 6 a.m. glared back at her in red. She reached above the bed to close the blinds and tried to sleep for a few more minutes. Her quilted bed was so warm and comfortable, she didn't want to budge. Up late the night before riddled with anxiety, she tossed and turned until finally she just got up and changed in and out of different outfits trying to find the ones she looked her best in. It was three in the morning the last time she looked at the clock.

She pulled herself out of bed, and all she could think about was a cup of hot coffee. She glanced over at her Bible sitting on the night stand. She usually read it in the mornings while drinking coffee, but didn't pick it up as usual. The phone rang. "Who's calling me at six in the morning?" Looking at the caller id, she thought, "This girl is crazy." It was her close friend, Carla. They had been best friends since high school and she has always been as loud, wild, and unruly as a woman can be. Carla still lived in California so they didn't get to see each other often, but talked on the phone nearly every day.

Carla was a biker chick. Her skin was smooth and midnight, like an islander. She was tall, lean, and very eccentric. She kept her hair short in a fade like a guy's and it looked fabulous on her. She wore tattoos for jewelry and rode a big clean Harley Davidson. She and Cynthia were so opposite, even they themselves couldn't believe they had been friends this long.

"Hello. Girl, why are you calling me this early?"

Carla's screams can surely be heard in the apartment next door, "Girrrrl, I just got home from my date last night and I remembered you was takin your virgin ass up to Vegas today. I had to call and cheer you on."

Cynthia responded, "You know what? You are certifiably crazy. What do you mean you just got home from last night's date?"

"No babe, we can talk about that story another time. We're talking about you. So you gonna give him some?"

Cynthia blushed. "No . . . I mean . . . I don't think so . . . I don't know. I'm scared. I haven't been with anybody but Darren in over a decade, and I wasn't with very many guys before that. I'm thirty five years old and I feel like a teenager. I'm so freakin nervous."

"Mmm . . . hmm." Carla just listened.

"I mean, I don't want to end up hurt again. I don't think my heart could take it. He's been such a good friend, and I really like him, you know? We get along so well. It's odd but we have this vibe like we've known each other forever. I don't want to risk losing that by screwing around. On the other hand, when I think about him . . . Ugh . . . I just melt!"

Carla answered, "Then drip drip." They laughed. "Seriously though. You are being way too uptight. Just go up there and relax. You're going to Vegas, let the chips fall where they may. Whatever happens, he's the lucky one."

"Thanks, girl. Listen I gotta go. I have to work til one before I head up there. I'll call you when I get back."

"Girrrl, you better."

"I will. Love you, bye."

"Love you too. Be careful."

Cynthia ate breakfast, tidied up a bit and threw a few extra things in an overnight bag. "Let's see, do I have everything?"
She took a look in the mirror to finish her make up, paused and said, "I sure hope you know what you're doing."

This whole thing was far out of the little box of safeness she had been living in for so long. She headed out to her car and quickly turned around. "Oh shoot, my cd's." The drive to Vegas was about an hour and a half and she definitely couldn't do that without her oldies.

Work was slow, it seemed an hour had gone by but when she looked at the clock it had only been about five minutes. Her assistant, Pauline, was being nosy and sat down at the desk next to her. Smiling and raising her eyebrows she questioned her. "So you're headed up to Vegas again, huh?" Pauline was about five feet tall, very round, and cute. At the time she was stuck in a bad marriage of her own. Watching Cynthia start over, offered her a glimmer of hope for the future.

Cynthia looked up from her computer. "Yea, I'm really nervous, and this day is dragging."

Pauline suggested, "Well, go ahead and go. I can handle it from here."

"No, you think I should? It's barely eleven o'clock, we have two more hours."

She threw her right hand out like shooing a fly and insisted, "Just go. We'll be alright."

"Thanks girl, I'm outta here"

Cynthia started to clean up her desk and thought, "I better call him first if I'm gonna be early." Just as she reached for the phone she heard, "Cynthia, line one."

She picked up the line, and in her professional fake phone voice said, "Thank you for holding. This is Cynthia. How can I help you?"

"You can help me by getting up here."

Realizing it was DL, she lowered her voice and spoke softly. Her desk was right behind the teller line and they all listened like she was disclosing secret stock tips.

"Hi DL. I was just going to call you. I'm heading out in the next five minutes. I'll call you when I get through the Dam."

"YAY! I can't wait to see you."

She answered, "Me too. Bye."

"Bye baby."

Cynthia quickly stacked her scattered paperwork into a pile and shoved it into her top desk drawer. She locked it and motioned to head out when her cell phone rang. She paused, then thought, "Oh shoot, I'll check it in the car." She shouted aloud as she exited the office, "Okay, I'll see you guys on Monday. Have a good weekend."

The sun was bright and the weather was perfectly mild. When she got to the car she saw that it was Darren who called. "What does he want!" Just then, he called again. Thinking there may have been a situation with the kids, she answered, "Hello."

"Hey it's me."

"Yea, I'm at work. What's up?"

"Oh okay, um, we're at the park across the street from your place. I thought you might want to watch my softball game with the kids."

"Uh, no thanks. I'm at work, and I'm headed out of town after that. You guys have fun."

He asked, "Oh? Where you headed?"

She had a feeling he would get suspicious and jealous, and thought about telling him a lie. Even though it had been months since they were together, she knew the anger he was capable of and that made her uneasy. Then she thought, "Why lie? Forget him." She said into the phone, "Excuse me? Out of town. I'll talk to you later, bye."

"Whatever, bye."

She drove out of the parking lot, stopped to get gas, and hopped onto the freeway. Trying to carefully shuffle through her cd's while driving, she thought, "Where is my Earth, Wind, and Fire?" She pulled the disc out of the case, popped it in, and was on her way. About fifteen minutes on the highway, with music bumping and the sun shining, Cynthia inhaled the freedom like a pleasant aroma.

She loved long drives; there was something therapeutic about them. Her Mustang took on the two lane highway like The Roadrunner escaping the grasp of Wile E. Coyote. Her cell phone rang, it was Darren again. She turned it off and put it in the glove box. Then mumbled, "He has Mom's number if it's an emergency." But she knew it wasn't.

One of the songs that came on started to take her back to a time when she and Darren were briefly semi-happy. However, whenever she thought they were happy, she would always find out at some point that he was hiding something. Like three years ago, she was under the impression they were having a good year. He suggested they go on a Caribbean cruise for their wedding anniversary. They planned from February through July, and in August they went.

Her feminine intuition was telling her the whole time something was not completely right. When they returned home, Cynthia retrieved the mail and saw their cell phone bill was over $400. In the two years they'd had cell phones, never, not even once, was the bill over $100. When she examined it, she saw that he was spending hours on the phone with his ex-girlfriend from high school. She counted almost one hundred calls between them in just that one month. Most of which were held between the hours of twelve and five in the morning.

Just then, the song on the cd changed. She shook her head and decided not to allow her mind to wander about him today. She popped in her 70's disco tunes. As she listened to Gloria Gaynor sing "I Will Survive," her spirits lifted and in no time she was pulling through Hoover Dam. She turned on her phone to call DL. He picked up and spoke like talking to a baby. "Hi baby boo boo, pumpkin pie."

She said with excitement, "Hi, I just came through the dam. I'll be up there in about thirty more minutes."

"Okay babe."

Cynthia saw on the display of her cell that she had four missed calls and three text messages. All were from Darren. She scrolled through to read them, "Honey call me asap . . . need help with car. Got a flat."

"Honey why aren't u picking up? At the park with flat tire."

Then her phone rang, it was her sister, Mona.

She answered, “Hello.”

In frustration, Mona said, “Hey, do you know your ex dropped your kids off at Mom and Dad’s?”

Cynthia questioned, “What? I just took them over there yesterday. He’s supposed to have them until Wednesday. Did Mom say why?”

“He gave her some cockamamie excuse.”

“He’s been trying to call me for the last hour. I shut my phone off...I told him I was leaving town. You don’t think he would try to follow me, do you?”

Mona said, “No. He’s not that smart. Well, I was going to help Mom and Dad empty their storage unit today, but that’s hard with the kids running around.”

“I’ll call him and tell him to pick them up. This is his week!”

Mona replied, “No, he’s up to something. I’m just going to pop up at his house. I’ll call you back in a little bit.”

As Cynthia exited the freeway, she thought, “I should stop somewhere and check myself. I can never be too careful.” She pulled over to a restaurant to use the restroom. She took a thorough look at herself in the mirror. She was wearing an off-white, cotton, form-fitting top that tied around the waist and caressed her bosom, and Capri jeans. “I can’t believe I’m in a six.”

Though most of her life people complimented her looks, beauty wasn't always what Cynthia saw when she looked in he mirror. She'd see the pimples that still seemed to pop up around her chin every month even though she was in her mid-thirties, and her round nose that to her, was a little to big for her face, and since having three kids, her figure wasn't at all what it used to be. “Oh whatever, this is me.”

She slipped on her black wedge, open-toed heels to show off her freshly done French pedicure, and put her tennis shoes in a bag. She adjusted her blouse and ran her fingers through her curled hair. “I hope he thinks I look pretty.”

Insecure about her breast size, she adjusted her bra trying to make them seem smaller. “Ugh, I wish I could get a reduction.” She put on a denim jacket and buttoned it up, then turned and examined her back side. She dabbed on a little smell good and cherry lip gloss. “I guess this is about as good as it gets.”

Mona called back just as she was getting into the car.

She answered, “Hey, what’s up?”

Mona, laughing and loud, asked, “Girl, do you know I knocked on his door and he had a woman over there?”

Cynthia was shocked. “What? Are you serious?” She exploded in laughter.

Mona continued, “Yea, some biggo Mexican chick She looked scared when she saw me. I just ignored her and told Darren that he had to come and get the kids because we had plans. Then he said, ‘Oh okay, we’re going to church. Do you mind if I come and get them after that?’ Then I asked him, ‘Oh, the kids can’t go to church?’ He didn’t answer. So I just said, ‘Well, please pick them up by three o’clock,’ and left. He was obviously about to start lying and I didn’t want to hear it.”

Cynthia was tickled. “Church? He’s still using his old tricks. He hasn’t been to church in years, probably since he found me there.”

Mona answered, “Girl, you sure picked a real winner with that one.”

Cynthia replied, still laughing a little, “I sure did, didn’t I? I hit the jackpot! Anyway, thanks for taking care of that. I’ll call you tomorrow.”

“Alright. Be careful, you don’t know that idiot either.”

“I will.”

Chapter Eight

As Cynthia approached DL's apartment complex, the chills set in. She drove through the large black gates in the front. "Nice place. Ugh, I have butterflies." She found his building and parked. As she walked toward his front door, she inhaled very deeply then exhaled and knocked.

DL opened the door almost immediately, smiling. "Hi baby. I'm so glad you made it. Come in." He took her bag and walked over to the end of the couch setting it down.

A bit shy and nervous, Cynthia looked over at him. Through the eyes of love she saw the lips and body of LL Cool J and the smooth demeanor of Denzel Washington. "He's so fine." she thought. They hugged and the scent of her vanilla body lotion peaked his senses. "You smell really nice."

She smiled, "Thank you." She looked around at his photography framed on the walls nodding her head in approval. "Your place is decorated very tastefully. Especially for a bachelor." She thought, "I better be careful, he's definitely a player."

"Thank you, but you've been in here before."

"Yea, but last time it was dark, and I didn't stay very long." She grinned and added, "Now in the afternoon light I can see how you really live."

"Oh, is that right?"

Cynthia pointed to a trio of photos hanging above the couch. They were bright and colorful pictures of a nature not easily captured on film. A clean white gazebo just beyond a crystal clear lake surrounded by plush greenery, with a cloudless blue sky as a back drop. "Wow, those are so beautiful. Where were you?"

"Thank you. I took those in Singapore while I was in the service. I rarely do color shots but I especially liked these. I didn't even Photoshop em. They're straight from film."

"You don't care for color?"

"Well mostly black and whites . . . Like this over here." He pointed to another photo of a wide stone path leading through an overgrown forest.

"Wow. That is very nice. The black and white does add something. You definitely have an eye."

"Thank you. Here let me show you around my place. It's small but it works." He motioned to the right and said, "Kitchen . . ." They walked back through the living room and through the short hallway, ". . . and here is the bathroom, and the bedroom is here."

DL stepped aside and allowed her in first. Cynthia placed one foot inside the room and peeked her head in. It was very inviting. The bedding was a fully matching taupe and off white Bed-in-a-Bag type set, and there was a mosquito net style canopy that draped from the ceiling down over the sides of the king-sized bed. His computer was set up on the desk in the corner by the window, and he had Cynthia's picture displayed as the screen saver.

Shocked to see it she softly grabbed his arm, "You're crazy!" It kind of broke the ice.

They sat down on the couch and started to talk. DL's mind began to wander as he thought, "She's too good for me . . . So classy, but still down to earth . . . Does she even realize she's out of my league? I think I actually have butterflies." Overcome by her beauty, he loved her eyes, her dimples, her hair, the cleft in her chin that appeared whenever she smiled. "She's so sexy." The chemistry was almost too much for him to bear. He gazed at her as she talked. Cynthia noticed, "What is it? Why are you looking at me that way?"

He answered, "I'm just trying to figure out what the hell is wrong with your ex!"

She shyly giggled. The physical attraction between them was intense. DL tried his best to appear patient. He asked, "So it's early, you hungry? I skipped breakfast."

"Yea. Let's go get something to eat . . . Oh wait!" Cynthia's eyes widened, and smiling, she leaned over searching through her purse on the floor. DL, still seated next to her on the couch, looked and saw a black thong rising from the back of her jeans as she fished through her purse. His eyebrows scrunched inward and he bit his lower lip as the blood rushed from his brain. He thought, "Damn!"

She sat up and said, "Guess what?"

He shook his head briskly and tried to re-focus. "What's up?"

She held up an envelope in excitement. "I have a fifty dollar gift card to Claim Jumpers."

Eager to get the day going, DL popped up from the couch rubbing his hands together. "Cool, let's go. I've never been there."

As they exited the apartment, his cell phone rang. "Damn! Hold on." He took the call. Then asked, "Babe, do you mind driving so I can drop my truck off with my brother and he can drive himself to his gig?"

"Sure that's fine. So you want me to follow you over there?"

"Yea." He got back on the phone. "Alright man, I'll be there in a minute."

Cynthia hopped in her car and followed. They arrived at Roger's about fifteen minutes later. "Come on up, you can meet my brother."

They entered the small bachelor place and there was a bigger than life poster of Jimi Hendrix on the living room wall and a full bar near the window in the corner. Other than the array of musical equipment scattered about, everything was obsessively neat. DL introduced them and Roger shook her hand.

"Come on in, have a seat."

Cynthia sat on the couch and DL reclined next to her. He leaned back to see if he could sneak another glimpse of that thong. He couldn't seem to take his eyes off of her. His cell rang. He looked at it then shut it off putting it back in his pocket. Cynthia caught that. "If you need to answer your phone, I understand."

"No babe. It's cool. I'm with you." He called out to Roger, "Isn't my girl beautiful?"

Roger stepped out from the bathroom brushing his fade. "Yea, gorgeous . . . Let's have a threesome."

DL jumped at him, "Shut up asshole!"

They wrestled like all of the sudden they were kids again and Cynthia wasn't there. She giggled, then cleared her throat.
". . . AHEM."

They broke apart and straightened out their clothes. DL said, "Alright dude, we'll be at your show later." He dug into his pocket and handed Roger his keys with hesitation. "Man please, please, be VERY careful. Please."

Roger snatched the keys, "Man, I know how to drive. I'm not going to hurt your precious truck!"

They headed for the door. DL looked back worried, "Man please be careful."

Roger pushed him out. "Stop being paranoid. You know I'm not drinking no more. Go have fun with your girl. I'll see you guys later."

DL and Cynthia trotted back down the stairs. She handed him her keys, "You should drive, I don't know my way around here that well."

His face lit up as they got in. "Nice car. What year is this?" He asked while revving the engine.

Cynthia looked nervous. "Thank you. It's a sixty six."

He picked up her cd case and flipped through it. "Let's see . . . Earth, Wind, and Fire, Super 70's, The Commodores, Barry White, Teena Marie. Janet Jackson...." He paused and stared over at her. "Rhythm Nation and Control? These are the newest ones in the case."

She giggled, "What can I say? I like old school. Most new songs don't have the lyrics old ones do. I love the music, the beats."

He popped in Super 70's, AWWWE Freak Out . . "It's cool, we can do old school."

DL revved the engine again then screeched out of the parking lot with full speed abruptly stopping at the corner. Cynthia looked over at him, as if daring him to do that again. "Uh . . . Okay now."

"Oops, sorry. Just testing out the power."

She asked, "You do have a license, right?"

They headed over to Claim Jumpers and parked. DL hopped out and Cynthia sat. He started toward the restaurant then looked back seeing her still in the car. "Damn." He jogged back and opened her door. "Sorry bout that babe. That was rude of me."

She smiled and said, "Naw, it's okay. I was just testing you."

He grabbed her hand. "I hope I passed." He laughed and added, "You're crazy girl. You know that? I gotta stay on my toes."

They went inside and had a delicious leisurely lunch, did a little sightseeing downtown, and then went to see Roger's show at Barry's Nugget, a locals' casino. They listened to music, drank, and mingled. DL was across the room talking with some friends while Cynthia sat in the booth listening to the band, and sipping her Merlot. The band took a break and Roger came over and sat with her.

"So . . . Are you enjoying the show?"

"Yes, yes I am." She smiled and added, "You play the guitar and the crowd very well."

He shrugged his shoulders and spoke like JJ on Good Times: "Well you know . . . What can I say?"

Cynthia smiled. “You’re a little crazy, I see.”

“Yea, just a little. So, where’s my brother?”

“Oh, he just went over there to say hi to some guy.”

Roger looked over and nodded at DL then scooted closer to Cynthia as if to make him jealous putting his arm around her shoulders he leaned in and whispered in her ear, “So you really diggen my brother? Or do I have a chance?”

Cynthia raised her eyebrows and looked over at him. She could see he was kidding and leaned in closer. “Well, sir. If I hadn’t met your brother first . . . Maybe.”

Roger got surprised and his voice went up an octave. “Really?”

Cynthia moved his arm gently from her shoulders. “Uh, nn-no! Sike.”

They laughed and Roger said, “I like you. You’ll be good for my brother.”

“Well, thank you. How long is your break?”

“Oh, bout twenty minutes.”

DL approached. “Man, I hope you ain’t trying to get at my girl.”

“Yep. We’re hookin up later, after we drop you off.”

“Naw, there you go over there.” DL looked toward the entrance and they saw Cecilia entering the lounge.

Roger looked over, “Man, damn! Did you tell her nosy ass I was here? She's just tryin to mess up my game.”

“Naw, that Earth, Wind, and Fire suit you got on el take care of that.” DL responded.

“Shut the hell up.”

Cecilia approached them. “Hey, what’s up?”

Roger popped up. “What’s up babe? I gotta get backstage. I’ll talk to you later.”

DL introduced her: “Hey, Cee. This is my girl, Cynthia. Cynthia, this is Cecilia. Roger’s son’s mother.”

Cynthia held her hand out. “Oh, okay it’s nice to meet you.”

“Thank you. You too.”

DL asked Cecilia, “You want to chill with us?”

“No, I’m cool. I’m heading home in a few. I’m just going to chat with a few people first. I’ll talk to you later.” She walked across the room.

“Babe, I think she’s upset,” DL said. “Let me go talk to her a minute. I’ll be right back. Is that okay?”

“Yea that’s fine. I’ll be right here.”

As Cynthia sat, the band started their next set with The Commodores’ “Brick House.” She felt a stare and saw in the distance a strange looking man glaring over at her from the bar. He was about seven feet tall, and skeletal thin. His skin was like chalk, and he wore all black. Despite the warmth inside the lounge he was draped in a long dark overcoat that dragged along the floor as he sauntered towards her. She thought, “Oh no!” Cynthia looked away hoping he would disappear. Her head spun around the room hoping to find DL. Too late; the peculiar stranger had already sat down across from her and started to speak.

His shoulders were hunched and his head was cocked awkwardly to the side. He said, "Hey baby. I've never seen you here before."

Cynthia's head was in motion still looking around for DL. "Uh, no. No you haven't."

The stranger's odor was of garlic and some sort of drugstore musk. It was so strong she could taste it at the back of her throat. Her head jerked back abruptly and she frowned, cutting her eyes his direction, in an attempt not to stare directly at him. Uncontrollably, she looked anyway, then had to suppress her laughter. She put her hand over her mouth when she noticed his severely receding hairline and the way the back of his hair draped his shoulders in an oily Jerry Curl. "Is he a vampire?" she thought.

He kept his voice low and deep like Barry White. "You alone sweetheart? May I buy you a drink?"

Quickly and nervously, she replied, "No, uh . . . No thank you. My boyfriend is around here somewhere."

Just then she saw DL across the dance floor looking and laughing. Her eyes batted as she looked away in embarrassment. Leaning her head down and tucking one side of her hair behind her ear, she mumbled, "I'm going to get him for this."

"Oh, well, okay baby. But let me give you my card. If you ever want to have some pictures taken, give me a call. I'm a photographer."

She swallowed the lump in her throat while noticing his hands as he placed the card on the table in front of her. His nails were black from bruises, not polish. She thought, "Is he still alive?" Trying not to be rude, she picked up the card and said, "Thank you."

She then dashed from the table and headed toward DL. Her eyes were wide open and she had a silly grin on her face. DL was bowled over in laughter. She smacked his back and laughed. "Ugh! I'll get you back for that one. You were just gonna leave me there, weren't you?"

DL said while still laughing, "No, I was gonna come over. I promise." He hugged her. "I'm sorry, but it was funny. Now we're even. The birthday restaurant thing . . . Remember?"

Cynthia pouted, "Tss. That's not fair. At least you got a free dessert out of it. All I got was a stomach-ache. He stunk."

He kissed her forehead still chuckling, "I'm sorry. Come on let's get out of here. You want to go get some ice cream?"

"Okay . . . And maybe some Tums."

Chapter Nine

When Cynthia and DL arrived back at his place, it was after ten. They fell into the door laughing and chatting like they had been friends for twenty years. Cynthia's mind wouldn't settle down: "I can't believe how much I like him. I never felt this way with Darren. He's so funny and sweet . . . But should I be here? Maybe it's too soon . . . Ugh! Just relax, relax."

Cynthia collapsed on the couch. "Do you mind if I take my shoes off?"

DL called back from the kitchen. "No go ahead babe. Would you like something to drink?"

"Uh yea, some water would be nice." She leaned forward and picked up the case of cd's under the glass coffee table. "Let me see what he's got. Nas, Tupac, Jay-Z, Xzibit." She paused and flipped one over reading the case,

"Parental advisory. Contains explicit lyrics . . ."

DL walked over handing her the glass. "I hope tap is okay? I don't really drink water."

She sipped. "This is fine, thanks. Just checking out your music collection."

He chuckled. "Uh . . .Yea, we don't want to listen to those right now."

He opened the cabinet below his TV where he kept a large collection of dvd's, "Want to watch a movie? I have a lot of comedy."

"Yea, let's watch something funny."

He popped a movie in and plopped down next to her. "Are you comfortable? Do you need anything?"

"I'm perfect. It's sweet, but you don't have to make a fuss. I like your brother. He's funny."

He responded, "Yea. Hilarious."

"You guys seem to be really close. That's good."

"Yea. He gets on my nerves, but I love him."

"Are him and Cecilia still together?"

"Ha! I don't know what they call it. They've been on and off for like eight years."

"Wow, no wonder she looked upset."

"Yea, I don't know what my brother's doing. Anyway, let's watch the movie."

DL put his arm around Cynthia's shoulders and they got cozy. She scooted over and laid her feet across his lap and he massaged them. "Your feet are so cute babe."

She smiled, "Thank you."

"I'm having a really good time with you. I'm glad you came up to see me. I wish I could see you more often."

"I'm having a good time with you too."

“I like you, Cynthia. I like that we vibe the way we do.”

“Yea, it’s weird huh?”

He agreed. “It is. We can talk about anything. I dig that.”

“What do you mean?”

“Like when we’re on the phone, the conversation just flows. You memorize funny lines from TV shows and movies and repeat em all the time. I thought I was the only one that knew the Friday movie word for word.”

She laughed, “I love that movie.”

“I know. My ex-wife hated it.”

“Really?”

DL went on, “Yea. I just feel like I can be myself around you cause you're so real....I've never had a conversation with a woman that comes so fluid. Even stuff I feel bad about I can tell you, and you say things to make me feel better.”

Cynthia said, “Well I try not to judge. We've all made mistakes. We all have regrets.”

“See? Like that. It’s cool you understand that.

“You’re being so sweet D.”

“Thank you..... I just think it’s so rare that you meet someone you’ve only known for weeks, but it feels like you’ve known them forever. You’re just what I needed right now, Cynthia. Most of the women I’ve come across lately are so temperamental. I feel so comfortable with you.”

"Thank you D. I love that you can tell me what you feel so easily."

"I do?"

"Yea, you do."

He asked, "Can I tell you something else?"

"Sure."

DL moved closer and lowered his voice speaking softly. "You're really special to me Cynthia." He pecked her lips gently.

She answered, "You're special to me too."

"Can I say one more thing?"

"Yes."

"That celibacy thing is kinda deep."

Slowly DL leaned toward her and kissed her lips for the first time. Unable to resist Cynthia kissed him back. Electric currents exchanged in seconds. He sat back and watched the television. He thought, "YES! She's feelin me."

Cynthia was nervous, trying to deny it; she felt what was coming. About halfway through the movie she excused herself to the bathroom.

While she was in there, DL ejected the movie and scurried into the bedroom. He quickly turned the dimmer switch on the lights, then hesitated thinking, "What if she gets mad?" Then folding back the covers, he heard the bathroom door open . . .

While in the bathroom Cynthia looked in the mirror and contemplated the night. She brushed her teeth and dabbed on lip gloss. "I shouldn't be here . . . Huh! Just relax." She could almost see a little devil on her left shoulder and a little angel on her right one. Her anxiety was building; she took a deep breath and came out. DL reached for her hand and gently guided her into the bedroom.

Cynthia looked up into his eyes as if she could read his mind and said, "Remember you said you would be a gentleman."

"I know, I will. I just think we'll be more comfortable in here." He looked at her and smiled. "I'll be good. I promise."

She walked ahead of him and mumbled. "That's what I'm afraid of."

He looked over at her. "What? Did you say something?"

She quickly replied, "Uh . . . No."

DL smiled and it made her feel weak. "Oh, he must have cutest smile in the world." she thought. As she got comfortable, he went to the bathroom.

Cynthia got under the comforter, but being nervous she purposely laid on top of the flat sheet, all the while wondering what she was doing. DL returned to the room, laid down, then scooted up behind her. He realized the sheet was separating them. "What the hell?"

She looked back and giggled.

"You're crazy, girl."

His dimples ignited her heart. He gestured to turn on the TV and put the movie back in, but Sanford and Son was on TV Land.

Cynthia popped up. "Oh, wait. I love this show." She lay back down and they spooned.

She could feel his body pressed against hers. The thump of his heart pounded against her back; hers began to beat faster than normal. He leaned over and kissed her cheek and it burned like fire. "Is this too soon?" she thought. But impulsively she turned her head and their lips came together like magnets. Softly and slowly, they engaged in a long passionate kiss. Her heart could not take this pace.

Cynthia turned over and DL brought her body closer to his. Far from the apprehension she felt, he burned with anticipation. Inside he screamed, "YAY!" All of the sudden, they heard the raspy voice of Fred Sanford say, "You big dummy!" They stopped and laughed. DL reached back for the remote and clicked off the TV.

They began again. His heart pounded rapidly like a drum. He thought, "Why does she feel so damn good, so familiar, like we've been here before?" Cynthia turned over on her side facing him and he moved even closer. He pulled back the sheet between them, gently embracing her waistline and patiently, as if they had a lifetime, he kissed her neck, her lips. His hands began to explore her body. He lifted her blouse and she let him.

"Oh, my goodness! Double d's!" he said in his mind. He leaned down and caressed them, kissed them.

She whispered, "I'm scared."

He paused in her ear. "Me too." He asked, "Do you want me to stop?"

In a sigh of relief she answered, "No."

He moved his body gently over hers. He stroked her hair and lifted her head up to his, their tongues met and their lips touched in breathless passion. There was no past, there was no future, they were locked in time. He used his fingers to trace the lining of her panties and guided them to the floor. His embrace calmed her in a way she had never felt before and she lost all inhibition. He touched her body as though he were blind, trying to find his way around every curve.

They pulled his shirt from his body; in lust, she used her tongue to taste his chest. Her soft skin felt pleasant against him. He kissed every inch of her, starting with her neck, then her shoulders, tasting her breast, her stomach, and slowly finding his way between her thighs. She felt the pleasure of his tongue inside of her. She tried to hold back but could not. She arched her back in complete pleasure, and the moonlight shining through the window shadowed her silhouette like a portrait no artist could capture.

He stopped just before she could climax. He positioned his body over hers. Then she remembered, “A condom, put on a condom.”

He thought, “Damn!” But said, “Okay.”

He rolled over briefly and came right back. With his tender lips pressed against hers, he put himself inside of her, and she received him like a dying woman accepting healing. Their bodies came together like the ocean and sky in a beautiful beach sunset. Like waves and water, they became one in movement, and she was pleased by his size. She massaged his back with her hands, reading every muscle with her fingertips. She pulled him in closer, deeper. Unable to resist the strength of his thrusts, her hips gave in to the rhythm as they created their own symphony.

Cynthia’s eyes closed, she could feel his breath on her neck. DL inhaled her delicate scent. It affected him like a sedative, and she felt as soft as fine silk.

He lifted his head and looked at her face, he was weakened by the connection he felt. He thought, "I don't deserve this." Her eyes opened and met his. She held on as if for her life not letting go. Moans of passion fell from her lips.

In his ear she whispered, "Oh . . . Oh . . . DL . . . I'm cumming."

Her sultry voice pushed him into complete ecstasy and he released control. They climaxed at the same time, the first time. He lay there one with her unable to move, paralyzed by her love. They slept.

Cynthia opened her eyes and saw that an hour had passed. She kissed his cheek and in his ear softly said, "I'll be right back."

He turned on his back and watched her walk away. He admired her feminine physique, and called out, "Must be jelly, must be jelly." She crawled back into bed, and nestled up close to him.

Her head on his chest, his masculine scent aroused her and she started to kiss his pecs. He could not resist her and he didn't want to. They started all over again, and again, and again . . .

When the sun rose she counted seven sessions, and multiple orgasms. They kissed and he looked into her eyes. He said, "What did you do to me? When I was inside you, I felt like I was home." She smiled innocently. He held her closely in his arms while they slept.

When Cynthia awoke again, she was alone. She looked over at the clock: 9:34 a.m. Her limbs weak from complete satisfaction. Her heart, body, and mind were one as she thought, "I didn't even feel like this on my honeymoon."

There was a pleasant smell floating in the room, she freshened up and went into the kitchen. DL was cooking bacon and eggs and there was a fresh pot of coffee brewed. Putting the spatula down he reached for her. He put both arms around her waist, pulled her close and kissed her on the forehead. He looked at her, and saw a sparkle in her eyes that gave him goosebumps, like a young boy with a crush.

With a huge smile he said, “You fooled me, I thought you were worried about what I might do, you were worried about what you would do. Damn. You’re insatiable.” They kissed again. She looked up into his handsome face and said, “Thank you.”

“For what?”

“For being such a perfect gentleman.”

He grinned a devilish grin and kissed her again. “I told you I would be.”

When she left, DL’s condition, his mindset, his thoughts about relationships were not the same. Somehow this was different. He knew it. It was raining, and he lay in bed that Sunday afternoon still feeling Cynthia, smelling her. Desiring her to come back.

Chapter Ten

Cynthia drove home trying not to be distracted by the experience. She had been away from the dating scene for so long and didn't want to be disillusioned. When she arrived home, she wanted to call DL but instead she decided to call Carla.

Carla answered, "Hello."

"Hey girl. It's me. Whew."

"What girl? What? What?"

"We did it."

Carla screamed, "Oh shit, girl, tell me all about it! Was he good?"

Cynthia started to talk like she was exploding, "Oh my goodness! I don't even know where to begin. He was incredible! Seven times, we did it seven times."

Carla asked, "What? In two days?"

"No girl, in one night!"

"Damn! Superman. When did you get home?"

"About twenty minutes ago. Why?"

"You didn't call him yet, did you?"

"No. I was, but I called you first."

"Good. Good. Don't call him. Let him call you first."

"What? Girl, you know I'm not good at playing games. I just didn't call him cause I needed to think some first."

"Just trust me okay? Let him call you. So what happened? I want to know everything. You didn't think about Darren at all?"

Cynthia laughed, "What? Girl, please. No."

Carla giggled. "Well, I know the first man I was with after leaving Donald was hard for me."

"Well, maybe Donald was a good lover. You know I never felt close to Darren. I always felt like I was giving one hundred twenty percent and he was giving like ten. Now that my head is a little clearer, I don't even think he loved me . . . Plus, Darren always seemed rushed when we made love. I was always so uncomfortable. He seemed so freakin frustrated all the time."

"Oh yea! You told me about that."

"You know, I could never hardly ever, well uh . . . Finish with him."

"Ha! That's right! You told me you could count how many you had in ten years. Like ten?"

Cynthia laughed, "Ha! Ten? No! It was two . . . Two times in ten years."

"Girrrl, among all the other reasons you should have left him, he wasn't even a good lover? Why did you put up with him so long?"

"I don't know. I don't think it was that he was a bad lover. I just couldn't trust him. So I couldn't connect on that level."

"Whatever. Anyway enough about Darren. Tell me about DL."

"Carla, everything came together so naturally. I felt so relaxed. It's hard for me to even explain."

"Girl, just tell me."

"Okay. It was almost nostalgic. Like going back to your home-town after being away for several years and feeling comforted by all the things you've missed. Kinda like that."

"Wow. Really?"

"Like at one point our eyes met and it felt like he could see right through to my soul and I could see his."

"I know exactly what you mean."

"You do? Cause I don't think I've ever felt this before. But I don't want to be naive. I really think it's too soon for me to get involved with someone right now. What if he doesn't feel the same?"

"Cynthia, you worry too much. Just take one day at a time."

"Carla, you know no man has ever been faithful to me. I'm finally getting out of that crazy marriage. I could end up hurt all over again. I don't know if I could handle that right now."

"You don't have to handle that right now. DL just screwed your brains out, and right now you feel like a queen. You had more orgasms in one night than you had in ten years. All you need to do, right now, is bask in the afterglow. Shit."

They both laughed aloud.

Cynthia asked, "How are we friends? You're such a devil."

"You need me. If it weren't for me, you'd probably be living in a convent somewhere."

"I know. That's why I feel a little guilty. I really like him, but I'm struggling with my morality."

They were on the phone for over an hour when Cynthia heard her other line beep. "Wait a minute, hold on Carla. I have another call." She looked at the display. "It's DL. Let me call you back."

"Girl, call me back!"

Cynthia clicked over to answer trying not to disclose her excitement. "Hello."

"Oh good baby, you're home. I can't stop thinking about you. I can't even wash my sheets."

She giggled. "Uh, why?"

"Because they smell like you."

"You're so crazy."

"I even just spent the last thirty minutes writing a blog about you online."

Cynthia laughed, "You did?"

He became serious. "Can I ask you something?'

"Absolutely."

"I wanted to know how you felt about it just being me and you?"

Cynthia paused, taken aback, not really expecting that. Over the last couple of months, she'd told DL all the struggles in her marriage.

She replied, "I like you, I really do. This weekend was wonderful, but I'm afraid of this."

He asked, "Why?"

"Last night, when we were together I said I was scared and you did too. I know what I meant, but what did you mean?"

He answered, "I guess I know how quickly these things can go bad. We seem to get along so well. I was kinda thinking that if we slept together I might lose you as a friend."

"Yea, me too."

"But I really want to be with you, Cynthia."

Her voice weakened; she couldn't help but consider the past. "D, you know how my ex was. He lied so much, it's hard for me to trust any man. Every guy I've been with has lied and cheated. I can't go through that again."

DL was calm and sincere. "Baby, I know you've been hurt, but I also know what we have is rare. I mean, I like you. The women I've been with before, I didn't feel like this. I like being with you, joking with you, talking to you, and now I know the sex is out of this world . . ." Without breaking his sentence and with excitement he continued on, ". . . but it's not just the sex. You're smart and funny, you work hard, and you're so beautiful. I want to be with you and I promise, I won't mess up." He spoke confidently and with passion.

Cynthia sat on the edge of her bed, and she could feel her anxiety worsening. But she also yearned so badly for this to be real. "I want to believe you, with all my heart I do. But how do I know what you're saying is true and genuine?"

"All you can do is allow me the chance to show you."

She asked in insecurity, "But we live so far from each other. How will that work? You'll want to see other women, I'm sure."

"Babe please, you're it. You have all I need. I can wait a few weeks in between."

"And you promise you won't lie and cheat?"

"I promise."

"And if later on down the road, you find that you have a change of heart you'll tell me? You won't just ignore me and act like I don't exist?"

"Baby, that will never happen. I promise."

Cynthia felt as though she were climbing out on the limb of a huge redwood tree, with no safety net underneath. But her feelings had become so strong that she had to follow them. She decided to trust him and took him at his word.

"Alright."

"So, it's me and you?"

"It is."

He cheered, "YAY!"

When they got off the phone, Cynthia logged on to her computer to read DL's blog spot. It read:

"*Thank you Cynthia.........*
I had someone tell me this weekend that I was a special person. That means a lot coming from her, because I know that she would be with me through thick and thin. We can discuss anything and everything and I can be myself. She's such a beautiful friend and that's just what I needed right now. Thank you, Cynthia."

Chapter Eleven

It was Wednesday, and Cynthia needed to pick up the kids from Darren's house. Usually she would pick them up from school, but she had gotten off from work late. She pulled up to the house thinking, "Ugh, I do not feel like dealing with this man." As she walked up the stone path to the door, she looked around in frustration noticing the fields of weeds that had grown up through the rocks of the once lovely desert landscaping. She knocked. Darren opened the door smiling. "Come in, the kids are getting their stuff."

Cynthia stepped through the door and stood in the foyer. It felt odd not living there. They had just bought the house a year and a half earlier, brand new. It had high vaulted ceilings, granite counter tops, and ceramic tile floors, and an awesome custom-built fireplace and mantel accented the great room. She had been gone about five months now and it looked so drab. The walls needed to be cleaned. The great room and kitchen were a mess. There was a bad smell, and from the looks of the kids, the laundry hadn't been done.

The children ran up to her. "Mommy!"

Cynthia opened her arms and leaned down to hug them. "Hey guys. I miss you so much!" They kissed repeatedly. "Okay. Grab your stuff, let's go."

The kids ran back to the room. Cynthia looked over at Darren in the kitchen. He was never a small man but he had gained more weight. He stood at about five foot ten, 240 lbs, and had a football player build. He kept his head bald and was growing in a beard.

He walked over towards her drying his hands with a kitchen towel and asked, "So how was your little weekend trip?" She ignored him.

He moved closer and peered at her as if he could smell another man. Throughout the marriage Cynthia had always been faithful. Even when they had separated before, the thought of another man never crossed her mind. It was as though Darren sensed it, like a bloodhound. Cynthia was a horrible pretender and couldn't lie.

He asked with disappointment, "Cynthia, are you seeing somebody?" He looked confused; he thought she would eventually come back to him, that she wouldn't go through with the divorce. His dark eyes were piercing and Cynthia fumbled through her purse pretending to look for something.

"Why do you care?"

He could read her face like an open book, she would not quite look him in the eye. "Honey, are you seeing somebody?'

He moved even closer touching her wrist with one hand and lifting her chin up with the other, trying to look into her eyes. Cynthia's head hung and her eyes locked in on the hand touching her wrist. His skin was like a raven's and contrasted hers so drastically. She used to love the look of that, now feeling his touch repulsed her and she pushed his hand away.

"Actually, yes. I have met someone. Obviously, you have too."

"Naw, she's just my friend."

"Ha. Whatever. I don't even care . . . Summer! Lil D!"

He asked, "So . . . Is it serious?"

She saw a look of pain and anger come over his face. He just stood there motionless, in awe. Not sure of what he might do, she wanted to get out of there. “Lil D! Summer! Let’s go!”
Cynthia scurried them to the car. Darren called out to her as she pulled away. “Cynthia! Honey, please . . . Wait!” He tore back through the house to the garage, then jumped into his car speeding after her.

Cynthia parked in the driveway outside her apartment. It was evening and it was cold. The valley wind had come up and was blowing about forty miles per hour through the open walk ways of the apartments. She handed Lil Darren the key. “Hurry. Go inside guys and get ready for bed.”

She stood outside near the edge of the walkway with her arms wrapped around herself, withstanding the force of the wind. Darren parked and got out of his car, the back of his long black coat was blowing upward as he walked toward her. Cynthia spoke loudly trying to speak over the howls of the wind. “Why did you follow me?”

“Honey please, we’re not over!” The stress of losing her was all over his face.

“What Darren? Be real with yourself. You have never been faithful to me and you’re abusive. Did you honestly think I’d live like that forever?” She felt her courage building.

“You weren’t abused.” He would always say that.

A look of perplexity was on her face. “You have beat me, you have slapped me, cursed me, pushed me, spit on my face. That’s not abuse?”

“You act like it happened every day.” he responded.

“Just cause it was two or three times a year, that makes it okay?”

Just then the wind caught more strength. The trees surrounding the building were leaning, a strong gust tore through one of them breaking off a heavy branch. It blew past the two of them striking the neighbors door. They jumped. Cynthia headed toward her front door.

Darren shouted, "You can't divorce me, Cynthia. We're Christian."

She shouted back, "Have you lost your mind? You know what? It's cold and dangerous out here. I'm not having this argument with you anymore. I'm Done! Leave!"

A feeling of strength that she never had with him came over her. Darren moved in front of her door and blocked it. "Who's gonna want you Cynthia, with three kids? Plus, you're . . ."

"Plus what? Plus I'm what? What can you say? I was nothing but a good wife to you, Darren. What have I ever done?"

"You're arrogant, Cynthia. You think you're better than me."

"What? That's it? That's why all the cheating, lying, and abuse? You're crazy. Move away from my door!"

She noticed that his fists were tightly in a ball and he was shaking. He lowered his voice and looked intently into her eyes.

He scowled, "If I can't have you Cynthia, nobody will!"

She saw a demon behind his eyes, but glared right back at him. She held her cell phone up. "You move! And you leave, or I will call the police. I swear, you won't hurt me again without consequences. LEAVE!"

As Darren stood there breathing heavily, Cynthia could see the simmer of his pain and anger about to boil over into an uncontrollable rage. Her fear was taken over by determination and she did not look away. She raised her cell and pushed the nine and the one. "I just need to push one more button." He stepped away from the door, paused, then left.

Cynthia blew inside the apartment and shut the door. She quickly locked it and leaned against it. Her heart was racing, and she was unsure if he would stand behind that threat. He worked as a probation officer for the county they lived in. She thought, "Surely he won't do something to jeopardize his job." But she never knew what he may or may not do. Trying to figure that out was like trying to figure out when an earthquake would hit or where a tornado might land.

Immediately, Cynthia checked on the kids. She knew they had heard some of that argument and reassured them that everything was fine. "They've been through enough." she thought. She took a shower and felt her heart beating in panic, like it did whenever she and Darren had fought in the past. Life with him had been a horrible, endless roller coaster ride and she wanted off. She prayed as she lay in bed in the dark.

"God, please forgive me. I know I don't always make the choices I should. I fail every day, but please help me, and protect me. Please keep us safe." She turned and a tear rolled down her cheek. "I'm so tired."

Cynthia tried to sleep but she was afraid. She got up and checked that her doors and windows were all locked. Summer called out to her from her bed.

"Mommy."

She cracked her bedroom door and peeked in. "Yes, sweetpea?"

"Is Daddy still mad?"

She walked over and sat down on the edge of the bed. "Maybe sweetie, but he's over at his house so we won't worry about that tonight. Okay."

Summer started to cry. "But I don't like when you guys fight."

Cynthia held her closely. "Oh baby, I know. Mommy's not going to fight with Daddy anymore. Okay."

She kissed her forehead and held her, singing a lullaby until she fell asleep. When she stepped out of Summer's room she peeked in to check on Lil Darren and saw he was up. "You okay mister?"

"Yea."

"You sure?"

"Yea."

"You know if you need to talk or if you have any questions you can ask me, okay."

"Okay."

Cynthia turned to leave and he stopped her. "Mom Why is Dad always mad?"

Cynthia went over and sat on the chair at his desk. "I don't know baby. Maybe one day he'll get some help. But it's important that you know none of this is because of you or your sister, okay. We both love you very much." She looked into his eyes, brown and watery.

"Do you think you guys will get back together?"

Sadly Cynthia answered, "No baby, I don't think so."

"Will you marry somebody else?"

"Oh, I don't know . . . I don't know."

"Will your last name stay the same as us, or will you change it?"

"What do you want?"

"Well . . ."

"It's okay, what?"

"Can you leave it the same as us?"

"Okay mister. I will."

"Dad told me this was all his fault. He told me that he wasn't a good husband to you and he told me not to do the things he did. He said that he was very sorry."

"Well, I'm glad he admits that. But don't worry about Daddy, he knows how to get help if he wants it. You just always be the good boy you are. Those are grown-up things, you just have fun being a kid, okay?" She patted the top of his head. "You okay?"

"If he's sorry, can't you get back together?"

"Oh baby, sometimes grown-up things aren't that simple. I wish they were, but they're just not. I promise you'll understand better when you're older. But just trust Mom for now, okay?"

Lil Darren was trying not to cry and his voice cracked. "Daddy prayed with me and Summer that you would move back home."

Cynthia was infuriated inside by that. She thought, "He's such a bastard." But was careful not to show her anger. "He did, huh? Well baby, then Daddy understands that God allows some things, and some things God does not allow. If he's praying then he knows that he has done some things that God does not allow. And when you do that, even though God will always love you, you have to face the results or consequences for what you've done. Like if you steal something from a store and get caught by the police. You might be sorry but you still have to go to jail. Does that make sense?"

"Yea, I understand."

Cynthia went over and hugged him. "You sure?"

"Yea. I do."

"Everything will be okay, I promise."

"I know. Love you Mom."

"I love you too mister. You get some sleep. But anytime you have questions you can ask me, Okay?"

"Okay." He smiled.

"Goodnight."

Cynthia went back to her room and the phone rang. It was DL. She answered and told him what happened. "Baby, I'm really tired. Do you mind if we talk more tomorrow?"

“You sure you’re okay? I wish I was there with you.”

“I wish you were too. But I’m fine, I just need to rest. I’ll call you if anything else happens.”

“Baby please do. Goodnight.

Chapter Twelve

Cynthia climbed back into bed and clicked off the lamp. She lay there, her mind drifting back against her will. It had been nearly ten years since that first incident, but it stayed in her mind like it was only yesterday. No matter how hard she would try to forget, it remained.

It was a Friday and both she and Darren had the day off of work. Darren had left in the morning and was gone all day. He came back home about six in the evening only to shower and get dressed to leave again. Already insecure because he had done this so often, Cynthia started to question him and that led to an argument in the hallway. Their voices escalated.

"Where you been all day?" she asked.

"None of your business Cynthia. Leave me the hell alone!"

"It is my business! I'm your wife. Where are you going?"

"Leave me alone, Cynthia!"

Cynthia, suspicious that he was with another woman insisted: "No! Where?"

Darren's anger possessed him like an evil spirit. Lifting his fist, he punched her in the face and her body slammed against the wall like a rag doll. Her vision went black. He grabbed her by the arms, throwing her to the ground. He stood beside her and kicked her repeatedly, cursing and screaming. Cynthia struggled to break free, her eyesight returning in a blurred state. The force of his foot pounding against her side stung like a heavy whip. He lifted her and shook her, then slammed her back to the floor. Against his strength she was powerless.

He ran to the kitchen. Her back in pain, she tried to flip over and crawl into the bedroom and lock the door. Before she could, he grabbed her by the shirt and threw her over onto her back again. He knelt over her and held a large butcher knife to her neck. She could almost still feel his saliva dripping onto her face as he yelled violently, "If you ever fuckin make me this mad again, I'll kill you!"

Cynthia thought she was going to die that night, and tonight those words exploded in her mind like a bomb as she reflected on the look on Darren's face when he left her apartment earlier. The fear she felt at his hands was far more incredible than being attacked by any stranger in the street.

She turned on the TV hoping to drown out the voices, the screaming, those memories that often tormented her at night. It didn't work; she tossed and turned. Relentlessly, the past kept flashing through her mind like lightening bolts. She clicked the lamp back on, leaned over, and searched through the drawer of her night stand for her journal. Sometimes writing helped to get things off of her mind. She found an older journal and started to read it:

Saturday January 2,
Darren and I had another fight today. He was mad because I spent money to join a weight loss program. I'm only about 155 pounds, but he thinks I'm fat. I thought rather than argue I'd do whatever I could to lose weight. He got so upset when I told him how much it cost that he spit in my face and threw me out of the car......

Cynthia stopped reading and remembered that day. Darren pulled the car over to the curb and screamed, "You're so stupid! Why would you spend money on that?"

"It was a hundred and fifty dollars, and I know I'll lose weight." He reached across her lap opening the car door, he hacked up mucus and spit it directly onto Cynthia's face, then pushed her.

"Bitch, get out."

Cynthia fell out of the car and feeling embarrassed, she got up from the ground quickly, using her blouse to wipe off her face, then started to walk home. Unable to stop crying, she walked through a small park and found a bench and sat for a while. Nearly thirty minutes later Darren pulled up beside her, his face covered in tears. He hopped out and got on his knees. "Honey, I'm so sorry. I can't believe I did that. Please forgive me! Please . . ."

"God, I'm so tired, my heart feels like it's bleeding from all of this pain, it hurts so much." Cynthia popped up from bed and grabbed a box of tissue off of the dresser. They were not enough. She got a bath towel from the linen closet. She sat up in her bed, and in the fetal position, she sobbed into the towel to muffle her cry. "Why was he always so unhappy? No matter how hard I tried."

She recalled a time when they were at church and they had been arguing all morning because he had come in at four that morning. He'd gotten so angry he threatened to hit her in the back of the room, then moments later went up to the stage and sang a song for communion. Her mind felt scrambled as she recalled memory after memory. "The few times he did seem happy he was apologizing for being angry so much. Huh! Just madness."

Giving up on rest, she found more journals she'd kept throughout the years and continued reading through them. "God, I feel so stupid, so defeated. Why didn't I ever have him arrested?"

Confusing God's definition of submission with her own, she had tolerated far too much. "I never even cursed at him, or called him out of his name. He cursed me out all the time." The insults echoed in her mind. "All those names calling me stupid, bitch, fat. Why did I let it go on so long?" She looked in the mirror, "I'm not even fat; he's crazy."

Moment after moment, hour after hour as she read her own words, the memories flooded her mind like raging waters. She'd lived it, but somehow reading the experiences on paper this way brought the pain back to the surface and she realized clearly for the first time how insane her life with him was.

She got up from the bed and paced. Still holding on to the journal, studying each day, each year of her life with him, flipping the pages one by one. Reading of incidences that she was struck and belittled in front of her children. Her self esteem and confidence had been chipped away with each chapter:

Wednesday June 18,
Another argument again today. Darren said he would go to Carla's wedding with me, but instead he made plans with his friends. I couldn't understand that. We've been planning on going to this wedding today for months. He got on the phone and made sure I heard him canceling his plans, telling his friend that I was trippin. So I told him to forget it, to go with his friends. As I walked by him, he grabbed the big glass vase by the kitchen, the one I keep the eucalyptus plants in. He held it up over my head with one hand and held on to my shirt with the other. That glass is about an inch thick. I begged but he wouldn't let go of me. Lil Darren and Summer watched in fear as he threatened to bash it over my head. I yelled for the kids to leave the room and pleaded for him to stop. As they scurried past us, he let go of me and grabbed Lil Darren, and commanded him, "No, you stay and watch. I want you to know how you treat a bitch when she gets out of line." God, he's only six! I pray he forgets this . . ."

Cynthia paused, still sobbing. She looked up from the journal and thought about the look on Anthony's face when finally, at about age thirteen he'd tried to break them apart. Then at age fifteen he took a swing at Darren punching him in the jaw. Being that Anthony was his stepson, Darren always seemed to have a coldness toward him. Darren screamed at Cynthia, "Either he goes or I go!" Cynthia ran into the bathroom not knowing how to handle that. She still felt cowardice thinking about it. "I should have thrown him out then." she thought. Instead, Anthony left and moved in with her brother. She's yet to know how much this cycle of abuse has affected his life.

Reading on, Cynthia envisioned the other women Darren had been with, and wondered if they were some how better, or more beautiful. All of her life she had been a strong woman and she turned the page, reading of the night her spirit finally broke:

Tuesday September 14,
Lord, three days ago I listened to the messages on Darren's cell phone. I don't know if that was stupid or smart. But I couldn't believe what I heard. Her voice was soft and sexy. "Hi Darren. It's me. I guess I missed you. Call me later tonight. I miss you. I love you." I confronted him with the message God. I screamed at him to move out. When he left, my body was shaking like I had a cold chill. I haven't been able to eat, and I've already lost almost fifteen pounds in just a few days. I'm sorry about last night Lord. That was dumb. My sorrow has become so unbearable. I don't think I really want to die, but I took the pills because the pain and anguish are so unrelenting. I just want to escape it somehow. My mind is in absolute turmoil, Lord. My heart is so broken. I was afraid that I wouldn't wake up today. I know it's only by your mercy that I did. I'm so sorry. I wish I could just check into a hospital for a few weeks . . .

Cynthia carried the burden of his childhood. She knew that Darren had been so abusive to her because of the abuse he suffered in his own life as a child. For so many years, she allowed that to be an excuse for what he inflicted upon her. The pain in her heart was overwhelming and the tears flowed from her eyes like blood from a gunshot wound. She prayed that someday she would never have to feel this agony again. She closed the journals and put them away. She cried out for peace, for rest, but it never came that night.

About six in the morning, only by the strength of God was she able to pull her body out of bed and get ready for work. She looked in the mirror, trying to figure out how she could hide the puffiness under her eyes, and if she did, would she be able to hide the misery in them. "At least I'm not living in it anymore." After she showered and dressed, she woke the children. Seven thirty, they headed out for the day.

When Cynthia got home from work that evening, there were two dozen red roses in a crystal vase on her dining room table. "Oh my goodness!" She read the card, they were from Darren "How in the world did he get in here?" She was frightened and upset. Just as she was looking for the phone it rang. It was him. She answered, "Hello?"

"Hey hun. Did you get your flowers?"

"How did you get in my house when I wasn't here?"

"What? Don't I get a thank you?"

"Don't you ever come in my house when I'm not here, Darren!"

"Calm down honey, your mom let me in."

"Well, I'll just have to talk to her. I don't want these flowers. Don't do anything else for me! We have the kids and that's it, nothing else!" She hung up.

Twenty minutes later there was a knock at the door. She saw it was Darren and cautiously answered, "What is it?"

He said, "I just wanted to say hi to the kids. I tried to call you back."

Cynthia called out to the kids. "Guys, Daddy's here." She turned back around and told him, "You can stay for ten minutes."

The kids scurried to the door and visited with him while she sat over in the dining area and held on to the phone. A few moments later, Summer came over and said, "Mommy, Daddy wants you." Cynthia walked toward the front door making sure to keep the phone close.

"What is it?"

He was holding a folder, the type used to turn in a book report.

She repeated, "What is it?"

His eyes were open wide and welling up, and his voice was low and calm.

"Please, can we talk?"

With reluctance, she said, "Alright, out here on the patio."

They walked through the living room. Cynthia slid back the glass door and pulled out the folding patio chairs. The night desert sky was black and so clear that every star was visible. They sat. Cynthia was obviously uncomfortable. "What is it? I don't have a lot of time."

Darren started to explain. "Uh, I've been seeing a doctor, and he wrote me a diagnosis. I'd like you to read it."
She became concerned. "Are you sick?"

He handed her the folder. She opened it and started to read with an intense look. Then her face changed and she frowned in confusion.

It read something like . . .

To whom it may concern:

I have been seeing Darren Wilson in psychiatric sessions, twice a week for the last three weeks. I have diagnosed his condition as bipolar. He also suffers from escalated testosterone levels. These conditions may cause sudden mood swings, irritation, and uncontrollable anger. He has been given a prescription and upon taking it his behavior should change considerably.

Regards, Dr. such and such . . .

Cynthia was puzzled, her voice went up an octave. "Why did you bring me this? It sounds like you had the doctor write you a note excusing you from school or work. You want this to excuse you from the last eleven years?"

Darren was hunched over in the chair as she read, and looked up at her as if to solicit sympathy. "I wanted you to know that I'm seeing a doctor. That I'm getting help."

She stood and replied, "Well, that's good. I'm glad you're seeing a doctor. But how many times have you done that before? I think at least three. And every time I believe you, you stop. I'm done Darren."

"But I'm serious this time, Cynthia. I promise."

"You promise? Ha, your promises have been broken way too many times. I'm done. You have to see a doctor for you, not for me." Cynthia saw he was sweating and the look of desperation he showed made her uneasy.

"Please stop pursuing me, Darren. We have the kids to talk about, that's it. The way you're acting makes me nervous. I hope you continue to get help. But as for us, I've had enough. I won't do this to myself anymore."

He responded, "Alright. I understand."

She escorted him to the door and said goodnight. He kissed the kids and left. She thought, "Did he actually think that three weeks of therapy and a doctor's note were going to excuse the hell he's taken me through?"

She grabbed her phone and called Mona. She wanted her to know what had been going on the last couple of days so she could be aware if Darren did something stupid. A little later DL called and they talked for a while, he was always so encouraging and supportive.

She told him, "Babe, you're so sweet. You're just perfect."

He replied. "No, I'm not perfect."

"Perfect for me . . . Babe, I'm so drained. I think I'm gonna turn in early."

"Alright baby, sleep tight."

Chapter Thirteen

Nearly seven o'clock that same evening, DL had the night off. He didn't have to take Roger anywhere and was actually refreshed by the fact that he had nothing to do. He went into the kitchen and poured a bowl of Captain Crunch Berries with no milk and sat in front of the TV eating it like popcorn. His home phone rang, he ignored it. Then his cell rang, it was Leslie. He answered, "Hello."

"Baby, where have you been? I haven't heard from you."

His response was uncaring, "Just been busy."

She asked with desperation, "What are you up to? Can we hang out?"

"Uh, let me call you back."

"Are you going to call me back?"

"Yea. I will."

"Alright bye."

DL hung up and tossed the phone down on the couch. He couldn't even answer for himself why he kept these women around him. He really didn't know anymore. He knew he didn't care for them like they thought he did, or the way they deserved. On the surface he was a player, but truly inside that wasn't what he desired anymore, but it seemed out of his control.

He picked up a small framed photo he had of his parents on the end table next to his couch. Overcome with grief, he tried to hold back tears as he gazed into his mother's eyes. But like a heavy rain down a glass window, they flowed down his cheeks anyway. She was so lovely and he missed her terribly. He was very close to her growing up.

He was the baby and she had gotten pregnant with him while she was still on birth control pills. So she always called him her little miracle, her special gift from God. He thought about the way his father treated her and his heart filled with stressing pain. He reflected on what a beautiful person she was, how hardworking and dedicated she had been to their family, and how his father was never faithful to her. He and his brothers all knew about it. He knew the undeserving agony she'd lived in because of it. Although it distressed him, he thought about the two broken marriages he now had under his belt. He seemed to be walking the same path with women his father chose, and he hated to think about it.

He glared at his father and his mind was strained by the bad memories. He could feel the spirit of hostile animosity seeping through his being like a serpent slithering toward its prey. The almost daily beatings his father had inflicted on him and his brothers had been severe. The abuse was demeaning and at times he felt emasculated.

The unforgettable images flipped through his brain like pages blowing in the wind. He was drowning in an ocean of shame and embarrassment, and he couldn't swim. What made it worse was that he still loved his father—and not understanding why or how he could. At times the torment in his mind gave him night terrors where he would wake up in a cold sweat and feel the humiliation as though he were a child all over again.

An unfaded memory seemed to always make its way to the surface whenever his life seemed to calm down. He was about nine years old and getting in from school. He heard his mother crying bitterly when he entered the house. She rushed toward him her eyes blackened from smeared mascara. She leaned down, kissed his cheek, and told him, “Keep your jacket on baby. Wait here.”

He was afraid and asked, “What’s wrong Momma?”

“Shhh. Just wait here.” She put all five of the boys in the car and they listened while she and his father screamed at each other. She shouted, “I’m sick of this Billy! I’m taking the boys and I’m leaving right now!” She had clothes packed and shuffled to throw suitcases into the trunk.

The young boys sat in the car with an inexpressible joy. “We’re leaving!” they cheered. But his father stopped her at the door. Holding on to her he pleaded, “Please Terri. I’m sorry. I love you. I promise I’ll change. Don’t go. Please.” And like so many abused women believing in the man she loved, she stayed.

The gloom and sorrow that came over DL from having to walk back into that house that night never seemed to leave him. His thoughts became too heavy and he just pushed the feelings deeper inside. It was as though he were filling an overstuffed storage box and putting it in an attic. He had become an expert at that. However, as he got older, sometimes it felt as if any day now the lid was going to blow off and everything inside would come exploding out through the roof.

He put the photo down, turned on his X-Box, and started to take his aggression out on his Mortal Combat enemies. Later that evening, he heard a knock at the door. He wasn’t expecting anyone.
He grumbled, “Shit, it’s probably Leslie.” He looked through the window next to the door and saw a man he didn’t recognize standing there. He called out, “Who is it?”

The man answered, “Uh, you don’t know me. I’m Cynthia’s husband.”

DL muttered, "What the fuck!" He spun around to his coat closet and fumbled to find his baseball bat. He picked it up as though he found a treasure and leaned it next to the door. He reached for his phone and called Roger explaining quickly, told him to stand by, then hung up.

He stood next to the door and, without opening it, said, "What's up?"

Darren, hearing the muffles of all of that, answered, "I'm not up here to fight you man. I was just hoping we could talk."

DL answered, "Just a minute." He was unsure, his adrenaline rushed. It had been a long time since he had a good fight, and knowing how this man had treated Cynthia, this could have been a serious problem. He slipped on his pair of K-Swiss and cautiously opened the door. He looked him in the eye with boldness. "What's up?"

Darren looked him over and then answered, "I guess I just needed to meet you for some reason." He held his hand out and introduced himself. "My name is Darren." He had heard nothing about DL, but DL knew all about him.

DL answered, "Yea, I know your name, my name is Darren too." But he didn't shake his hand. He felt himself calming down and had confidence that if he needed to, he could take him.

"Hold up." DL grabbed a jacket that was thrown over the back of his couch, stepped outside and shut the door behind him. They walked over to a short brick wall that lined the walkway and sat down.

Darren started to talk. "So your name is Darren too? Did Cynthia trip off of that?"

DL chuckled and said, "Yea. Actually we both did . . ." There was an uncomfortable silence.

"Listen man, why are you here?"

Darren didn't quite know what to say. "I guess I wanted to meet the man I'm losing my wife to. How did you guys meet anyway?"

DL answered, "We met at a casino when she was up here a few months ago."

Darren asked DL a few more questions, and DL answered them with no problem.

Darren was studying him as he talked. He would never say it out loud, but he saw DL was handsome, tall, and had an athletic build. He felt intense jealousy and a sense of loss. He thought, "No way will I ever be able to get Cynthia back after being with this dude." He knew he was beat and asked him, "Man, can you do me a favor? Can you just back off from her for a little while? Let me have the chance to see if I've really lost her?"

DL answered, "Man, I don't have anything to do with you losing Cynthia. The problems you guys had, have nothing to do with me. I think she made her decision long before I came along."

Darren replied, "I know, but I just need one more try." Then he made up a lie. "Plus, about two weeks ago we made love and I know there's still something between us."

DL didn't believe him for one second. His eyes rolled upward and he thought to himself, "She was up here with me two weeks ago."

Darren was feeling desperate, he started to tell DL things that were obviously evidence that his mind was slipping. He said he had Cynthia's phone tapped, that he watched her apartment at times. Then he asked DL, "Man . . . Have you slept with her?" Darren moved one side of his jacket back to reveal the badge he had on his hip.

DL answered, "I care for Cynthia. I'm not gonna disrespect her." Darren, making sure the badge was visible again and trying to intimidate DL, said, "I need you to step off for a minute, and I have ways of getting what I want."

DL knew that he was a probation officer and that it was not a police badge, but sensing that he could flip at any moment, he stood up and said, "I think it's time you leave." Leaving no opportunity for reply DL shot into his apartment and called Roger, then grabbed his bat. Darren hopped into his car and drove off.

Seven o'clock the next morning, Cynthia was preparing to leave for work when her phone rang. She answered, "Hi baby. You're calling me early."

DL replied with his voice low, "Yea, I need to talk with you a minute. Do you have time?"

"Yes, of course. What is it?"

"I think you should know your husband was up here last night."

Immediately Cynthia felt a mix of panic and fear. "WHAT? How in the world does he know you? How did he know where you live?"

"I don't know, but I wanted you to know . . ." DL went on to explain all about the conversation he had with Darren.

She stood there perplexed, "That's it! I'm getting a restraining order. Is he crazy? He went to my sister's job yesterday and held her up for almost an hour trying to convince her to talk to me. He called Carla the other night, trying to get her to talk to me . . .This is nuts. I don't know what he'll do next!"

Cynthia's mind was in motion as she tried to figure out how Darren knew who DL was. She said, "The only way he could have found out who you are is by snooping through my apartment. I have your address on the back of a receipt in my nightstand, or maybe he's been in my email." She continued in panic, "Baby, I'm so sorry. Are you okay?"

"I'm cool. I'm worried about you. I think I'm going to buy myself a weapon though. I don't like the fact that he knows where I live. It's clear his head ain't right."

"D, I'm so sorry you're mixed up in this. I would understand if you want to put us on hold right now, this is a lot."

DL responded, "Baby, as rough as this may be, that's not the answer."

Unsure of that, Cynthia looked at her watch and said, "Babe, I'll talk with you later. I've got to get going or I'll be late to work."

On her drive to work Cynthia felt more and more ill at ease, remembering Darren's threats, his looks, the things he'd said and done over the last week. All of it, added to the fact he drove all the way up to Las Vegas and knocked on a man's door he didn't even know, equaled crazy. Cynthia knew that he wanted her to be scared, and it all began to overwhelm her.

Then it dawned on her. "Darren put his car in the shop yesterday. He must have driven his work car up there." She realized he would risk his job. She got to work and called her supervisor immediately to tell her what had been going on. She felt she needed to leave that day and have an Order of Protection placed. And that's what she did.

Chapter Fourteen

Cynthia and DL didn't talk for three days. It was torture for both of them. It took all of her strength not to call him, so she sent him an email instead:

Hi DL,
I just wanted to reiterate that I am so very sorry that you ended up in the drama that has become the definition of my life. I never meant for any of this to happen. I think when we first started talking I said I was afraid to include anyone in my life seriously right now because of my situation. But I guess I started caring about you before I could do anything about it. D, if I never see you again, I will at least always have the time we shared in my heart, and be able to know that there is a good man out there.
Take care of yourself, Cynthia

With sadness and a lump in her throat, she pressed the send button. It was a about fifteen minutes later that she received this reply:

Baby, I don't even want you thinking like that. I'm not giving up on you, or us. I do plan on seeing you again . . . I want you in my life and I don't want it to end . . . I care too much about you not to fight for this. You know I'm here for you . . . and I love you . . . I just want you to be safe . . . And if that means backing off for a moment until things are settled, I can do that. I just want you in my life. You are my best friend & the love of my life. I'm gonna be waiting on you baby...And we are gonna make it through all of this TOGETHER . . . So don't even make it sound like this is the end . . . Because it isn't . . . I'm here for you . . . I love you too much to just let us go like that.... DL

Cynthia read the email and was touched by his emotion for her. "He said 'I love you'" she thought. She called him at work.

He answered, "Tech Support. Darren Lewis."

"Hi, it's me."

"Oh baby. Why did you send me that email?"

She said in nervous excitement, "You said you love me."

"I know, because I do. I need to see you, Cynthia. I miss you."

"I can come up there Friday night."

"YAY! Listen baby, I'm in the middle of a work ticket, I gotta go."

"Okay, I'll talk to you tomorrow."

He answered, "Yes, definitely. I love you baby."

"I love you too."

Cynthia said it and realized it at the same time. She sat on her bed, opened the night stand drawer, pulled out her journal and began to write. Her notebook was sitting next to her on the bed, and she heard a Ding indicating she'd received a new email. She plopped the computer onto her lap to check it and saw it was from Darren, it read:

Honey, I hope you get this today. I've submitted a petition to the court requesting to lift the Order of Protection, and we have to appear in the morning at ten. They should be contacting you if they haven't already. Your "boyfriend" got me fired. He called my job and told them about me driving the county vehicle up to his house and I was let go. The only thing I can do right away is go back to my job at the prison, but they won't hire me back with a restraining order. I want you to know that I'm sorry. I know I've been behaving irrationally. But I love you so much. I couldn't imagine you and I really being apart for the rest of our lives. It was just too much to bear ......"

The email went on for about three pages and was full of I'm sorries and regrets. Cynthia couldn't continue reading, it made her ill. Not one word was anything he hadn't said to her countless times before. She thought, "This is the same old song he sings year after year. I don't even have the energy for this crap anymore." She closed it out and mumbled, "My boyfriend got you fired. You drove that car up there knowing you weren't supposed to. He's always blaming somebody else for his mistakes." She started to reply to the email then said, "Forget it. It's a waste of time."

She opened her Word program and remembered that she had been working on a poem since the last time she and DL were together. She started having flashbacks of being with him. The way he touched her, the gentle way he made love to her. She thought about him saying he loved her. Her spirit lifted and she thought she could finish the poem.

She loved to write. All through high school and college it had been her favorite thing to do. She had written numerous short stories and poems, but during her marriage it had come to almost a complete stand still—only spewing out a few bitter poems here and there, or journaling her sorrow most of the time. But this poem was different. It was inspired by one of the three things Cynthia felt really good poetry is: hate, love, or intense pain brought on by hate or love. This one was inspired by love:

"My Lover is Mine"

My lover is mine and I am his.
an untainted and
beautiful embrace this is

His strong arms caress me
like the scent of fine cologne

His hands protect my heart
with a strength few know

His body covers mine
like a mist from an ocean spray

When his tender lips touch mine
I'm left with no words to say

I held him so close
not letting go
until I felt the warmth
of his love inside me

I am winter melting in the spring suns glow

Oh, I am his and my lover is mine
His cream fills my glass
and cheers me like wine

My legs are weakened
and I can not open my eyes

Our spirits as one fly
as precious memories through time

Oh lover be mine only and only will I be yours

Kiss me, and I am kissed
Touch me, and I am touched
Bless me, and I am blessed

His love strengthens me
and I am strong

Even after he leaves this earth
his embrace will move me on

When he holds me through the night
I am carried through the day

His love comforts me like money
my worries drift away

He has stolen my heart
my lover
my friend
let each day be as blissful as this

My lover is mine and I am his
his physique perfection
I delight in his kiss

Come to our room
my lover,
and close the door

100 princes could desire me
pursue me

But I will only be yours.

Friday morning, Cynthia got to work at eight, she poured her coffee and made her way to her desk. “Good morning, Pauline.” Pauline emptied the bags from the night depository. “Whew We have about fifty bags today . . . Good morning.

Cynthia smiled and said, “You’re a pro. You can handle it.”

“I’m giving you half.”

“Uh, nope. I have to leave for a little while. I’ve got to go down to the courthouse. I’ll be back about eleven, or maybe twelve. I’ll probably have lunch before I come back.”

“What are you going to the courthouse for?”

“The restraining order thing. Darren’s trying to have it lifted.”

Pauline asked, “Oh. What are you going to say?”

“I don’t know. He can’t work with it against him. I know he has to work. I guess I’ll let the judge decide. It’s been two weeks and he hasn’t violated it.”

“Well maybe you finally involving the court woke him up.”

Cynthia said, “I don’t know. I hope. My mind has been spinning around like a carousel all morning and I have a bad headache. I don’t know what to do. Pray for me.”

“Well, I don’t pray really. But I know you and you’ll be alright.”

“Pauline, you don’t pray?”

“Not really.”

Cynthia asked, "Why?"

"I didn't grow up doing the church or God thing."

"Well, we'll have to talk about that sometime."

"Yea, maybe."

"I gotta go. Try and pray for me anyway." Cynthia smiled and added, "I'll pray for you too."

"Thanks. I'll need it around here."

Cynthia arrived at the courthouse and wandered around trying to find the right room. She and Darren appeared before Judge Ross, a family judge who had the reputation around town for favoring men. They were sworn in and the judge brought the proceedings to order.

"Mrs. Wilson, we will begin with you since you placed the order. What happened? And I should say, although you two may have a lot to express, please try and stick to what is relevant here."

Cynthia explained, "Well in short, I left my husband about six or so months ago because he was abusive and unfaithful. He recently found out that I've been seeing another man, and he flipped. He threatened me saying that if he couldn't have me, nobody would—"

"—I didn't mean it like she's saying," Darren interrupted.

The judge stopped him. "Order, Mr. Wilson. Do not interrupt. You'll have an opportunity to speak momentarily. Mrs. Wilson, please continue."

"Um . . . All I can tell you is that, after saying that, he then drove his company's car—that he's only supposed to use for work—up to my boyfriend's house in Las Vegas and threatened him. All the while he has a girlfriend . . ."

Darren again spoke out of turn, "That's not my girlfriend!"

"Mr. Wilson, if I have to stop you once more, your petition will be denied. Mrs. Wilson."

"He was trying to scare me, Your Honor, and I didn't feel safe. So I placed the order."

"Do you feel it's safe to lift it now?"

"I don't know. I know he has to work."

"Okay, Mr. Wilson, I'll hear your response now."

"Thank you, Your Honor. I'm sorry about that. Let me just say that I did do some dumb things. I wanted my wife and family back, and maybe I got a little desperate. But I understand that I was wrong."

The judge asked, "Why do you need this order lifted?"

"I lost my job with the county, and I have an opportunity to go back to my old job as a correctional officer, but I can't do that with an Order of Protection against me. I am really sorry Your Honor. I never meant to hurt my wife. I did a lot of stupid things and I don't have a girlfriend, she's my babysitter."

"Mr. Wilson, I'm going to stop you. I'm sure you have a lot of things you would like to say, but we have to stick to what's relevant here. I'm going to lift this Order of Protection with a warning. I'm going to believe that, in losing your wife, you had a case of temporary insanity, that this is not something that will happen again. If it does, and you appear before me on anything having to do with this matter, I will have you jailed. It's clear to me that your wife has made up her mind to divorce you. When people do that, there's nothing you can do. If she wishes to see other men, that's no longer your business."

She looked over at Cynthia, "Mrs. Wilson, if he in any way makes you feel that he is a threat, you call the police."

Cynthia left the courtroom as soon as she could. Darren called out to her, but she quickly got on the elevator and headed for her car. She was full of mixed emotions. She felt that all the things Darren had done through out the years carried no consequences, and that was her own fault. It made her feel so unimportant, so small, and there was nothing she could do about it.

Darren phoned her when she got back to work.

"Cynthia, line one."

She picked up the line. "Thank you for holding. This is Cynthia."

"Hey, it's me."

"What Darren?"

"I'm sorry, honey."

"I really don't have time for this."

"Okay . . . Okay. I miss the kids. I'd like to pick them up after school, til Wednesday, like before."

"Fine. I'll call the school."

When Cynthia got in from work that evening, she called Darren's house to say goodnight to the kids. He answered, "Hey honey."

"Darren, please stop calling me honey. I just want to say goodnight to the kids."

"Alright, Cyn-thi-a. Hold on."

Lil Darren got on, "Hi Mom. We got some pizza and Daddy rented movies."

"Oh good, I was just checking on you. You have my cell number if you need anything, right?"

"Um . . . Is it 895-3123?"

"Yep, you remembered. You're so smart. I love you put your sister on."

"Okay, I love you too."

"Alright, bye."

"Bye mister. Be good."

Summer got on, "Hi Mom. I miss you."

"I miss you too, sweetpea. I hear you got pizza."

"Yep. It's goood."

"Summer, eat the whole thing not just the cheese off the top."

She laughed, "Okay, Mommy."

"Be good, sweetpea. I love you so much."

"Okay Mommy. I love you too, bye."

Cynthia's phone rang as she was putting it down. It was DL. She answered, "Hi baby."

"Hey babe. You almost here?"

She giggled and replied, "No, I'm barely home from work."

"Awe, hurry, hurry. I'm frying us some chicken."

"Ooo, you are? Thank you."

"What do you want with it?"

"Um . . . Maybe some green beans and . . . can you make biscuits?"

"Baby, I'm from Georgia, you know I can make some biscuits."

She laughed, "Mmm good. You want me to bring something?"

"Just your sweet face . . . Oh, and I bought water for you."

"Awe, thank you D. Be there real soon, bye."

Chapter Fifteen

Over the next few months every other week when the kids were with Darren, visiting DL had become Cynthia's routine. She and DL fell deeper in love. They went to movies, played together, they laughed a lot together, shopped together, cooked together. DL had a poor diet and Cynthia was always trying to get him to eat better.

When she would try to feed him something healthy, he would scrunch up his face and hold his mouth shut like a rebellious little boy. She would say, "Come on babe, try it. It's good for you. I need you to eat better so you'll be here with me until a ripe old age."

Then he would try it, and he would like it. They got to know each other's family and friends. DL had gone down to Arizona a few times and met her mom, dad, and sister. But most of the time, Cynthia preferred to go up to Vegas.

One weekend she didn't go up because it was her family's annual trip to Disneyland and they usually stayed there for a few days. While she was asleep in the hotel room, her cell phone rang at about five thirty in the morning. She crept out of the door so she could talk without disturbing the kids.

"Hello."

DL said excitedly, "Baby, it's me. Guess what?"

"What?"

"I just got home from work and found a thousand dollars laying on the ground outside my apartment! Just waving in the wind."

Cynthia got a little loud. "Shut UP! You did? Just waving in the wind?"

"Yep! I got out of my truck and started walking toward my door, and I thought I saw money over on the ground near the bush. I hurried and picked it up and counted it inside. It was four hundred. Then I went back out and looked under the bush. There was more. So I picked it up and hurried back inside. It was another six hundred!"

"Oh my goodness! Only in Vegas. You're so lucky baby. Who has ever heard of that?"

He laughed. "I know, huh. I'm going to save it until you come back so we can spend it together."

"Oh baby. That's so sweet. But shouldn't you turn it in at the office? What if somebody's looking for it?"

DL replied, "Shiiiit. I'm not taking this money to no office. It's my money now. Finders keepers."

As the summer weeks zoomed by, their hearts for each other had become inseparable. When Cynthia's birthday came in July, DL had a dozen long-stem red roses, mixed with beautiful freshly cut Cali Lilies, delivered to her job. She placed them proudly on her desk, and smiled all day bragging about how sweet he was to her customers and co-workers.

Sometimes, they would just take drives around the city, occasionally going through neighborhoods, looking at houses for sale, and complaining about how over-priced they were. Once they drove up to Red Rock Canyon and watched the sunset over the mountainous horizon.

He said, "Next time we come up here, we should go rock hunting."

Cynthia looked confused. "Rock hunting?"

"Yea, you know. Like the white people do."

She asked, "Why would I want to shoot a rock? Wouldn't it ricochet?"

"Cynthia, please say you're kidding."

Other times they would just go to the park and sit and feed the ducks at the lake. Cynthia would read or just write as DL snapped pictures of everything he could. Sometimes he would snap pictures of her. "Smile baby." She would flip her head back and give a goofy smile. "Smiling."

They would go visit Roger and listen to all his woman trouble. He was always mixed up in some crazy drama. Listening to his stories, and the animated way he told them, they thought was better than watching stand up comedy on HBO. DL would always prompt him to tell the one about how he discovered that one of his girlfriends had hair around her nipples. "Man, what's up with Tonya?" Roger got loud. "Man, I ain't messin with that hairy skanch. I almost choked last time. I had a hair stuck in my throat for two days. Plus, she looks like a man when she wakes up in the morning."

They had a taken a few weekend trips, one in particular to San Diego. Cynthia's sister, Dana, lived there with her husband, Bernard, and their five children, all teenagers. They had just bought a new home and invited Cynthia and DL to come and visit. DL had never been to San Diego and had always wanted to see the city. Late in July they drove down to visit for few days.

When they arrived, they entered the home and admired how lovely it was: high vaulted ceilings, custom crown molding, granite counter tops, the whole bit. Her sister had the same designer's touch Cynthia did and the decor was flawless. As Bernard showed them around, Cynthia was eager to get to the pool in the backyard. She knew how much DL had talked about living near the water someday and thought they could go in and have fun. Once they were settled, Cynthia changed into her swim suit, and ran out and jumped in. She tried over and over urging DL to join her, but he wouldn't.

She flopped in and out of the water, like a mermaid. "What's the matter? Come on baby!"

He leaned down next to the side of the pool, admiring her pink two-piece swim suit. She swam up next to him and blew water into his face. Out of breath and gasping, she pleaded, "Come on. Get in!"

His voice low, he said, "I can't swim."

"What! But you always say you want to live near the water. You can't swim?"

"No, I never learned."

"Well come on, get in on the shallow side. You can walk around. I'll show you what to do. It's easy."

Firmly he answered. "No."

She could see he was scared, and she was tickled by that. "What about the Jacuzzi?"

"Okay, the Jacuzzi is cool."

They cuddled up in there and talked as Dana and Bernard got drunk and cooked bar-b-que. Anthony came down from school to join them and met DL. They hit it off.

Anthony pulled Cynthia aside and told her, "Mom, I'm glad you've met someone nice."

They hugged. "Thank you, baby."

Dana's kids frolicked around the pool too. They made DL and Cynthia seem old as they chatted about all the new singers and songs that were out. Her niece had just gone to see Chris Brown the night before and was crazy about him. She couldn't stop talking about the show.

Cynthia looked over at DL. "Who's Chris Brown?"

"Some new little rooty poot singer. You know that song, You makin me wanna say yooo, excuse me miss I saw you from across the rooooom."

"Oh, oh yea. Next time just tell me, don't sing it."

"Tss, forget you."

Cynthia interjected as the kids went on and on, "I don't care what you guys say, nobody's better than Michael Jackson!"

DL looked over at her. "You know you're old, right? Anyway, Prince is better."

"Oh, here we go. Will that argument ever be laid to rest?"

The kids looked confused. Her niece asked, "What argument?"

DL and Cynthia looked at each other. She said, "I guess we're both old."

It was over 100 degrees and too hot to continue to sit outside. Hungry and tired, they went inside to eat, but Dana wouldn't turn on the air conditioner so it was pretty warm in the house too. DL asked Cynthia quietly, "What's up with the air conditioner?" "I don't know, let's see if we can find the thermostat."

They looked around the house like secret detectives on a hot case. But it was large, over 3500 sq feet, and they had trouble finding it. Up the stairs, then back down, then up, then back down. Looking unsuccessfully in and out of hallways and rooms. When they finally found it, Cynthia moved the needle. They leaned their ears in and listened closely a minute, but nothing happened. They both peered at it, eyes squinted, and picking it apart on the wall. They fiddled with the pieces inside as if doing surgery.

"I think it's broken," she said.

DL jerked his body. "Daaaamn!"

As the sun went down, somehow the house seemed to get warmer than it was outside. Dana had opened the windows but that didn't seem to do anything. DL and Cynthia were trying to get comfortable on the couch but the heat seemed to escalate. The covers had been kicked to the floor and they were lying as bare as they could in someone else's den. Cynthia tossed and turned.

About four in the morning, she got up to use the bathroom. When she got back she sat on the edge of the couch, sweating and sipping a cold glass of water, trying in a failing attempt to cool off. DL sat up.

She whispered, "Are you up baby? I thought you were sleeping?" He was clearly very irritated, but tried to keep his voice low. "How? It's too fuckin hot in here! I was about to get the floaty thing and go sleep in the pool. Shit!"

Cynthia choked on her water and it came spitting threw her nose in laughter. "You can't even swim!"

They got up and sat in back and watched the sunrise. Cynthia laid her head on his shoulder. He said, "Let's go somewhere so I can take some pictures."

She asked him, "Have you ever heard of Coronado?"

"No, where's that?"

"It's a small island off the coast. Maybe about forty five minutes from here. We'll go for the day. You'll get some beautiful pictures down there."

They ate breakfast and drove down. Once there, they found a nice place on the beach to park near the old famous hotel Del Coronado. As they entered, Cynthia told him about the old wives' tale that it was haunted, and DL tried to startle her at almost every turn. She just shook her head at him. "Pathetic."

They went inside the main lobby and it was magnificent. The ceilings were so high you almost couldn't see the tops, like the inside of a cathedral. The walls and hallways were detailed with statues and hand carvings. DL snapped his camera excessively.

They walked along the beach holding hands and collecting sea shells. The temperature was a perfect 78 degrees and the blue sky was a work of art. They sat for a while on the sand and talked while watching families play in the water. DL stared over at her. The gentle wind blew just softly enough through her hair to lift it a little from her shoulders. He said, "I love your hair." Sometimes she wore it natural and curly. Other times, long and straight, like today.

"You're so pretty, baby." He would always tell her that.

She just smiled and said, "Thank you."

He leaned over and kissed her lips. She cherished the moment in her heart, while wrapping it up in her mind as if it were a priceless gift to have forever. How many times she had been down to that island in her life, and couldn't recall any of them. But somehow, this visit she would never forget.

One Saturday night they were at DL's place and after watching a movie they fell asleep. Even though at her house it had happened quite regularly, it hadn't happened when she was with DL. Cynthia had fallen into a deep sleep and began to stir in the in the bed while having a nightmare about Darren.

She was running from him down a long dark hallway. She turned a corner and stumbled to the ground. He was standing over her with that same large butcher knife, that she couldn't seem to forget, pointed down toward her. The blade shining in the moonlight. Just as it was coming down towards her chest, she cried out in her sleep.

DL reached over to her in the darkness. Without saying a word, he grabbed her and pulled her close to him. He held her securely in his arms for the rest of the night. In the morning they woke, still wrapped in each other's embrace. The desert morning rain pounded against the window like a soothing drum. They lay in each other's arms just talking. He asked her, "Am I being a good boyfriend, baby? Are you happy?"

"I am happy, babe. You're such a good boyfriend. Thank you for asking me that." She paused. "Oh, I hate to go home." She took his hand in hers and started to tenderly massage his palms and fingers one by one.

His voice faded into a trance because it felt so good, he whined, "Don't talk about that, you still have a few more hours."

"Aren't you sick of me yet?" She grinned up at him.

He held her tighter. "You know what's funny? When I was with my wife, I was in Singapore for six months and sad to say, but I never missed her. When you're gone for a few days, I miss the hell out of you."

She leaned up and kissed him. "Thank you baby."

"Just being real."

She said, "Babe, do you realize we've been seeing each other for seven months and we've never had an argument?"

His eyebrows lifted. "Yea, that's true. Wow. That's because I like you."

She answered, "Isn't that just weird?"

"Yea, I guess that is a little strange."

She added, "I mean, it's not like we try not to argue, we just haven't . . ." She paused, then continued, "Babe, you know my ex has been telling the kids that I have a boyfriend?"

He answered, "Uh, huh."

"Well, I guess when I first thought about it, I figured I wouldn't introduce them to you until we were together for maybe a year at least. But since he told them about you, they've been asking me about you."

DL just listened. "Hmm, oh yea?"

"Yea. How do you feel about that?"

He replied. "It is up to you babe. I'd love to meet your kids, but whenever you're ready."

"Well, I'm not sure. It's already August, maybe around the holidays?"

"Whenever you're ready, babe."

She turned over and straddled his lap, then leaned down and kissed his lips. "You're so handsome, baby."

"Thank you."

"And you're so perfect."

He answered, "No, I'm not perfect."

She hopped up and added, "Perfect for me." Then she went into the bathroom, calling out, "I'm gonna hop in the shower."

"Okay!" DL clicked on the TV and started to watch a ball game when his phone rang. He looked at the caller id: "Holly Kelly"

"Hello."

"Hi baby. Are you busy?"

DL leaned up and looked to make sure the bathroom door was closed. "No, I'm cool, what's up? I haven't heard from you in awhile."

"I know, I've been traveling. Do you work tonight?"

He answered. "Yea, at five thirty. Why?"

"Can I come visit you? I'll bring you dinner."

A slew of emotion rushed through DL's mind and body, he blocked it out. "How long you in town?"

"About a week."

"Yea, that's cool. I'll call you when I get to the office."

"Okay. Miss you, bye."

"Me too, bye."

Chapter Sixteen

September 2 was a Saturday and DL's birthday. Cynthia couldn't go up to Vegas because she had the kids and also had to work. She called him first thing in the morning.

He answered, "Hi baby."

"Happy birthday. I'm so sorry I can't come up. Did you get the card and candy I sent?"

"It's okay, babe. Yea, I did get them. Thank you, that was sweet."

She asked, "So what are you doing today?"

"Awe, just relaxing right now. Some of my co-workers are taking me to lunch. Then probably going to Roger's show with his ex-girl, Cee. You know his son's mom."

"Oh, cool. I'm so glad you have plans. I didn't want you to miss me too much." She snickered.

"No matter what I'm doing, I always miss you babe."

"You're so sweet. Well, I better finish getting ready for work. Have fun today. I miss you."

"I miss you too baby. I love you, bye."

Cynthia got off the phone feeling disappointed that she couldn't go up, but she was also refreshed by the fact that she felt she could trust DL. With Darren, whenever he left the house, his guilt was written all over his face when he returned. As she cleansed her face in the sink, her eyes zeroed in on a very tiny scar she had on her neck. No one would ever notice it because it was so faint now, but she remembered when it was put there.

Once during an argument with Darren she stormed out of the house and drove over to her parents' house. She went into Mona's room—who still lived at home at the time—and sat at the edge of the bed. With her head in her hands, she was trying not to cry and to keep her composure.

Shortly after she arrived there, Darren knocked at the front door. Cynthia's dad let him in, not knowing they had been arguing. Darren made his way down the hallway and opened the door to Mona's room. He was sweating and desperate as he sat down on a chair next to the bed. Trying to keep his voice low, he spewed out pleas for her to come back home. "Please, honey. I'm so sorry. Let's just go home and talk."

"I know you, Darren. You're hiding something. Tell me the truth! Did you cheat on me again?"

Suddenly, in anger, Darren leaped from the chair, throwing his whole body toward her. He grabbed her neck with both hands and forced her down on the bed. Snarling, he shook her head back and forth, his thumbs pressing against the area in the middle of her neck. Wildly, she kicked her feet at his groin, and felt the sting of his fingernail scratch against the side of her neck when she pushed him off. Her father heard the thump when the chair tipped over and fell to the floor and he busted into the room. He wailed out, "Oh hell no! Not in my house!" He threw Darren out.

Cynthia slammed the bedroom door behind them, not wanting her father to see her neck before she could. Breathing heavily, she rushed over to the dresser mirror and closely examined it, then wiped the trickle of blood away with a tissue. The damage to her skin was insignificant, but to her heart, detrimental. She convinced her father that was the only time he had become violent.

For years now, the mark on her neck was a little reminder. Anytime those horrible memories would rear their ugly heads, she would think about DL, and her heart almost felt like it was mending. She finished getting ready and left for work.

Chapter Seventeen

About nine o'clock that night, DL was headed through the crowded streets of Vegas to go hang out with Cecilia and celebrate his birthday. Monday was Labor Day and a three day weekend was a good excuse for the tourists to pour into the city. He pulled into the parking lot of The Golden Goose, a little hole in the wall bar/club off the strip. Roger would play there in between real paying gigs. It was small, dark and smoky. By midnight it was as packed as a sardine can, and smelled a lot like one too.

The whole place knew it was DL's birthday because Roger would periodically yell it out from the stage between songs. When the band was taking a break, Roger came over and sat with DL. He leaned over into his ear and asked, "Man, was that who I thought it was sitting with you earlier?"

DL answered, "Oh, Holly. She's down here from Portland for a few days."

Roger said, "I hope you ain't getting involved with her again. You know she's crazy."

"I'm cool."

DL threw back his fourth shot, sipped his second beer, and found himself unable to turn away. When Holly returned to the table, his resistance was low. Her blonde hair flowed over her tanned, freckled shoulders. Her skirt was too short and her blouse was cut too low. It was as if she counted his drinks, because right around his sixth shot she leaned over and whispered into his ear, then scooted closer. Her big blue eyes called out to him for satisfaction.

"You've missed me. Haven't you?" Putting her hand under the table she massaged his manhood, and leaned in, kissing his neck. She then stood up and reached for his hand. DL fought the logic and reason of a conscious trying to warn him. He was lead by the irresistible power of seduction and followed her, disappearing into the crowd. Cecilia noticed but, being distracted by another friend, she was pulled away. About an hour later, she was ready to go. She looked for DL unsuccessfully.

Cecilia found Roger and asked, "Where the hell is your brother? I'm about to go."

Roger replied, "I don't know, he's supposed to take me home." They looked around a bit more.

"Well maybe he left." She looked at Roger. "Well come on, if you're ready, I'll give you a ride."

They said a few good nights and left. When they stepped outside, they saw DL's truck was still parked across the lot. Roger walked over. Just as he got close, he saw the blonde's head pop up and he quickly turned away. "Oh shit." He jogged back over toward Cecilia. "Just give me a ride. He might be a while."

Five in the morning the sun was just barely peeking over the horizon, and the sky was still mostly black. DL woke up in the back seat of his truck to the sound of sprinkling rain tapping against the windshield. In a drunken stupor he looked around realizing where he was. His mind in a haze, he couldn't recall a lot. He looked down and saw a used condom on the floor of his truck. He sat up, leaned over and put his head in his hands. "Shit." He felt the sobering pain of regret pounding in his brain like a bass line. He reached into the glove compartment to find a napkin. Then he stepped out to discard of the souvenir his intoxicated evil twin had left behind.

He walked over to the mini market next door to where he was parked and bought a hot cup of coffee. He climbed back in his truck and fumbled around to find his cell. He saw "1 voice mail" across the display. It was Cynthia, she had called at midnight. He listened. She was singing, "Happy birthday to you, happy birthday to you, happy birthday, my baby, happy birthday to you." She giggled. "Hi baby. Missing you. Just wanted to say it again before your day was over. Hope you're having fun, call me tomorrow. I love you. MUAH!"

When he finished listening, he tossed the phone over onto the passenger seat and saw there was a note lying there. He picked it up and read it: "Goodnight, sorry I had to rush off, I had a flight to catch. I'll call you about the photography thing. Hope you had a happy birthday. 503-555-6222 my new cell. XXXOOO Holly :)"

DL wished he could wake up and start yesterday all over. But life's a bitch, and that was never going to happen. He drove home, and when he got inside, he immediately disrobed to take a hot shower. The water fell over his body and he wished it was hot enough to rinse away the night before. He thought about Roger's warning. "Why didn't I listen?" He thought about Cynthia's call. "She called at twelve . . . Maybe if I had heard my phone?" The regrets of his poor choice started to make him feel dirtier as he washed. He tried to talk himself out of feeling worse as he thought about Cynthia. "She's not my wife, shit." He dried off and climbed into bed. He slept until one o'clock. His phone rang, it was Cynthia.

He answered, "Hi baby."

"Hi baby. How was your birthday?"

"Awe, nothing special. It was okay." He needed a new word for the guilt he was feeling—"dog" just didn't seem accurate.

"Baby, you sound sad. Oh, are you still asleep? I'm so sorry I woke you."

"No, it's okay."

"Guess what?" She said in excitement. "You're off work tonight, right?"

"Yes."

"Well, my sister-in-law and her friend are out here. She had a fight with my brother. They want to come up there tonight and party, so I thought we could go see Roger play. Is that cool?" Her enthusiasm poked at his heart and he felt worse.

He answered, "Absolutely, baby, I'd love to see you. I miss you so much."

"Me too. I can't stay all night though, because they have to get back. Where's he playing?"

"Um, he's at the MGM, or Caesar's. I'll find out and call you back."

"Okay. Love you."

"Me too."

As Cynthia exited the freeway in Vegas, it was about eight o'clock. The streets along the strip were packed with cars. Groups of people scurried around the sidewalks like party animals in a zoo. They parked at the MGM and entered the casino.

She called DL. "Hi baby, we're downstairs on our way up there. Look for me, it's crowded in here."

He answered, “Okay.”

A few moments later DL’s cell rang again, he stepped over into a corner where he could hear better. Not really recognizing the number, he usually didn’t answer. But he thought it looked familiar so he did. “This is D.”

“Hi, it’s me, Holly.”

He looked over and saw Cynthia standing just outside the entrance to the night club. “Damn! She looks good,” he thought. Then said into the phone, “Oh, hey, what’s up? I’m out right now. Can I call you later?”

She answered, “Oh, okay, bye.”

Quickly hanging up the call, he turned the phone off, then approached Cynthia with a kiss and wrapped his hand around her waist. “Hey baby, that hat looks good on you.”

She was wearing a smooth black suede brim. She smiled. “Thank you.”

He loved her dimples and the way her nose perked up when she smiled.

DL lead them over to the table he had saved. Cynthia looked around. The club was filled with ambiance: there was a colorful Egyptian theme, and the tables were decorated with large dark purple candles as center pieces and golden table cloths. There was a small covered bridge that lead from the seating area over to the dance floor. Smoke from the dry ice under the bridge gently blew over onto the dance floor like a soft wind. Cynthia introduced everybody, trying to speak over the music. “This is my sister-in-law, Jennifer, her friend, Kari, and you already know Mona.” Everyone shook hands and said hello.

They all got cozy and ordered their drinks. As the music bumped, the night began to spin like a good record. Cynthia had brought her digital camera and they snapped shots all night. Roger played with two or three different bands, and tonight he was playing with The Snazz Band, a group of very talented musicians. The lead singer was a sight; he wore a weaved ponytail that hung out of the back of his black brim, and his white suit was a bit too small, but he seemed confident and completed the ensemble with a sequenced fluffy blouse underneath, white socks, and black patent leather loafers.

Mona leaned over and said to DL, "Is he for real? He looks like he got on a train in 1986 and never made it off. I can't figure out if he's Prince, Michael Jackson, or Rick James."

Throughout each song he would just repeatedly shout out of nowhere, "Snazz Band!" Very sharp and quick, over and over. Cynthia laughed and looked at DL. "What is wrong with him? He sounds like he has Tourette's Syndrome."

He answered sarcastically, "He's from Cali. You know how you guys are."

"Whatever!"

The band began to play a medley of smooth R. Kelly hits. Cynthia jumped up and grabbed DL's hand and said, "Oooh, come on baby, it's 'The Steppers Groove.' We have to dance." He didn't like to dance but her dimples persuaded him to get up. He followed her out to the floor where they danced as if no one else were there.

DL leaned down into her ear and said, "I must really love you because I don't dance."

She smiled and turned around pulling him close to her back side. "You're doing good. You dance well."

He spun her back around and said with confidence, "I know. I just usually don't want to."

She looked up at him. "And what makes you want to tonight?"

He saw that sparkle in her eye again, and the goosebumps came back. "You."

As they chatted and danced, DL's back was toward their table. That's when Cynthia saw Mona pop up out of her seat and rush toward someone in anger.

Cynthia dashed back over the bridge, and wailed out, "OH SHOOT!" DL followed seeing the disruption. "What the fuck?" He grabbed Mona and tried to guide her back to the table, but failed to calm her down. Mona tried her best to pull away. She shouted, "Move . . . Fuck her! I'll toss her ass over that bridge."

Roger watched from the stage, trying to keep playing as though nothing were happening, but the whole band was completely out of tune. Cynthia was in the path of a large, six foot tall blonde woman who was aggressively trying to get around her. As she tried to talk her down and hold her back, security approached. They managed to calm the scene down before it got any worse.

DL spoke to Mona as if talking to a small child. Calmly, but with frustration, he said, "Babe, you can't fight people here, they know we're guests of the band. They won't be able to play here anymore."

Mona tried to collect herself. "Sorry! But that bitch was getting on my nerves."

Cynthia plopped down in her seat out of breath. She asked Mona, "What did she do to you?"

Mona answered, "Nothin . . . I just didn't like the way she was actin . . . So when she walked by me, I stuck my foot out and tripped her."

DL said, "What the hell?"

Cynthia looked at him. "Sorry, I guess I should have warned you, my sister can be a little street."

He answered, "Yea, just a little." They all busted out in laughter.

Chapter Eighteen

October went by as if it only lasted a day and it was almost Thanksgiving. Cynthia spent a Monday morning in court with Darren trying to mediate a custody agreement. The kids had been going back and forth between them every week since the separation, and Cynthia thought that was too unstable. The two of them agreed to share legal custody, but Cynthia wanted residential custody; having them live with her, mostly during the school year. She thought they could then split time during the summer, holidays, and weekends. But Darren wouldn't agree to anything that made sense.

Cynthia explained to the mediator, "He doesn't take care of them properly since I left. The kids tell me he leaves them home alone a lot."

Darren pulled out a folded sheet of paper. "No, I have a babysitter now. I have the times written here with her signature."

The mediator stopped him. "As I explained in the beginning, Mr. Wilson, we don't take any documentation in mediation. We only try to assist in helping the two of you reach a mutual agreement."

Cynthia said, "He doesn't have a babysitter, Ma'am. That's his girlfriend. And with the hours he works, he leaves the kids alone as early as three and four in the morning, until well after they get out of school."

Darren interjected, "No! She's not my girlfriend. Cynthia hasn't even met her. She's my babysitter."

The mediator asked him, "Are these your work hours?"

He answered, "Yes."

"And you have a sitter that covers those hours?"

"Yes."

"Stop lying, Darren. That's your girlfriend."

"It's not. "

Cynthia asked, "How much are you paying her then?"

Darren was stumped, "Uh . . ."

The mediator asked, "Is there compensation involved?"

"Well, no. I help her with her kids."

Cynthia blurted, "Thank you! That's his girlfriend. What babysitter shows up at three in the morning and doesn't get paid? And if he's leaving my kids with some woman, and I'm at home and available to be with them, that just doesn't make any sense."

The mediator looked at Darren and asked, "Are you willing to agree with that?"

"No."

Cynthia was annoyed. "That's because he's just thinking about himself. He's controlling. He thinks the only way he could stop me from moving out of town after we're divorced is to fight a custody agreement."

Darren raised his voice. "That's not true!"

Cynthia went on, "Well, not entirely. He also told me he would never pay child support. He knows with the kids switching back and forth. He can avoid it."

The mediator stopped them, "Okay. It's obvious there's more here that the court needs to consider. I'd like to speak to the children. I'll set the appointment for January. Both of you should receive the date in the mail."

It had been a long morning, Cynthia left the courthouse feeling defeated by Darren once again. The court always gave her the impression that they thought she was lying about the abuse, and she was completely drained. "Lord, I just want out of this marriage."

Mentally worn out and famished, she stopped at a small Chinese restaurant to grab some lunch before heading back to work. As she sat there, the guy who delivered the bottled water to the bank came in. He recognized Cynthia and stopped by her table. "Hello." His accented voice soothed her ear drum.

She looked up in nervous shock. "Uh, oh hi. Cedric, right?"

"Yes."

Cedric didn't know, but every time he had come into the office, all the women would woo over him because he was so gorgeous. Six foot five, cinnamon brown skin, the body of a well-trained athlete, the beautiful face of a model, and with those shorts the uniform required, Cynthia thought, "He could stop traffic on a freeway."

He asked, "May I sit down?"

She answered while trying to swallow the bite of Chow Mien she had just taken, "Uh sure, please."

He initiated a conversation. "Are you okay? You don't have that usual lovely smile I'm used to seeing every week."

Her spirits lifted, she was floating on a cloud. She thought, "Wow, he noticed my smile." She answered, "Yea, I'm in the middle of a divorce. I just left court, it wasn't fun."

"Oh, I'm sorry."

"No, it's okay. I'll be alright . . ." She chuckled and added, "I'm just happy I'm finally getting out of that marriage."

Cedric appeared pleasantly surprised. "Oh yea?"

Cynthia couldn't resist asking, "Where are you from? Jamaica?"

"No. I am from The Virgin Islands."

She smiled. "Wow, okay . . . I bet it's beautiful there."

"It is. Maybe someday, you'll have a reason to visit."

She giggled. "So, how's the water business treating you?"

"Oh it's okay, but I only do this part time. I actually own my own pool cleaning business."

"Oh wow, are you a swimmer?"

"Yes. I love the water, but my business is slow this time of year, so . . ." He paused, looked at his watch, and stood up. "Man, I'm sorry to rush off, but I've got to finish my route."

"Oh okay. It was good seeing you."

He began to walk away then hesitated, he appeared to be nervous. "Uh, maybe if you're free, we can go out for lunch, or maybe dinner, next week?"

Cynthia's shock was evident, and she paused. She was very tempted as she looked at his tight shirt clinging to his chest, with the sleeves rolled up showing off his biceps. But she couldn't help but think about DL. "Um, that's really sweet of you to ask, but I can't. I'm actually seeing someone right now. I'm sorry. But, thank you."

"No, it's okay. I should have known someone would have snatched a lovely woman like you up already. I guess I'll see you at the bank."

"Okay. Thank you again. I'll see you soon." She thought to herself, "Dang, he's so fine. But DL is so sweet to me. Why would I jeopardize that?" She watched Cedric walk out. "Whew."

After work Cynthia went home and called Mona, trying to go through their holiday plans, when Darren called. "Let me call you back." She clicked over to the other line.

"Hello."

Darren said, "Hey, um, Thanksgiving is in a couple of weeks. I wanted to see how we're going to work that out?"

"Well, the kids are with me that week, so if you want to come get them for a few hours during the day, that's fine. Maybe from twelve to four or five?"

He answered with no argument, "Okay, that'll work."

"Okay bye." She quickly hung up.

She called Mona back, who asked, "Hey, what's up?"

"Nothing, that was Darren, trying to ask about Thanksgiving. It's funny how he'll work something like that out with no problem, but he won't work out the day to day custody."

Mona responded, "You know he's crazy. Why do you keep expecting him to act like a normal person? Anyway . . ." They went on to talk about the relatives that were coming out, and made the necessary plans and arrangements.

Cynthia hung up and thought about DL. She knew his parents had passed away and, except for Roger, what family he had were all in Georgia. She figured it would be nice if he could spend the holiday with her family and finally meet the kids. She called and invited him, and he happily agreed.

Chapter Nineteen

DL drove down to Arizona the day before Thanksgiving. When he arrived, Cynthia greeted him outside. They hadn't seen each other for two weeks. He hugged her closely and kissed her. "I miss you baby," she said.

His embrace warmed her like a security blanket. "Me too."

She pulled him by the hand. "Come on, come in. You can meet the kids."

When they entered, Summer and Lil Darren were in the living room. They looked at him in suspicious bewilderment and said, "Hi."

DL shook their hands and felt their distress. "Hey guys, I brought some games." He unpacked his X-Box.

Lil Darren's face lit up. "Awe, cool!"

After hooking up the game, he turned on his laptop for Summer and she got online and played games on the Disney website. While they sat there playing, Mona came by to visit. Cynthia turned on some music and started to cook dinner. She prepared lasagna and the aroma from the simmering garlic, onions, and peppers started to float throughout the house. DL hollered over from the couch, "Baby, that smells so good."

Summer sat down next to DL and started to look him up and down. She was only eight, but at times it seemed as though a wise old woman dwelt inside her body. Her face looked as though she had a million questions. DL felt her stare, paused the game and asked, "What's up baby?"

She asked boldly, "How old are you?"

He looked curious. "Why?"

Without hesitation she responded, "Cause you look like my brother Anthony's age, and he's only eighteen."

They all laughed. DL didn't answer. Cynthia looked over at him from the kitchen. "You better answer her. That's all I need is for her to go telling daddy that I'm dating an eighteen-year-old."

DL looked at her and chuckled. "No baby, I'm thirty two."

Summer approved. "Oh, then that's good."

She went back to playing on the computer. As she played, DL looked over at her as if in a trance for a few moments. "How old are you again?"

Summer answered, "Eight."

"You're the same age as my son."

"You have a son?"

"Yes."

"Why didn't you bring him? He could play with us."

"He doesn't live with me. He lives with his mom in Washington. He's too far."

"He's too far? Do you miss him?"

"Yes, I do."

"What's his name?"

"Kylon."

The last time DL had seen Kylon, the boy was only four. Realizing that pulled at his heart strings. The first two years of his life, DL worked nights, took care of him during the day, and had bonded with him very closely. Though he missed him, he had become very skillful at burying painful feelings.

Cynthia set the table and there was a knock at the door. She went to answer it. "Hey Mom, Dad, come in. We're just about to eat dinner. Want to stay?" They all ate and chatted while the music played. Cynthia's dad was sixty five. He had suffered a heart attack and a stroke a few years prior, and it was a little harder for him to get around now. DL helped him over to the couch and sat with him. They talked about the time they had both spent serving in the armed forces. Cynthia's dad had spent four years in Germany; DL spent two years there. Somehow, that time period seemed to be the highlight of their memories.

After her parents and Mona left, Cynthia tucked the kids into bed, and it was after ten o'clock. DL and Cynthia retreated to her room. He plopped down on the bed. "I love your bed. It's so big and comfortable."

"Thank you."

He patted the bed next to him. "Come lay with me. Thanks for dinner, it was good." He kissed her forehead. "And your kids are great."

"Thanks baby. I think they like you."

"Yea, kids love me."

"Oh yea . . . I stink, I'm gonna take a bath."

"Yea, you kinda smell like peppers."

"Tssst . . . Forget you."

While Cynthia was in the bathroom, DL lay there watching TV and thinking. He had been moving around so much and it had been a long time since he felt the love of a real family. It felt good and at times he longed for it again. His mind started to drift back to when he was a kid and how he loved going to his Grandma's and Grandpa's house, especially on holidays. He felt so safe with them, away from his father's rage, that he never wanted to go back home. Being around Cynthia's parents brought back that same feeling of reassuring comfort he used to get from them. He tried to fight off the truth, but the reality of the rolling stone he had become tore at his heart and mind. "She's so sweet, what am I doing?"

Just then, Cynthia came out of the bathroom; the scent of her vanilla body wash floated right through him. Her hair was still damp and with her bath towel wrapped around her body, she crawled up next to him. Her soft skin brushed against his as she started to kiss his neck. The fruity strawberry scent of her freshly washed hair was weakening and her kisses affected his body like a muscle relaxer.

She paused and said, "Here, let me turn off the TV." She walked over toward the armoire and shuffled through her cd's to find the one with love songs DL had made for her a few months earlier, and popped it into the player.

Then she lit a few candles. He watched her as she stood there, holding on to her towel with one hand and lighting tea lights with the other. It seemed that somehow the more beautiful she was, the worse he felt.

Cynthia could sense his distance, but reasoned with herself that he was probably tired from the drive. She reached over and got a bottle of body oil from her dresser. She stood next to the bed and said, "Take your clothes off baby, and lie on your stomach."
He did. She warmed the oil in her hands and starting with his scalp, she gave him a long tender massage.

As he felt the strength of her hands rubbing his neck, his shoulders, and his back, he started to fall into a trance. She continued down his lower back and his legs, taking her time with each muscle. She used her nails and scratched his back, then his scalp. Gently she turned him over and massaged his chest. Straddling his lap, she opened the bath towel and dropped it to the floor. Her breasts were as perfect and lovely as succulent fruits; he reached up and massaged them tenderly. Her caramel skin glowed in the candlelight like a goddess.

She leaned down and started to kiss his neck and his chest, slowly making her way down his abs. When she licked around his navel, he couldn't open his eyes. His heart pounded and the blood rushed from his brain, as her lips made their way lower, and lower. She used her tongue like a magic wand, savoring each taste like fine wine. He felt his breath leave his body. She did it so well, it was as though this were his first time. She stopped and positioned her body over his, she held him, stroked him, then put him inside of her. He looked up at her face as she moved passionately up and down over him.

Her eyes closed, she leaned her head back and it rolled to one side, uttering moans and sighs to express the gratification words could not. She opened her eyes, and looked into his while licking her lips. She softly blew him a kiss. He was hypnotized. He held her hips in his hands like treasure, admiring and cherishing her body like a rare jewel. As the love songs played, his emotions were overwhelming and he knew he loved her. His mind could think of no one else. Never had he felt such pleasure and such pain at the same time.

She began to whisper all the right things into his ear. He lifted them both up and laid her down on her back. They could see their reflection in the large mirror on the wall next to the bed as they made love. Softly in her ear, he said, "I love you Cynthia." He drank her in until he was fully intoxicated. They slept in each others arms until the sun rose.

Early in the morning, Cynthia got up to put the turkey in the oven. As she was stirring around in the kitchen the phone rang, it was Darren.

She answered, "Hello."

"Hey, do you mind dropping the kids off at my house at noon?"

"No, I don't mind. Why?"

He paused a moment. "Um, I'm just a little caught up right now."

"Okay, whatever. I'll drop them off."

Cynthia sensed that something was a little strange about that request, but she didn't really care enough anymore to give it much thought. She started to prepare the meal when DL came into the kitchen and kissed her.

"Good morning baby."

He started to help her. He wasn't a bad cook either and began to give her some useful tips. Her brother and sister arrived from California at about eleven o'clock and everyone was talking, drinking, laughing, and having a good time.

At a quarter to noon, Cynthia called out to the kids so they could head over to Darren's. DL rode along. When they arrived in front of his house, it looked desolate. Cynthia told Lil Darren, "Go and knock on the door."

He did, and knocked a few times, then yelled back to the car, "He's not answering!" Then he went around the back to see if that door was open.

While Lil Darren was checking, Cynthia tried to reach Darren on his cell phone a few times and left a message. "Hey Darren, not sure what's going on, but you aren't here and it's about ten minutes after twelve. I'll wait a few more minutes, then I'm heading back home. Just call me when you get this message." She called Lil Darren back to the car. "Come on babe, let's go. Maybe he'll call later."

They headed back.

Around two o'clock, Darren called.

He said, "Hey, it's me. Where are the kids?"

"What do you mean? They're here. Didn't you get my message?"

He answered, "Yea, but why didn't you just leave them here?"

Cynthia was shocked. "What? You wanted me to drop them off and leave them at your house by themselves, and on Thanksgiving? What are you talking about? That's crazy."

"Well, whatever. You're overreacting as usual. I'm here now. Can you bring them back?"

"Uh, no. You'll have to come and get them. I have family here. I'm not leaving again."

"Alright, I'll be there in a few minutes. Listen for my honk."

A few moments later there was honk outside, and the kids scurried to the door. Cynthia leaned down and kissed them as they left. "I love you, be good. I'll see you guys later."

They ran out. "Bye Mommy."

About seven o'clock, the children returned and immediately they wanted to go next door to see their grandparents and the relatives that were visiting there. It was dark out as they rushed back through the front door and Cynthia yelled out, "Wait! Let me get my shoes and walk you over."

But they didn't hear her and flew out the door like bats out of a cave. Cynthia's father came in while she was exiting and said, "Hey baby girl, did you know Darren is outside with the kids?" She answered, "No, I thought he left."

When Cynthia stepped out, Darren didn't see her and she listened at a distance. Apparently, while the kids were with him during the day, they must have mentioned to him that DL was over. He was obviously jealous and was questioning the kids about him. It was clear that he was trying to hang around and get something started. Cynthia looked the other direction and saw his car parked next to the apartment. There was a female waiting inside.

Cynthia thought, "No he's not questioning the kids about my boyfriend being here and his chick is sitting in the car!" She was upset.

She approached him. "What are you doing here, Darren?" He raised his voice and answered, "I was leaving when I saw the kids running around in the dark! If you're not gonna watch them then—"

She cut him off. "Lil D, Summer, go over to Grand Mommy's." Lil Darren ran off but Summer stayed next to her. Cynthia raised her voice,

"Just leave Darren. You know they were just walking over to my Mom's. You're just trying to start some mess!"

An argument began to brew, but Cynthia looked down and saw Summer's little face looking up at her with sadness, and she stopped herself. She took her hand and leaving Darren standing there, they started toward her door. She said over her shoulder, "You know what? You can stand out here as long you want." When she opened the door it hit DL; he was standing on the other side like he was ready to jump out at any minute.

"What are you doing?"

DL answered, "I heard you guys. If he did something stupid, I was ready."

Chapter Twenty

The day after the holiday DL headed home. His cell phone rang during the drive. He answered and talked almost the whole way. When he got back into Vegas, he got off of the phone and threw it angrily down onto the floor of his truck in distress. “Fuck!”

He stopped at Roger’s since he had promised to bring him left-overs. Cecelia was over visiting with Lil Roger. Even though she and Roger weren’t together at this time, they had managed to remain friends, and she was like a sister to DL. They kicked back on the couch and started to watch TV.

Roger warmed up the food, and plopped down next to DL. “Man, this turkey is good, and these greens. Mmm mm.” He paused licking his fingers and smacking his teeth. “Did Cynthia cook this?”

DL answered his mind distant. “Yea, I helped her a little bit, but she cooked it.”

Roger replied, “Damn, she’s fine, plus she can cook too. You need to keep this one for real.”

DL looked over at him. “I know, huh.”

Roger added, “Plus, she’s just cool people.”

Cecilia joined in. “Really? I can’t wait to meet her.”

DL said, “You met her at Roger’s show over at Barry’s Nugget a few months ago.”

Cecilia tried to remember. "I may have met her, but who can keep up with your women? I don't know which one she is."

DL looked over at them with a strange look on his face, and he was sweating a little.

"What's up man? What?" Roger insisted.

DL leaned forward and put his head in his hands. "Man I fucked up." Roger put his turkey leg down, chewing and wiping his mouth with a wash cloth. He asked again, "What?" But he knew that look from experience all to well. "Is she pregnant?" He asked as he patted DL's back. "It's cool man, she's good people. It'll work out." DL looked over at him. "Man, Cynthia's not the one that's pregnant."

Roger paused and asked, "Then who? Please don't sit there and tell me you got Leslie's ass pregnant?"

"Man, HEEEELLLL naw!"

"Then who? The Asian?"

DL was unable to look up. "No man, Holly."

"Awe dude. That crazy bitch? Damn!"

Roger shook his head slowly in denial as he felt the air of maturity come over him. He had three daughters of his own by two different women and one son by another. He knew first hand the torment of his brother's regret. His role as the eldest brother took over.

"Man damn. Cynthia's a good woman. You gonna tell her?"

Cecilia interjected, "Why the hell would he do that?"

To DL, even the thought of telling Cynthia ripped him to shreds. "I really care about her, I can't tell her this. Not after what she has already been through . . . I can't tell her this." There was a lump the size of a lemon in his throat and his heart felt like it was attacking him for being so careless.

"Well, what the fuck man? I don't know what to tell you. I told you needed to tighten up your game."

Roger felt horrible; he knew how good Cynthia was to him, and being older, he knew how hard it was to find a woman like her. But telling DL all of that now would be like pouring hot coals on his head. He just repeated, "I don't know man. Damn. You sure it's yours?"

"Pretty sure."

"You better get that test man. Get that test."

Cecelia glared at him. She was a short, round, fiery Latina woman who had grown up with a loving father and a strict mother who didn't take any BS, so it was hard for her to tolerate BS. Holding both hands up in confusion, she threw her opinions at DL like darts at a board: "Well, if you care about her, why were you fuckin around? And if you knew you were going to fuck around, why didn't you wrap your package? I swear you two act like sixteen year olds!" She went into the bedroom frustrated and cursing in Spanish. She grumbled,

"Malditos hombres. Eres egoista todos los perros en celo!"

DL didn't answer her. The room was silent for a few moments. With his voice low, and his elbow propped up on his knee, he massaged across his forehead and announced, "I'm moving up to Portland."

Roger stood up. "What man? Why would you do that? You're gonna adjust your whole life for that bitch? Get an abortion!"

Cecelia yelled from the other room, "That's your answer, huh? That solves the problem?"

Roger hollered back, "Shut up! Mind your own business. Damn!"

DL, trying to speak and think clearly but failing, admitted, "Man, before my brain even had time to register the fact that she's pregnant, she told me that she won't have an abortion. I already have a son I don't know. I don't want to do that again."

"You know she did this on purpose! I told you she was messed up, didn't I? Damn. When are you moving? You just moved here!" Roger loved having DL close by and hated the thought of him leaving.

"Uh, probably the end of January sometime. She's due in July."

"And Cynthia, she loves the hell out of you, man. What are you going to tell her?"

"I don't know, I'll think of something. Or maybe I'll just disappear. She'll be better off anyway."

"You damn right she will. I haven't been a knight in shining armor myself. But you fucked up this time, lil bro. All I got is three letters for you: D-N-A."

Chapter Twenty One

During the Christmas holiday, Cynthia thought it was important to spend it with her children. DL told her he had plans to be out of town. He explained to Cynthia, "An old friend of mine knows a guy who owns an art studio in Portland. I gave her some of my photos to show him. He really liked them."

Cynthia said, "Really? That's great baby. What friend? I never remember you mentioning anybody from Portland?"

"Oh, Holly. She's an old girlfriend of my brother's, Holly Kelly."

Cynthia joked, "You sure she don't like you baby? You are fine, you know?"

"Naw. I'm cool, she's like forty three years old. Anyway, she showed her colleague some of my pictures and he's interested in possibly displaying them in his gallery. So I'll probably be there for a few days."

Which was a true story, there was a friend with a gallery that was interested in displaying his work, but DL conveniently left out the part about him screwing Holly. He called Cynthia throughout his trip. On Christmas Eve she was up late wrapping gifts when the phone rang.

She picked up. "Hello."

"Merry Christmas baby. I miss you."

She answered, "Oh baby, I miss you too. I wish you were here."

"Me too."

She asked, "So how's your trip going?"

"Well, we had a good meeting. His gallery is very nice. He's going to put my work up soon. When he does, I may have to move up here for a while. I could make a lot of money . . . But this chick Holly is getting on my nerves."

Thinking that was strange, Cynthia asked, "What do you mean?"

He answered in irritation, "She's just crazy. She's really pissing me off. Every time my phone rings, she's asking who it is and shit."

"Really? Why?"

"I don't know. We keep arguing about everything."

"Well babe, be patient. She's doing you a favor by introducing you to her friend. Don't let personality clashes get in the way of a possible blessing."

"You're right babe."

"So, you would move up there if he displays your work?" Cynthia knew his career was important and didn't want to get in the way of his dreams, but she couldn't help but feel disheartened.

"Yea, it would be a good opportunity for me to market my own photography, and possibly open my own studio."

"Baby, I'd hate to see you move, but you know I would support anything you feel would help you better yourself. Your photos are beautiful. I know you could be successful."

"I knew you'd understand, babe."

"I'd miss you, but do your thing. Do you . . . Listen, I really hate to go, but I want to finish wrapping these gifts and go to bed. I'm so tired. I'll call you tomorrow, okay."

He whined, "Noooo, stay on the phone. I miss you."

She laughed. "You're so crazy," she said, and then remembered, "Hey! When are we going to exchange our gifts? New Year's Eve?"

He answered, "Yea, that sounds good. What did you get me?"

"It's a surprise. Anyway babe, Merry Christmas. I'll call you tomorrow. I love you."

"Alright, I love you too. Goodnight."

Cynthia got off the phone and contemplated life without DL. It was a rough thought, and it hurt. But oddly, over the past few weeks she had been feeling guilty about sleeping with him and not being married. She loved him, but was nowhere near ready for that commitment again. She'd been praying about her life, what she wanted from it and what it actually was. Since the separation from Darren her personal life was kind of an organized mess. She had a lot of debt from her marriage and three children that needed her attention. Her spiritual roots seemed to be pulling her in the opposite direction than she was going. She thought, "Well, if he moves, then we can just be friends and I won't have to feel guilty anymore." But they got along so well, and he had become her best friend, that it pained her to think of living without him.

New Year's Eve, Cynthia headed up to Vegas about nine in the morning. She missed DL—they hadn't seen each other in over a month. She had shopped for hours the week before trying to find the best gift for him. She knew she had spent too much money, but thought her choice was perfect. Mona, and Denise, her other sister from California, and Mona's best friend, Sandra were all coming up to Vegas later that night to party with them at Roger's show at the New Orleans Casino, and bring in the new year.

When she got to DL's place, she parked and started up the walk way. He dashed out of the front door as if he were on fire. He grabbed her around the waist and forcefully walked her into the house. Kissing her passionately, Cynthia couldn't resist as he backed her onto the bed. He never seemed shy or inhibited with her like some guys have and she liked that. The excitement was overwhelming.

She stopped him. "No wait. We have to wait until midnight." He replied, "Babe, I've been waiting a month. I need you." Gently biting and sucking her neck, he said, "Oh my goodness you taste so good."

She couldn't stop him. She said teasingly while he kissed her neck, "I've got your present. Don't you want to open it?"

He stopped, and turned into a six-year-old kid. "Oh yeah! YAY!"

He popped up from the bed. "Wait, let me go get yours." He opened the closet door, and pulled a fancy pink gift bag down from the shelf. "Here, open yours first."

Cynthia reached for it smiling. "Thank you baby. You're so sweet." The bag had an assortment of Victoria's Secret lotions and body washes, but there was also a separate wrapped box. She opened it and inside was her favorite scent that she had not been able to purchase in years because it was so expensive

She wailed out, "Oh baby, Chanel! Thank you! Oooh, you got the big one, too." Thank you so much!" She kissed him repeatedly. He also enclosed a card. She handed him a small wrapped gift box and while he opened it, she read the card.

He opened his gift with excitement. “Damn! Diamond earrings! Baby, can you afford these? Thank you so much.” A smile spread across his face and he immediately jumped over to the mirror and put them on.

His card touched her heart. It had a long Hallmark love poem, but he also wrote in his own words:

Baby, I’m so glad you are in my life. I have never had a more beautiful relationship, and I love you so much. I know this next year will only bring us more joy as we grow closer together and more in love. Merry Christmas and happy New Year.
Love, DL

She got up and hugged him as he admired his new bling in the mirror. “Baby, thank you for being such a sweet man. You make me so happy. I love you.”

DL turned and kissed her forehead, putting his arms around her waist. “You make me happy too, baby.”

About six that evening, they drove over to Roger’s apartment to follow him to the casino in order to make sure they had no trouble at the door getting in. Roger’s current significant other, Marisol, was there to give him a ride. They followed, and Marisol needed to make a stop at her babysitter’s apartment first.

DL and Cynthia waited for them outside in the parking lot. It was dark and there were no other people around. Cynthia leaned over to DL’s ear and made him an offer he couldn’t refuse. When he was about half way to his boiling point, Roger and Marisol came walking out toward the car. Cynthia’s head popped up and they laughed.

DL was annoyed. “Shit, that man has impeccable timing.”

Cynthia kissed his cheek. "Don't worry baby, you know I'll take care of you later."

They arrived at The New Orleans Casino in full party mode. Mona, Denise, and Sandra joined them at the entrance. They found a table in the lounge where Roger was playing. New Year's Eve in Vegas, and the club was crowded. The atmosphere was like a blazing fire. Everyone was ready to shed the year like a snake sheds its skin. Cynthia fit her jeans very well as usual and wore her new Chanel fragrance like a queen wearing her crown. At eight o'clock, the band started and soon the obvious drunks were at full throttle. Everyone was on the floor dancing and having the time of their lives.

DL, Cynthia, and Denise were sitting this one out. Mona, Sandra, and Marisol were still on the floor. Mona was spinning her head around and dancing like a Soul Train regular when her hair piece flew off her head and slid all the way across the floor. Cynthia saw the hair piece in motion and tried to get up and help, but her laughter prevented her from walking upright.

DL and Denise hadn't noticed it fly off but saw it laying there next to them on the floor. Denise looked down in a drunken haze her body jerked in fear, and she shouted, "What the hell is that?" DL jumped out of his seat and squinted in confusion at the unidentifiable hairy object on the floor. "Is it dead?"

Mona quickly rushed over and retrieved it. She stepped away to the restroom and hooked it right back on her head, then returned to the dance floor as if nothing happened. They were laughing so hard they could hardly breathe. DL looked at Cynthia and said, "Your sister is crazy!"

Trying to calm her uncontrollable laughter she could barely speak, "I know!"

Just then, Sandra and Mona returned to the table. Sandra had brought along some very small "cigarettes," and whispered the offer to them. Mona popped up to join her. DL looked over at Cynthia like a child begging for a toy, and asked, "Can I, baby?" He kissed her cheek.

She reluctantly gave her permission. "Go ahead. It's New Year's Eve."

The three of them headed out of the casino and to the car. While they were smoking and talking, Mona looked over at DL in all seriousness and said, "You seem like a cool guy, and my sister really loves you. Please don't hurt her. She's been through so much." She paused and took another hit, "Plus, if you do, I'll have to kick your ass myself."

DL answered, "I love your sister too. You don't have to worry about that."

As they walked back inside, DL was behind Mona scoping out her size. He realized that if she wanted to kick his ass she could probably do it; she was a big girl. There must be something sobering in lying, because his high was coming down way too quickly. The reality of hurting Cynthia was too heavy to think about. He found a server and threw back a shot of tequila to sail him right back into fantasy land.

When it got close to midnight the MC began the count down. DL took Cynthia onto the dance floor and held her in his arms. At the stroke of midnight they kissed, as the band played "Auld Lang Syne." She looked up at him completely in love. There was no place in the world she would rather have been. She felt their relationship had been the perfect dream. "I love you so much, D."

He replied, "I love you too."

But Cynthia sensed something cold in his response, and she didn't feel the same connection she usually felt in his kiss. Her head tilted to the side and it was as if she had a big question mark above her head. This was the first time she'd felt a disconnection with him, and it threw her.

About one in the morning, the night began to wind down and everyone was ready to head home. On the way out, Cynthia quietly suggested to DL that they make a stop on the way home, and DL's face lit up like a neon sign on the strip. They said some good nights and headed out of the casino. Cynthia looked over at DL's face as they approached the car, and said, "Uh, I better drive, you're high." She reached for the keys.

He agreed, "Yea, I think you're right." He climbed in on the passenger side.

She pulled into the parking lot of an adult store and they ran in giggling like children headed for Chuck E. Cheese. They ventured around the store for thirty minutes, picking up stuff and laughing, trying to guess how they worked.

They found a few toys and headed back to DL's place. Anxiously, they rushed in the door. The sensation in their bodies was uncontrollable, and the high from the night was at its peak as they fell into the bed like two untamed animals. They messed around until almost five in the morning.

DL out of breath, said, "You know what? You're a freak. I never would have guessed that when I first saw you. I thought you would be more of a prude, but you're a straight up freak."

She giggled. "Uh huh, never judge a book by the cover."
They dozed off.

Later that morning, DL awoke before Cynthia. In the bathroom where he sat and did most of his thinking, he pondered about his life. He knew he didn't want to lose Cynthia. But it was too late for that now. He thought, "She deserves so much better than me. She's too good for me. She doesn't even curse!"

He reflected on his past, thinking of his two ex-wives and the different women he had dated. Every time the relationships ended, whether he cheated or not, he had always felt justified. None of his relationships were healthy, and actually all of them had displayed some form of disfunction. Either they argued all the time about everything, or the women cheated on him. His second wife wouldn't work—at home or at a job. A few girlfriends had psychological issues that made it obvious they weren't mentally balanced. One girl he dated in his early twenties still peed in the bed. He cut her off quick. Another woman had Post Traumatic Syndrome. If her stress level got too high, she would pass out completely in the middle of an argument. On one occasion, she fell and hit her head. One of the neighbors heard them yelling and called the police and DL was almost arrested for domestic violence.

But Cynthia had been so different. She was human, she wasn't perfect, but she was normal. He knew what they shared was something he had longed for all of his life. She had so many positive qualities about her that when he was around her, he could feel her making him a better person. He cared for her even with her flaws. She slept like a wild animal, and snored like a pig in a pen, and he didn't care. With any other woman that would have pissed him off, but with her, it was funny.

"How did I manage to screw this up so badly?" He opened up that storage box in the attic again, and stuffed more articles inside.

When he came out of the bathroom, Cynthia was in the kitchen, humming and making breakfast. Even in the morning with no make up on and her hair a mess, she looked incredible. He felt sorrowful, but hid it. She reached for him and held her cheek out for a kiss. “Good morning baby.”

He kissed her cheek. Then took a little nibble at it. “Good morning.”

“You want some coffee?” She poured him a mug.

He reached for it, saying, “Thank you baby . . .” Then took a sip. “UGH!” He spit it out.

“Damn! This is too strong. Is this espresso?”

She laughed. “No, you wuss, it’s real coffee, not that sissy apple crap you drink from Starbucks.”

“I can’t drink this, it taste like mud.” He laughed. “Another flaw” he thought to himself, “ . . . and it’s funny.”

“Forget you!” She grabbed his chin, wiggled his face, and spoke like to a baby, “I’ll make a weaker pot just for you, you big baby.”

She made their plates, and they got comfortable in the living room and ate in front of the TV. Cynthia looked over at him and studied his features.

“You’re so handsome, babe.”

“No, I’m not. I need a shave.”

“No. I like it when you have a five o’clock shadow at nine in the morning. It’s sexy.”

Cynthia was also avoiding bringing up his moving plans, but at the same time wanted to talk about it. She asked, “So have you decided for sure about moving?”

His heart pounded, he looked over at her and leaned back on the couch. “Yea, I’m gonna to move. Since he displayed my work I’ve sold a lot of pieces. I need to be there.”

Her face saddened. “Oh, okay babe. I understand . . . So when?”

“Uh, most likely by the end of the month.”

She hesitated, then asked, “So . . . What about us?”

He acted as though everything were fine. “We’re going to keep going just like we have.”

“Babe, we can’t do that. Portland is too far.”

He pulled her over to him on the couch and held her. “Yes we can.”

She asked, “Are you sure you want that?”

“Yes I do.”

He just couldn’t do it. He picked up their plates and took them into the kitchen. He washed the dishes and wiped down the counters. The apartment was too silent. The thought came to him that with any other woman there would have been an argument going on right now. But not Cynthia, she never asked too many questions or talked too much. She just took everything he said as the truth, and he knew that he had taken advantage of that.

When he returned to the couch, she was sitting there content, peacefully reading a book. He sat down next to her and reached for her legs, putting them across his lap. He smelled her peach-scented moisturizer and lifted her toes to his lips and kissed them. Then laid them back down over him. He picked up his X-box controller and asked, “You wanna play me?”

"I don't know how."

He handed her the other controller. "Here I'll show you."

Chapter Twenty Two

January 10, Cynthia had to bring the kids to mediation so that the court's counselor could talk with them. Having to put her kids through that was challenging, and now all she could do was wait for the custody decision at the divorce proceedings, which were scheduled for February 8. After they finished, she dropped Lil Darren and Summer off at school and headed for work.

Once there, she opened her email and saw that she was scheduled to go to New York in March. The bank she worked for was involved in a merger and needed experienced managers to go out and train the new staff. She had done this last year and was very excited to do it again. She called DL.

"Babe, guess what?"

"Hey baby. What's up?"

"I'm going to New York again in March."

Last year when Cynthia had gone she had only just met DL and he wanted to join her then, but she declined, so he was just as excited. "I'm going this time!"

She responded, "But you'll be in Portland by then."

"So? I'll fly out and meet you there."

"Okay, cool. I gotta get to work. I'll talk to you later."

As the days went by, it had become harder and harder for Cynthia to focus. She had a lot going on. Her divorce and custody, her career, and with DL moving, it just added to her anxiety. She found herself taking PM pills every night just to get enough sleep. It started with just one a night, a month ago. Now she was up to three.

She and DL had planned to see each other one more time before he moved. He came down to Arizona to be with her that weekend. They decided to drive to the Grand Canyon. He had never been and wanted to take pictures there before leaving. It was almost a three-hour drive from Cynthia's place, so they left early on Saturday morning.

The temperature was in the low twenties and snow-capped the mountains. The view was breathtaking. They walked around the canyon for hours and DL snapped tons of shots. He handed Cynthia his camera. "Here, take a few."

"I don't know how to use this camera. It looks expensive. What if I drop it over the canyon?"

DL's face fell. She giggled. "I'm just playin."

She got closer to the rail and he stood behind her. "Here, I'll show you."

She snapped a few shots. "Oh yea, this camera is easy. Here now, let me take some of you."

DL posed while she snapped shots of him. "Okay, your turn."

Cynthia made silly faces while he snapped shots of her. He leaned in and kissed her, "You're so pretty babe."

"Thank you."

The air was so crisp that even being bundled in coats, hats, and gloves, it still felt as though their bones had become icicles. DL said, "I never knew Arizona could get this cold. Come here, let's snuggle up."

"Yea. I'm freezing."

Finally, they ducked into a museum and learned from a tour guide all about the California Condor and how they were near extinction, but were being saved there in the Grand Canyon. Cynthia asked the guide, "If it's a California Condor, why is it being saved in Arizona?"

DL just shook his head, "Baby, I don't know about you sometimes."

"What? That's a legitimate question."

Finally they decided to leave and stopped in a small town to eat before getting back on the highway. They sat and talked in the restaurant, both trying to avoid reality. She had always been able to talk with him so openly, but today she felt a wall. She busted through it. She did not want anything to stop her from loving him every moment she could.

When they got back to Cynthia's place it was about four. They plopped down on the couch and slept for a couple of hours. Cynthia woke up and looked over at the clock, it read 6:22 p.m.

"You hungry?"

DL turned over. "Yea."

"I think I'll order a pizza."

He sat up scratching his head. "Yea, pizza sounds good."

DL went and showered then fell back down on the couch. He nestled up to Cynthia like a baby cub to his mama. She turned over and started massaging his scalp. She knew he loved that. She leaned her nose down to his neck and kissed it. "You smell good baby."

Then she sniffed her armpit. Her face soured. "Eve, I think I better take a shower too."

She got up wearing a black cotton tank top and panties. He slapped her booty, and said, "Mmm mm . . . Must be jelly, must be jelly."

"Ouch!" She giggled, then drug her tired body down the hall way. "Listen for the pizza man."

"Okay baby."

When Cynthia came out of the bathroom the pizza was there, so they ate and watched a movie. She motioned to get up. "I forgot to get us a drink."

He stopped her. "No, sit baby. I'll get it."

From the kitchen he called out, "Babe, you want water right?"

"Yes, please."

He poured her a glass of water then shuffled through the refrigerator. "Babe, I don't see any pop in here. Do you have any?"

She answered, "Oh, check in the laundry room. On the shelf above the dryer."

"Okay." DL opened the door to the small laundry room next to the kitchen. In shock he wailed out, "DAAAAAMN!"

Cynthia popped up and rushed over, “What!”

DL was standing there with his mouth hanging open. Mona had been over earlier that week using the washer and she’d left her bras hanging up. They were triple D’s. His eyes were wide open. “I’ve never seen a bra that big in my life!”

Cynthia pushed past him laughing. “Tss, be quiet! You scared me.” She reached for the soda and shut the laundry room door. He stood motionless then opened the door again to take a second look.

Cynthia chuckled. “You act like you’ve never seen a bra before.”

“Not that size, shit. Up until you, maybe a B cup is all I’ve ever had.”

She looked at him with pity, put her hand on the center of his back and rubbed it around in circles. “Poor baby, you’ve been deprived.”

They finished eating and watching TV, still not talking about the obvious. They climbed into bed and Cynthia turned on some music. They made love, and it was slow and sweet. Somehow when they were together, it was like they were set on cruise control, relaxing and enjoying the pleasure of each other’s bodies. Like a beautiful drive across the country taking in the view along the way as if it were their last. When they finished, Cynthia lay there with her head on his chest, and he held her closely. “Tender Love” played on the stereo, and Cynthia recorded the moment in her mind and heart knowing she didn’t want to ever forget it. She thought, “There could never be drug created that gives this kind of high.” She fell asleep and slept better than she did with the sleep aid.

Face to face, DL watched her for almost thirty minutes. He had been with her for almost a year now, and still every time he was with her he was just as excited as the first. A tear rolled from his eye as he gently touched her face, and slowly ran his fingers down the side of her cheek. He whispered, "I'm so sorry baby." Sleeping, she couldn't hear, but he'd hoped her spirit felt his. He kissed her lips softly. She opened her eyes just a little, still in dreamland. She smiled, turned over, and started to snore. He grinned and chuckled under his breath.

DL couldn't sleep. His mind was like a lab rat in turmoil, trying to find a way through this maze he had created. He knew he had to make an adult decision. But what? It was as though he heard 9,151,974 little voices in his brain all telling him different things to do. He was a boy who physically had grown into a teenager and then into a man. But mentally, he was still that little child who had been abused and neglected by his father.

At eighteen years old, he was sent out into the world to live his life unprepared. Now instead of living a life, his life was just happening to him. It seemed that every time he was right at the brink of happiness, like a mist of perfume sprayed from a bottle, it would blow away as quickly as it appeared. Cynthia remained a lovely scented fragrance he'd always remember. His heart felt like a hollow well, as though his spirit left him in frustration.

In the morning he woke up to an incredible sensation of pleasure. He looked down below his waist and saw Cynthia underneath the cover. "Oh my God! What are you doing to me?" When they finished, she nestled up under his arm and they lay and talked for hours, too weak and lazy to move.

"You know what's cool?" He asked.

"What?"

"It's just a boring day, but with you, I don't feel bored."

She said, "I know, huh." Then she brought the conversation around to the inevitable. "Baby, you know this relationship will probably fade after you move. I don't want to tie you down like that. I understand you're a man, if you ever want to see other people just let me know, okay?" She looked up into his eyes with sincerity.

He looked at her lovingly, stroking his fingers through her hair. "Baby, this is the healthiest relationship I've ever been in. I want to make it work."

She said, "I just don't know how we could do that. You'll be so far away."

"I'll fly down every chance I get. I'll be in New York with you in a couple of months. It'll work out. Don't worry."

He had a way of making her feel secure and she trusted in his words. "Okay."

Chapter Twenty Three

Midnight, February 8. Cynthia lay in bed riddled with anxiety. Divorce court was scheduled for ten in the morning. She had taken three sleeping pills but they had no effect. She tossed and turned remembering when she'd first met Darren. How in love they were at one time. How when they were dating he used to sing love songs to her. He had been so good at wooing her.

Even after they were married, every time he screwed up, he would say and do all the right things, apologizing to the point of tears. Each and every time for years, she would believe him. He'd turn into a model husband for about three months, sometimes even six. Then the same cycle of destruction would start all over again.

Cynthia questioned the dark night: "How did this happen? How did I get here? For so many years I loved him, now it's just dead." She thought through the memories, trying to recall some of the good ones. But then, right along with the few good ones, were trails of bad ones. Eventually, all there were, were bad ones outweighing the good at least 10 to 1.

She knew a divorce was the right choice for this relationship. Once her mind was made up the relief was like a one hundred pound sack of cement was lifted from her back. Not once after leaving Darren did she second guess her choice.
She slept a little then the alarm rang. As she pulled the covers back to get up

DL called. "Hello."

"Hey baby, just wanted you to know I'm thinking bout you."

"Thank you . . . I'm so nervous."

"Why?"

"I don't know. I guess just being in a court room in front of the judge again. My parents will be there. I just can't wait for it all to be over."

He encouraged her. "You're strong baby. Everything will be fine."

"Thank you babe."

"Your welcome. Call me as soon as you're finished, okay?"

"Okay, I will."

Cynthia got ready, then left. She stopped to pick up her parents then drove downtown to the court house. They were scheduled for ten o'clock. Cynthia checked in with the clerk. "Hi, excuse me. I'm Cynthia Wilson. I have a divorce hearing scheduled for ten."

"Yes. However, Judge Ross had to take an emergency case. Yours will be delayed until eleven."

"Oh. Okay, thank you."

It turned out they were delayed until after noon. When they entered the court room, the judge made it clear that she was working through her lunch hour. It was evident from her rash tone that she was hungry and irritable. Cynthia's parents sat in back. Darren had brought his current girlfriend along, and she waited in the hallway just outside of the court room. The judge hit her gavel and explained the order in which the proceedings would take place.

Cynthia was called to the stand first. She had made an outline of what she wanted to say, but her mind was so clouded that she forgot to bring it up to the stand with her. She spoke from memory starting with the abuse. She explained in detail what she had suffered throughout the marriage.

Her mother wailed out in shock, "Oh my God!" And started to cry.

Her father echoed, "Got dammit!" He held his head down as if somehow he were at fault.

When Cynthia fought to speak, the judge asked, "Mrs. Wilson do you need a recess?"

"No. It's just that I've never told my parents about this, I never wanted my family to know. Having to speak about it aloud is extremely difficult."

She was ashamed that she had allowed Darren to treat her that way, and for so long. She moved on from that and spoke about his philandering, also she added the fact that he had fifteen jobs during their eleven-year marriage, thus he was not stable enough to provide for the children. The judge interjected a question every now and then. When she was finished, Cynthia's face was swollen from crying and her voice was hoarse. They took a five-minute recess as Darren drummed up a cry, and stood in the hallway embracing his girlfriend.

When they were called back inside, it was Darren's turn to speak. He denied everything Cynthia said to be true. The judge asked, "Mr. Wilson, can you tell me about the physical abuse. Did that happen? Let me remind you that you are under oath."

He answered, "Yes, Your Honor. There was abuse, but it was mutual. Cynthia inflicted me with the same abuse she described. I was abused by her as well, Your Honor. It was mutual."

Cynthia's mouth fell open. "I can't believe what I'm hearing." She yelled out, He is lying!"

The judge interjected, "Order! Mrs. Wilson. Please do not interrupt again."

Cynthia fought her own will and stayed quiet in total disbelief as Darren continued to lie about everything on the stand. Then he stepped down. Cynthia's mind was in disarray. "All those years I stayed with him taking so much crap, believing that somewhere inside he was truly a good person. I've wasted a huge part of my life. He never loved me." The truth ran over her like a freight train.

The judge asked, "Mrs. Wilson, are you asking for your maiden name to be returned to you?" Before Cynthia could answer, Darren hollered out, "Yes! She doesn't deserve my name!"

Remembering the conversation she'd had with Lil Darren, she felt horrible.

She felt as though her throat had been sliced with that knife he held to it all those years ago. Cynthia struggled to remain collected and spoke softly, "Yes please, Your Honor."

The judge gave Cynthia back her maiden name of Stewart. She left the custody the way it was, granted the divorce, and shuffled them out of the court room like cattle, calling for the next case. It was a monstrosity.

Cynthia lost all control in the hallway and cried uncontrollably in her parents' arms. Darren walked over to her and tried to say something, but she turned and screamed, "Get away from me you bastard! You're going straight to hell for what you just said!" Her mother cursed him as well, while her father struggled to settle them both down. Finally, the clerk came out and pulled them into a private room. "Ms. Stewart, please come in here. You can sit as long as you need to."

Cynthia didn't want to see Darren or his girlfriend outside, she was afraid of what she might do. So she went into the room. Her anger boiled like lava as she remembered all that she'd endured with him. Her head collapsed down on the desk and she began to pray silently in her mind to God: "Lord, you know he's lying. Help me not to do something evil because of this circumstance. Please calm my spirit, and take away my anger."

The clerk brought her a glass of water and a box of tissues. A few moments later, she looked over at her parents, and said, "Let's go. I just want to crawl into bed."

Her mother held her as they walked. "He'll be sorry, Cynthia. Nobody gets away with treating another person so badly. He'll be sorry."

Cynthia climbed in bed as soon as she walked in the door. Not even removing her shoes she lay there for hours tossing and turning, replaying the scene over and over in her mind. Her head felt like it had been struck by a natural disaster as she tried to figure out what she should have said or done differently. None of that mattered now. It was done, and at least she was divorced.

A few hours had passed and her head continued to ache. Nothing she took got rid of it. Her phone rang, and she thought, "I don't want to talk to anybody."

She saw it was DL and let it go to voice mail. An hour later he called again, and this time she answered. Her voice broken and weak, she said, "Hello."

"Baby, you didn't call me."

"I know. I'm sorry."

He asked, "How'd it go?"

"I don't really want to talk about it."

"Okay babe. But are you divorced?"

"Yes, thank God, at least I have that."

"Are you okay? Do you need to talk?"

"No, but thank you babe. Some roads you have to walk with just you and God."

"Alright baby. Call me if you need to."

She regretted never having Darren arrested. She regretted ever meeting him. But the thought of her beautiful children pulled her through the night. She felt as though Darren still had suffered no consequence for his actions, and she knew that still, that was her own fault. Then she realized that wasn't up to her to worry about anymore. She picked up her Bible from the night stand and started to read, something she hadn't done in several months. She read a passage in Romans 12:17:
"Do not repay anyone evil for evil. Be careful to do what is right in the eyes of everyone. Do not take revenge, my friends, but leave room for God's wrath. For it is written: It is mine to avenge, I will repay, says the Lord.."

Also she read Matthew 6:14:
"For if you forgive men when they sin against you, your heavenly Father will also forgive you. But if you do not forgive men their sins, your Father will not forgive your sins."

She prayed, "God I know you've seen the years I spent in that marriage. I know you know the truth, even if Darren lied to the court, the judge, whoever. Lord, you know I gave everything I had to that man trying to save our family."

She felt comfort come over her spirit like the sun rising the morning after a long rainy night. One of her favorite hymns came to mind, "The Storm is Passing Over," and she started to sing it. She prayed to forgive Darren, and for her own forgiveness, then she let go of that burden. She felt strengthened and got up to eat.

Chapter Twenty Four

March. Cynthia had to leave for New York in a few days and arrived at work earlier than usual. She was going to be gone a week and a half and wanted to make sure everything was in order. It turned out to be a slow day, and she was getting a lot accomplished. Late in the afternoon she decided to take a lunch break. As she was exiting the office the water guy, Cedric, was entering. Quickly he put down the two five-gallon water jugs he was carrying on his shoulders, and rushed to hold the door for her. "Hello."

She blushed and walked through. "Thank you."

"You're welcome, lovely lady."

DL called while her face was still feverish. She got in the car and answered, "Hi baby."

He asked, "Hey babe. You all set to leave on Friday?"

"Yea, I think so."

"Baby, I miss you. I can't wait to see you."

"Me too, baby."

"Will you be working the whole time? Will we be able to do much sight seeing?"

"I'll be working a lot, but we'll squeeze it in, somewhere between work and lovemaking."

He laughed. "Yea, I know!"

"I guess I've got to get a room in Vegas the night before because my plane leaves at seven in the morning. I'd have to leave here by like three a.m. I don't want to drive up there that early."

DL suggested, "I'll call Cecilia, you know, Roger's ex. She's real cool. She'll let you stay at her house the night before."

"Are you sure? I've only met her once."

"Yea, she won't care. I'll ask her and call you back."

"Okay, let me know."

"Okay baby. Talk to you later. I love you."

"I love you too."

It was Friday, and although Cynthia had planned on heading up to Vegas at noon, the bank was too busy and she couldn't leave. She ended up staying until it closed at six. She called Cecilia, "Hi. Cecilia?"

"Yes, this is she."

"Hey, it's Cynthia."

"Oh hey. You still coming up?"

"Yes. Girl, this bank was a madhouse today. This town only has a population of about thirty five thousand and I think they all bank here."

Cecilia chuckled. "Really?"

"Anyway, I'll be there close to eight."

"Oh okay. I'll listen for you."

"Thanks again. I really appreciate you letting me spend the night."

"It's okay. Anytime."

When Cynthia arrived at Cecilia's, she was welcomed very warmly. They didn't know each other, so Cecilia made her a margarita and they ended up talking for a few hours. After chatting and laughing on and on about anything and everything, Cynthia looked over at the clock. "Whew, it's after eleven. I better go to bed."

"Alright. I'm glad you came and stayed with me. Feel free to keep in touch, okay?"

Cynthia said, "I will. Thank you so much. You've been so nice. I can't thank you enough for saving me that early morning drive."

"Oh, no problem. Anytime, I mean it. Goodnight."

Cecilia went to her room. She felt badly now that she had talked with Cynthia. She thought that she had a kind spirit about her and understood why Roger had been so upset with DL that night. She thought to herself, "That poor girl. She has no idea. He's such a punk." Cecilia wanted to tell her the truth about DL, but he was like a brother to her so she kept quiet.

In the morning Cynthia got up at four so she could get to the airport on time. Later that day she was in Minnesota on a layover. She sent DL a text message. He was in flight too and she wasn't sure where he was right then. He called. She answered, "Hi baby."

"Hi pumpkin, I miss you so much. I'm so anxious to see you. I don't know if I can live this far from you anymore."

"Awe, that's so sweet. I know." She heard her flight number called over the loud speaker. "I've got to go board. Call me as soon as you get into the city, okay?"

"Okay baby. Bye."

Cynthia arrived in New York, retrieved her luggage, and picked up her rental car. It was cold out and there was still snow on the ground. She drove carefully through the icy roads, and found her hotel. It was tucked behind the street surrounded by a forest of very tall trees, somehow still green and flourishing as if the winter hadn't touched them at all. The hotel was 18th century style and beautiful, like a Shakespearean castle. She checked in, and found her room, but it was rather plain. Nice, but not what she expected considering the extravagant lobby. DL's flight wasn't due in for another two hours, so she hopped in the shower and changed clothes. She wanted to look and smell her best. She was so anxious she couldn't stand it.

Finally he called, but she was already on her way back to JFK. "I'm almost there babe. What terminal are you in?" She hung up the phone and pulled into the airport parking lot. It was just past a year now since they first met, and this was the longest they had ever gone without seeing each other. Cynthia knew in her heart they couldn't do this very much longer, and it burned.

She parked and entered the terminal. She stood at a distance from the gate, so that she could see him before he saw her. Her mind flashed back to the first time she had met him at Arizona Charlie's Casino. She had done the same thing then. Time had flown by so fast. She stopped and bought a pack of gum and looked over at the people exiting the gate. Then she saw him. He was so handsome.

He wore a stylish knee-length, fudge brown leather coat, and his face was clean shaved and smooth. His hair was freshly cut low. She crept up behind him and grabbed his waist, his scent was a soft expensive cologne, maybe Bulgari. He turned around and hugged her as tightly as he could. He said, "I miss you so much." They kissed passionately.

When they got back to the hotel Cynthia attacked him, but DL was a little resistant, not at all his usual behavior. Her intuition was telling her that he was distant, she wasn't feeling the connection they once shared. They went out to eat and he took a call, obviously from a female. He did say to the caller that he was in New York with his girl. Later she couldn't help but ask him about it.

"D, who was that calling you earlier?"

"Oh, that was my friend up in Portland. It's nothing babe. She works with me. She knows about you."

But there was just something strange about the whole thing to Cynthia. She started to have the same feelings she had with Darren when he was messing around. But wanting to deny it, she convinced herself that DL would never treat her that way. She decided to push her insecurities aside and focus on having a good time. Over the next few days, they took in whatever sights they could when she wasn't working. When she was, DL just went out into the city and snapped photos on his own. He stayed with her for five days. The night before his plane was leaving they ate dinner in the room and shared a desert.

Cuddling up to her on the bed, he said, "I'm having so much fun with you, babe. I'm glad I could come."

"Me too. I wish you could stay longer."

"I know, but I have a wedding to shoot this weekend."

"I understand. "

DL popped open his notebook and started to download the pictures from his camera. She asked, "Did you get some good pictures?"

"Yea, I think so. I think I've taken like five hundred shots. My memory is near full."

"Oooh, I wanna see."

On their stomachs they lay side by side across the bed looking through them. They talked like the good friends they had become, and Cynthia sealed his face in her mind so that she would never forget it. As they chatted she massaged his hands, studying them, feeling as though this may be the last time she held them. She could feel he was different. Whatever window he had opened up in his heart for her months ago had closed along the way somewhere.

That night Cynthia couldn't sleep. She was in turmoil. It was like a war going on inside of her spirit. She wanted to talk to him, but didn't want to wake him. He felt her jostling around and reached over and held her. They spooned like that first night, and a tear rolled down her cheek. She wiped it off and fought the desire to cry. She knew it was over, but wasn't ready to feel the agony of another lost love.

Chapter Twenty Five

Early the next morning Cynthia and DL awoke and he made love to her, but it wasn't the same. She felt as though he had no soul. After work, she drove him out to the airport. When they got there, she got out and walked around to the sidewalk. They hugged and kissed goodbye. DL was completely shut down, and Cynthia felt it. Only she blamed herself, still oblivious to the truth, she just assumed that he had met someone else, perhaps he had become bored with her. She watched him walk into the gate, then drove back to the hotel. She fought the sadness like a prize winning boxer. She knew she still had a few more days to stay and work and she needed to focus. They kept in touch over the rest of her trip.

When Cynthia arrived home from New York she was bushed. She called DL the next morning and they talked for a few minutes. Over the next several weeks, the phone calls were less and less. They went from talking every day, to about once a week. She also noticed that she was making most of the calls. On a few occasions she tried to talk with him about how she was feeling, but he would just act like everything was fine.

In April Cynthia was about to purchase tickets for the annual trip she and her family took to Disneyland each summer. DL was supposed to join them this year. She wanted to remind him before buying the tickets to make sure he was still planning to go, so she called.

He answered, "Hey pumpkin."

"Hi babe. I have a question."

"Yea, what's up?"

"I'm online about to buy the tickets for Disneyland, but I wanted to make sure you were still able to go before I purchase them." She was ready to hear whatever.

He answered with excitement, "Yea, I am. I want to go."

"Okay, cool. I'll call you back in a bit."

Cynthia purchased the tickets, and called him back giving him the dates. May continued on with the same distant relationship. She knew she had to make a decision. He hadn't called her all week, and she didn't call him. She was not good at playing these types of relationship games. She was always one that said what she felt, and expected others to show her that same respect. Part of her knew what must be going on, but the other part didn't want to believe it was really happening. Friday afternoon she called him, thinking maybe he was on his lunch break.

He answered, "Hi baby."

She said, "Hey, I was just thinking about you. I miss you."

"Awe, me too baby. Can I call you later? I'm at work."

"Baby, don't say you're going to call me later if you're not going to call me later. I'm okay with you calling me in a few days."

He assured her, "No baby. I wanna talk to you. I'll call you tonight. I promise."

Later that night Cynthia waited on his call. But it never came. The same feeling of insecurity she had throughout her marriage started to infect her body like a bad disease. She pushed back the tears she felt welling to the surface, and could feel the cold chill of her heart hardening. That was Friday, and Sunday was Mother's Day. She thought for sure he would call to wish her a happy Mother's Day.

She and Mona took their mom out to lunch and to a movie. She made sure her cell was on, still DL hadn't called. She checked her phone when she got home. Nothing. She felt the all-to-familiar soreness of rejection settling in her chest like the flu. She knew in her mind that everything had changed, but her heart was still not ready to accept it. She got on her knees that night and prayed that she could face whatever the truth may be. That was very hard to do, because she believed in the power of true prayer.

Monday, as she was leaving work and setting the alarm for the night, her cell rang.

"Hello."

"Babe, it's me."

"What's up?" She spoke in monotone; it was as though her heart were dying.

"I'm so sorry." He quickly began to mutter an excuse, "My phone's been broken."

She was insulted and thought, "Does he think I'm that dumb!" She said in doubt, "Oh yea . . . hey, let me call you back. I'm trying to leave work. I'll call you when I get home."

When she got home she didn't call right away and deeply contemplated if she should. She loved DL and thought, "Maybe I'm over-reacting." Then decided, "I told him I would. Why should I play his game?" She called.

"Babe," she said calmly. "Are you cheating on me?"

He quickly denied it. "NO! Baby, I've just been really busy."

The phone went dead, and Cynthia tried to call back a few times.

Finally he did. "See? My phone is really broken."

She replied, "Look, you're way out there. It's obvious you're too busy. I'm busy, may be we should just put this on hold."

The line went dead again.

He called right back, "My phone is messed up." As they tried to talk the called dropped two more times. She waited and then decided to just send him an email. It read:

Babe,

Please bear with me here. First let me say that the last thing I want to do when we do get a rare chance to talk is argue about why you don't call me. The VERY LAST thing I want to do is argue about anything. I guess when you decided to move and we talked about making this relationship work, we didn't really talk about how to do that. Maybe I expected one thing and you another.

Or maybe neither one of us knew what to expect. A lot is going on in both of our lives and I MISS YOU terribly. What I miss most is being able to talk to you every night. I know what is to be busy. I have my children, their day to day, and this custody situation. Trying to keep my home in order, trying to get my life in order after that crazy chaotic marriage. Then there's work and the people and things I'm responsible for there. In all this I make calling you a priority because I want to, it's something you would never have to ask me to do. So when you say you have been too busy I wonder why you tell me you still want this. You are the sweetest man I have ever met. I thought what we've shared was very special to both of us.

Be real with me, D. If being in a relationship doesn't work for you right now, I understand. Maybe, it's the right thing at the wrong time. The last thing I want to do is hinder the advancement you're trying to achieve for yourself, or make you feel like "you better call me or else." But again, I truly do understand if it's just too much for you at this time in your life. I'm strong enough for you to tell me the truth even if it hurts. I would rather you tell me now than for things to just fall apart.

Love u sincerely,
Cynthia

After sending the email she called him. He answered, "Hey babe."

She said, "I sent you an email. Will you read it and then call me back?"

"Alright baby."

Chapter Twenty Six

DL never called back that night. The next day, Cynthia left him a message, then the next day . . . then the next. After about the fifth day, she realized that he was never going to call her back. For days she came in from work, checking her caller id, checking her email. Nothing. That evening she went online and sent him a final email, it read:

Babe,
Against all my hurt pride I have to send you one last e-mail because I care for you so much. You promised me that you would never do this to me. That if you wanted to break it off you wouldn't just ignore me, but that we would talk. I'd hoped that we could do this like adults and remain friends, because I thought what we had, in your words, was "something rare." Instead it's like you are choosing to completely shut me out, and burn all bridges. I opened up to you with all the pain I'd been through and you told me you would never hurt me this way. The worst is that I don't even know why? I love you D. Even though it didn't work out, at least I'll have one year in my life of knowing what a beautiful relationship could be.

. . . fighting tears, she pressed the send button. She remembered that shortly after DL moved to Portland he had started a website for his photography. She wanted to view it, to see if he had put up any of the pictures he had taken at the Grand Canyon and in New York, realizing she would probably never see all of them any other way. When she found the site she saw he had updated it with new categories. One was called "Nudes."

"That one wasn't there before." she thought. Her heart pounded nervously as she clicked the link. There she was. The nude body of a blonde, freckled, petite pregnant woman. Down toward the bottom of the page it listed her name, Holly Kelly. Cynthia remembered the name from his trip to Portland at Christmas time. Her back straightened, her arms dropped to her side, and her mouth fell open. She knew.

The truth hit her head like a hammer, busting it apart like a large rock and she thought she would faint. She looked at the tastefully posed photographs, examining each one in pain. The torture of viewing them was like being whipped and chained in a dungeon. Unable to bear it any further. She closed out the page, got up from the couch, and sluggishly moved down the hallway like a dead woman walking. She went into her bathroom and showered.

Cynthia tried desperately not to feel what had become a volcano in her heart for the last several weeks, now boiling over to eruption. She turned off the water and climbed out, then wrapped the towel around her body. She shut the bathroom door, then leaned her back against it. Powerless against the truth. Her body slid downward as if she were slowly being pulled by the weight of the agony. She fell to her knees and clutched her chest. Completely dejected, she lay prostrate on the floor and wept bitterly.

There was no way around her sorrow, no way to relieve it, no way to make it cease. There she was, naked and bare lying on her stomach, destitute. She remembered her prayer from the days before asking God to reveal the truth. She cried out, "Lord, I am so sorry! . . . I'm so sorry! . . . I'll never leave your path again!" Her cries grew stronger and her prayer got louder. She felt separated from God. She screamed in anguish beating her fist against the floor.

There was no way anybody on earth could understand this level of heartbreak. She was so ashamed that she'd ever believed him, and the humiliation over took her body like a fast growing cancer.

Rivers of tears flowed from her eyes as she wailed in unceasing misery, "Why am I so stupid? . . . How could I be so dumb . . . AGAIN?" She felt a horrible storm blowing through her body, as questions spun around in her mind like a tornado: "Why would he do this to me? Why did he think I deserved this? What did I do? . . . Do men feel? . . . Do they care?" Her spirit lamented as she continued to sob, "Oh God! I love him so much! . . . I love him so much!"

The pain was like a tsunami flooding her brain, and she couldn't stop weeping. Her throat was sore, her voice faded, and then her stomach began to convulse and cramp. She grabbed the toilet, slumped over it, and started to regurgitate. The memories sickened her, realizing she and DL hadn't used a condom in months. "How many women was he sleeping with?" She threw up repeatedly. Then she passed out there, nude on the floor.

She woke the next morning still there, shivering in a cold sweat with a fever. Her skin was clammy and her heart was beating as if she had just run a race. There was a foul stench and a mess on the floor as she had collapsed and passed out while vomiting.

She managed to pull her weak frame up and stood near the counter. Her throat was so dry she couldn't swallow, and her tongue was stuck to roof of her mouth. She leaned over into the sink and drank some water. She could feel her own fragility and got on the scale; she was six pounds lighter than the day before. Her temperature was 102 and she felt dehydrated. "Maybe I should go to the emergency room?" Catching her horrible image in the mirror and shaking her head she muttered, "What would I say? Doctor help me, I've been run over by a fast moving bastard?"

She thanked God it was Saturday and she didn't have to work. She thanked him that the kids were at Darren's this week. She bent over and laid her head down on the counter. While her whole body was shaking, she wept some more. She tried hard to stop, but unable to shut out the pain of the last twelve years, she couldn't. With visions of DL in her mind, her heart felt as though it were being squeezed in the palms of his hands. She washed in the sink, but was too weak to clean the bathroom floor, and too distant to care.

She slipped into her robe and just lay in bed all day, and the next. Not even eating or drinking, only getting up to use the restroom. Her blinds stayed closed and it was dark, she lost track of day and night. The whole house was deafly silent, she just stared at the clock. Her heart breaking more and more as each minute passed.

As she felt the shadow of gloom position itself over her, she could still hear DL's voice and pondered over his words, over the time they spent. She turned over in bed, and spoke softly, "Was all of it a lie? . . . Everything he said? . . . Everything we did? . . . He didn't mean any of it? . . . He knew what I'd been through. How can a man be this cruel and heartless?"

A single tear ran down her cheek and into her mouth. Too weak to wipe it away the stain from it joined all the others. If there were a thermometer to measure the degree of her misery, surely it would be recorded in the book of world records.

When she was with Darren, he was so angry all the time, so the progression their relationship took, though painful, was inevitable. She spent the last year believing what she and DL shared was so sweet, so peaceful. Her head ached wondering why he made this choice. It just didn't make sense.

"Am I ugly? . . . Fat? . . . Boring? . . .What's wrong with me?" She felt her soul spiraling down the same slide of despair it had in her marriage. She knew this was not going to feel better in the near future. The only medicine was time. She made a vow to herself that night: "I swear, this will never happen to me again."

That Sunday night, Carla called. Cynthia had let every other call go to voice mail, but she answered, her voice weak.

"Hello."

Carla asked in concern, "Girl, where you been? Is everything okay? I haven't heard from you all week."

Trying not to break down again she answered, "I know. I've been kind of in turmoil. Especially since Friday."

"What? It's not Darren, is it?"

"No." She was so hurt she just couldn't say it without crying, and she broke down sobbing again. "It's DL . . . We broke up!"

Feeling her best friend's pain as if it were her own, Carla held back her own tears. "Awe, babe. What happened? Don't cry."

Carla had known all about her marriage. She had really hoped that DL was as loving as Cynthia had been saying all these months. She was divorced for two years now herself, and her heart went out to her friend.

"Talk to me . . ." she said.

Chapter Twenty Seven

The days passed so quickly, though each night felt like an eternity. For weeks Cynthia couldn't sleep through the night, and nearly every morning she was up before the sun. Her heart forcefully battled the enemy of pain. Each time she thought she couldn't cry another tear, something would trigger it—a song, a place. Today, it was the mail.

Stopping at the box on her way in from work, she retrieved it. There was a manila envelope from "The Happiest Place on Earth." She opened it and looked through the package she'd ordered in April. His name was printed across his ticket. As she sat in her car and fished through the folder, she could feel her inner being hardening to numb the soreness, and this time she was able to stop the tears. On the radio, the DJ couldn't of had more perfect timing as he played the song she had dubbed her life's theme months earlier, when it started she couldn't help but be struck by the irony of the first verse:

"Broken heart again. Another lesson learned. Better know your friends or else you will get burned. Got to count on me, only I can guarantee that I'll be fine."

She stopped at her parents' apartment for a visit before going home. They hadn't asked about DL in a while and she didn't tell them. On a few of his visits to Arizona, he had spent time with them while Cynthia was at work. Her mom loved him.

When Cynthia entered the apartment her mother was cooking. "Hey Mom." She leaned over and gave her a kiss. "What you making?"

"Uh, just some meatloaf. How was your day?"

"Mmm, smells good . . . My day was okay. I got the Disneyland package in the mail."

"Oh great! Let me see." Wiping her hands on her apron she reached for it. She looked at her daughter's face and paused to ask,

"Is everything okay Cyn?"

"Yea, fine."

She sifted through the brochures and saw DL's name on the itinerary. "Oh, is DL still able to come? I'm so glad you finally met someone nice."

Cynthia answered short and quick, "No."

Cynthia's mother was a small Portuguese women with olive skin. She had a long braided ponytail, the color of amber wood. She hadn't cut in years and it was past her waist. It would always make it's way over to the front of her shoulder. She threw it back and turned toward Cynthia. "What happened?"

Cynthia's face saddened. She sat down at the round wooden table in the middle of the kitchen. She propped her elbow up and leaned the side of her face on her hand. Trying to speak without crying, she just spit out the best definition she could, her voice was low. "He's a dog, Mom."

She took off her apron and pulled a chair up next to Cynthia. With her own tears welling up said, "Awe, Cynthia. Really?" She put her arms around her, "You're such a sweet girl. Why does this happen to you?" She pulled her closer and held her. "One day, the right man will just knock on your door when you least expect it. You just wait and see."

"Thanks Mom. I know."

"Here, have some bread. I just baked it. It's right out of the oven."

Cynthia stood up trying to shake off another crying spell. "No thanks, I better get home. I have laundry to do before the kids get back."

She kissed Cynthia's cheek and brushed her hair back with her fingers. "Okay. Bring them by tomorrow."

They embraced again. "I will. Thanks Mom."

Cynthia went home thinking about what her mother said. Somewhere inside she wanted to believe that one day the right man would just come knocking at her door. But with her heart inflamed in misery would she be willing to let him in? She went into her apartment and dropped her work bag in the corner, then plopped down on the couch. She grabbed the phone and thumbed through the caller id. Her doctor's office had called. With her heart pounding, she listened to the voice mail:

"Hello Ms. Stewart, we see that you were not able to make your two o'clock appointment today. Please call us to reschedule."

Cynthia sighed. She remembered the appointment. She made it days after realizing what DL had been doing. But she was afraid. She started to read articles online about AIDS and STDs, and all the issues unprotected sex brings. It had been difficult to face. She leaned back on the couch and muttered, "How could I be so stupid?"

She called back, "Hello, this is Cynthia Stewart. I missed my two o'clock appointment today. I'd like to re-schedule. Do you have any open this week?"

The receptionist answered, “Hold on Ms. Stewart, I’ll check for you. . . Actually we have a cancellation for tomorrow at one o’clock. Can you make that?”

“Let me check my work schedule. . . Um, I can’t tomorrow. What about Thursday? I’m off work on Thursday.”

“Yes, we have a ten a.m. on Thursday. Should I put you down?”

“Yes please. Thank you very much.”

“Okay Mrs. Stewart, we’ll see you on Thursday at ten.”

As Cynthia was hanging up she heard a knock at the door. “Who is it?”

“It’s me, baby girl. Dad.”

She opened the door. “Hey Dad. What’s up? Come in.”

Cynthia’s Father moved very slowly since his stroke. He was tall and frail. His dark skin was like leather and he always sported an artsy cap. He called it his “Big Apple.” He came inside, leaned his cane against the wall, and sat on the sofa. “You busy baby?” He tossed his cap onto the coffee table. His head was bald and he rubbed it a few times.

Cynthia answered from the kitchen, “Not really. The kids will be here a little later, just straightening up. You want something to drink?”

“No, no thanks. Come sit with me a minute.”

Cynthia walked over in curiosity. Although she and her father lived close by, they never really had deep conversations. She sat next to him. “Is everything okay? You’re not getting sick again are you?”

"No, baby girl. Mom told about DL. I wanted to come talk to you, see if you're alright."

"I'm fine Dad. Don't worry about me."

"Well, I am worried and I need to apologize to you, baby girl. There was a lot I didn't do . . ."

Cynthia interrupted, "No Dad. Apologize for what? You're the best father a girl could have. You worked very hard, you—"

"That's just it. Now let me speak, cause I should of said this years ago. Listen up now. Okay?"

"Yes Dad."

"Now, I know I was good father. But none of us are perfect and I have some regrets. I made a lot of mistakes with you kids growing up. When I met your mother, she already had your three brothers. Now, I didn't mind that, but I was young. So I did what my father did. I worked. All the time. Before I knew it, you kids was grown and I missed a lot."

"But Daddy—"

"Listen, baby girl. You always been good. You always been pretty and you're intelligent. Even when you had Anthony so young, you didn't miss a beat. Now I should of said more then. But you didn't have a bunch of boyfriends, you didn't party. You went to school, worked, and took care of your baby. Me and your mother, we helped financially and we baby sat, but you raised that boy and you did a good job. Better than some grown women do."

"Thanks Dad."

"Now, somewhere I missed the chance to tell you how special you really are. And I don't think you know, cause that husband of yours was a horrible choice. Now, I thought maybe that was just another mistake. And now I hear about this DL guy, I need to say something baby. Now you stop it. You slow down and you wait. You'll know who the right man is when you meet him, and if you ain't sure, then wait some more. The right man ain't going nowhere. Your mother, she's a little crazy, she took me through some hell. But I made a promise to her, and all my life I did whatever I had to do to live it. I never put my hands on her and I never cheated on her. I take the best care of her I can."

Cynthia started to cry. "I don't know what I'm doing wrong, Dad."

"Come here baby." He put his arm around her and she laid her head on his shoulder. "You always been strong and smart, Cynthia. What these bastards do ain't your fault. Don't you blame yourself. Stop allowing just any man in your life just cause they say all the right things and make you feel good."

"Daddy!"

"No no, now listen. Men gonna want you, baby. Don't be so surprised by that. If you wait, you'll weed out the suckers and liars. I'm trying to tell you to choose men more carefully, baby. Life ain't no . . .What's that new cat's name that's makin those movies out of his plays? He dresses like an old sista? He's funny . . .Uh . . . Ty, Tyson?"

"Oh . . . Tyler Perry."

"Yea, that's the cat. Life ain't no Tyler Perry movie, baby girl. Now he's real funny. But ain't no black Prince Charming gone knock on your door, sweep you off your feet in a few days, and the two of you live happily ever after. This is real life. Now, you make the next brother wait, and if you wait long enough you'll know who he really is before it's too late. Within a year, you know who somebody really is. The way they work, live, and who they really are. They can fake it the first four or five months."

Cynthia nodded. He continued, "Be okay with being single for a while. Learn to love yourself. Too many young people today jump in and out of relationships and beds like it's a car wash. Marriage was meant to be a life long unity, not a train wreck. Now, you wait, and you be picky."

"Then people think I'm stuck up."

"Let em think it. Shit, you be it. It's somethings you have to be picky about, and a relationship is one. Now you figure what's good for you in a man and you pray and you trust God."

"Daddy? You never go to church."

"I know . . . Another one of my mistakes."

They laughed together.

"You hear me now, baby girl. You do what I say. And don't do like me and forget to tell my granddaughter the same thing."

"Alright, Daddy. Thank you."

"You're welcome, baby. I love you."

"I love you too."

"Daddy?"

"Yes."

"They don't make men like you anymore."

He hugged her again.

Chapter Twenty Eight

Thursday morning Cynthia woke up with the sun and climbed out of bed. She made a cup of coffee and stepped out onto the patio. She looked out over the morning desert sky. It was clear and the early morning breeze was already warm. June already; summer had fully arrived. She sipped and then reclined in the patio chair, thinking, "I wish I could fast forward my life just one year."

She knew her body felt different, that something wasn't right. She went back inside and looked at the small pocket calendar she kept near the phone and began to count the days since her last period. Her second one missed. It hadn't been normal in years though. She whispered to herself, "Don't panic."

Cynthia woke the kids and got them off too school. When she returned home, she hopped in the shower and got ready for her appointment. Looking into the mirror, she lamented, "Just one year ago you were deep in love. If someone had told you this would be happening in twelve months you would have never believed them. Was he worth it? . . . What if he gave me something I have to live with for the rest of my life? What if I'm pregnant? My God, what if I have AIDS?"

She started to worry so much that a pain grew in her lower stomach. Falling into the chair next to the closet, she bent forward pressing her hand against the cramp. She'd felt it a few times over the last couple of months but never this strong. Overwhelmed, she started to cry. Her head began to ache and she was unable to figure out what brought on the tears, the pain, or the oppressing feeling of loneliness and stupidity. Realizing how fragile her humanity really was, she pushed through but prayed, "God please help me."

She arrived at her doctor's office at 9:45 a.m. The lobby was full but she knew that making her appointment at the last minute would mean the wait would be long. She signed in, sat down, and pulled a magazine onto her lap. She looked at the countless brochures that lined the rack against the wall next to her. Ailment after ailment. "People suffer from all kinds of things."

Cynthia gazed around the room filled with people. Most appeared tired and broken down. One elderly woman sat in the corner, leaning her head against the wall. Clothed in tattered brown polyester pants and an old floral wool overcoat, her face carried the signs of a life long smoker, lined in wrinkles, and her skin was scorched by sun. She hacked and coughed profusely, quivering and holding her arms around herself, but failing to keep warm.

Cynthia thought to herself, "Shouldn't she be in the emergency room? How do you avoid it? How do you avoid getting sick?" She thought about the things she may have. "How could I have avoided it? I was so stupid to believe that man was only with me. What man is ever faithful?"

She started to feel angry. Angry with DL, angry with Darren, with any and every man who just couldn't love the one he's with. But none of that mattered now, and she was angry at herself. "I really can't blame anybody for the men I've chosen." As her animosity peaked, she yanked the pages of the magazine while flipping them. "Why didn't I stay celibate like I planned? Then none of this would be happening. Now he's gone, having a baby with some forty-four year old woman, and I'm here alone—scared for my life!"

She pulled so hard that one of the pages ripped. She felt a glare and looked back over her shoulder. A little boy was sitting next to her frozen in fear trying not to look directly at her. She forced a smile at him and got up, turbulently tossing the magazine on the couch. She paced back and forth with her arms folded and prayed in her mind: "God, whatever happens, give me the wisdom and strength to live with it or through it." Just then, a four foot four, very round woman stepped out from behind the door and called out, "Stewart . . . Cynthia Stewart?"

Cynthia scurried over. "I'm here." She followed the nurse through the door and down the hall. The nurse smiled and moved aside. "Right this way, Ms. Stewart. Room six there on your left." They both entered. The nurse flipped open her chart and begin to spill out questions like pouring water from a pitcher. "Let's see . . . You're here for a pap? Your last one was a year ago. Good. . . . You're thirty six? Three children." She looked up at Cynthia.

"Um, any concerns?"

Feeling nervous and awkward, Cynthia began, "Uh . . .Yes. I have some concerns. I'd like a pregnancy test . . . and I'd like to be tested for STDs and AIDS . . . and I've been having this severe pain in my stomach. It comes and goes, but earlier today it was really very strong."

The nurse was very dry and nonchalant as she jotted down notes. "Okay. I'll take your blood pressure and weight and let the doctor know." She strapped the monitor around Cynthia's arm. "Your blood pressure is a little higher than normal. Have you ever had problems before?"

Cynthia was shocked. "No. Never."

The nurse guided her toward the scale and weighed her. "Your weight is down significantly since your last visit. Are you dieting and losing on purpose, or is this sudden?"

"I think a little of both."

The nurse continued to write while leaving. "Okay Ms. Stewart, please disrobe completely. There's a gown for you on the table. The doctor will be in shortly."

Cynthia removed her clothes and slid into the paper gown that was left for her folded on the table. She caught a glimpse of her face in the mirror over the sink and noticed that it was abnormally thin and pale. Sickly pale. She moved in closer to the mirror and rubbed her hand over her cheek examining her face. Struck by fear, she sat on the table and contemplated the last year or so of her life, since she left Darren. She sighed. "I thought these worries would all be over when I left him."

She recalled sitting in her doctor's office years ago when she found out Darren was cheating. The dread and trepidation was just as strong today. She felt feverish and began to sweat a little. Now another bad choice in men had put her in the same predicament. "I must have some sign across my head or something: 'All no good cheating liars, come to me! I'm stupid enough to put up with you' . . . All the plans I had . . . My goals."

She swallowed the lump in her throat, realizing she'd allowed DL to blow through her life like a hurricane. "I let him totally knock me off course. Now he's disappeared into the night leaving me this mess to clean up all by myself. Meanwhile, him and the freckled blonde are living happily ever after. How did I get here? I'm thirty six years old; I know better."

Just then there was a knock on the door. "Hello?"

The doctor entered and said, "Hi Ms. Stewart? Dr. Khan is out today, so I'll be seeing you. I'm Dr. Beverly." Her pink face was small and scrunched like she had been sucking on a lemon. Her hair was pulled back in a bun but had wiry strays that wouldn't cooperate.

Cynthia answered, "Hi. Nice to meet you."

Dr. Beverly plopped the chart down on the counter and leaned her foot on the stool as she read through it. "Okay. It seems you've been healthy. But lately you've had some concerns. What has changed?"

Cynthia wanted to say, "Well Doctor, it seems that I've been duped by a bastard who told me he loved me, but screwed me and only God knows how many other women. And now I'm afraid that I'm pregnant and maybe dying of AIDS."

But instead, she said, "Well, not thinking, I had unprotected sex with a man I was dating, and I'm a little worried."

"When was your last period?"

Cynthia answered, "Um, the last week of March."

"So you didn't have a period in April or May?"

"No. But my period hasn't been normal for a couple of years now. Sometimes I skip one. I've told Dr. Khan but she never ran any test or anything."

With concern, the doctor questioned, "You've skipped one. Ever skip two?"

Cynthia was nervous. "No."

The possibilities crushed her heart like aluminum can.

Dr. Beverly looked over at Cynthia. Her little face seemed to really care and she put her hand on Cynthia's hand. "Well, in addition to your pap, we'll take a urine and blood sample and get you tested for everything. I'll put a rush on the results from the lab and get them back within a few days. We'll make an appointment for Monday and talk some more then. That sound good?"

"Yes. Thank you, doctor . . . oh, but the pregnancy test? That takes until Monday too?"

Dr. Beverly smiled while pulling on rubber gloves. "I can call you with that result later today."

"Alright, thank you."

After Cynthia finished at the doctor's, she drove home in anxiety. Though relieved that she finally went, she was still stressed having to wait for the results. At two o'clock she made some lunch and watched TV, anticipating the ring of her phone.

It rang and she thought, "That can't be the doctor that fast?"
It was Carla. "Hey girl, what's up?" she asked.

Carla always animated was upset. "Bout to fuck this man up!"

"Who? Your dude?"

"Yea. I can't do nothin without him thinkin I'm cheatin on him! He questions me if I walk out the door to get the mail. I'm tired of this shit!"

"Well, you do cheat on him, Carla. What do you expect?"

"I know, but he ain't my husband. Shit. I pay my own bills. You know what he did last night?"

"What? I need a good story to distract me right now."

Carla chuckled and said, “I got a good one for you. I was out at Dynasty—you know that little club in LA near the Forum?”

“Yea.”

“I met a nice guy there. We exchanged numbers. He asked me to call him when I got home, just so he knew I made it safely. I got in about two in the morning. I showered, got in bed, and called him. While I’m on the phone, this mutha fucka jumped outta my closet and screamed, ‘I KNEW YOU WAS CHEATIN ON ME!’ Girl I—”

Cynthia interrupted, “WHAT! He jumped out of your closet? How did he get in your house? Was he there when you left?”

“Girl, no! I don’t know how he got in here, but he scared the hell outta me. If I’d had gun I woulda shot his ass. It was a good thirty seconds before I knew what was going on.”

Cynthia was laughing hard. “Who does he think he is, hiding in your closet? R. Kelly?”

Carla laughed but was still irritated. “Shut up girl. He’s crazy! I gotta cut him loose.”

“Yea, you do, but you’ll be calling me with another part to the saga next week.”

Carla calmed down. “So, what’s up with you? How’d your doctor’s appointment go?”

“I’ll let you know when I know. They just ran a bunch of tests. I should know something by Monday.”

Carla asked, “Monday? Really? Are you okay waiting?”

"Do I have a choice?"

"Well the kids are at Darren's this weekend, aren't they?"

Cynthia said, "No. Why? I'm not driving way down there."

"No. I thought I'd ride my bike up there and we can do Vegas this weekend. We both need to exhale."

Cynthia thought about it. "You know what? That sounds like plan. My mom will keep them for the night."

"Cool, let's do it."

"Let me call you later. I've got to go pick up the kids from school. We'll smooth out the plans tonight."

Just as she hung up there was a ring, it was the doctor's office. Cynthia answered anxiously, "Hello?"

"Hello, Ms. Stewart?"

"Yes. This is she."

"This is Dr. Beverly's office. The doctor wanted me to call and let you know that the results of your pregnancy test were negative."

Cynthia responded, "Oh, thank you! I'm so glad to hear that."

"She also would like to see you on Monday. Is ten o'clock convenient for you?"

"Yes. Thank you. I'll be there."

Chapter Twenty Nine

Saturday rolled around in the blink of an eye. Carla arrived on her Harley at Cynthia's by nine in the morning. About an hour later, Cynthia was seated on the back of the bike and they were on their way to Nevada. They spent about two hours on the stretch two-lane highway to Vegas. The ride was smooth, and viewing the desert mountains and the clean blue sky from a motorcycle brought a peace and freedom very few things in life do.

When they arrived in Vegas, they checked into the Golden Nugget right in the heart of downtown. They shopped most of the day on Fremont Street, had some lunch, and then played some slots in the casino. As they roamed around, Cynthia thought of DL. This was her first trip to Vegas since breaking up with him and it was hard. She worked to push him out of her mind, and slipped five dollars into a slot machine. Carla went around to the other side and played as well. Cynthia's machine started to ring and whistle. She shouted, "Oooh, look! I won. I won!"

Carla got up and ran over. "How much?"

"I don't know!"

The machine spit out a ticket.

Carla snatched it. "Tss! Girl, you only won fifty bucks."

Cynthia grabbed it back. "Shoot, that's fifty bucks I didn't have two minutes ago."

Carla was tired. "It's almost four o'clock. Let's go take a nap before we go out. I'm sleepy from that drive."

“Yea, me too.”

Carla’s man called her cell as soon as they got up to the room. He was obviously unable to deal with her being in Vegas for the weekend and had been calling every half hour since she got there. Instead of taking a nap, Cynthia had to listen to the screaming and arguing of two people who made each other miserable.

She got up and took a bath while Carla called her man every curse word ever invented. God only knew what he was screaming back at her on the other end of the line. When Cynthia came out of the bathroom, Carla was sleeping soundly on the bed. She heard Cynthia stirring around in the closet.

“You done in the bathroom?” Her voice was peaceful, as if she hadn’t just spent thirty minutes yelling at the top of her lungs.

Cynthia, wrapped in her towel, sat on the edge of the bed putting lotion on her legs. “Yea, I’m finished.”

Carla sat up. “You know what? You really got skinny.”

“Yea, I know.”

“You don’t look bad. Actually, you look damn good. You’ve never been a big woman, but I’m not used to you being that small. How much do you weigh?”

Cynthia looked up. “I don’t even want to say. I think I lost almost twenty pounds in the last couple of months.”

“Well, be careful girlfriend.”

“I will . . . You be careful. I’m wondering which one of you guys is going to kill the other first.”

Carla chuckled. “Girl, if I didn’t argue and curse him out every now and then, it wouldn’t be love.”

Cynthia massaging lotion onto her hands. “Oh yea? I went through enough of that mess with Darren. I can’t live like that anymore. DL was the first guy I ever dated that I never had an argument with. I thought it was a beautiful thing. Obviously I was wrong. Maybe had I went off a few times, he wouldn’t be living in bliss with the blonde.” Cynthia was hit with grief and lay back on the bed. She sighed and said, “The same name thing was a sign from God. I should of known . . . Or, maybe I was just too boring.”

Carla looked directly at her. “First of all, you know damned well he’s not living in bliss with that woman. Second, you are peaceful, and that is a beautiful thing. He’s an asshole. He was an asshole before you met him, and he’ll probably die an asshole. That has nothing to do with what you did or didn’t do, or his name...And one thing I know for sure, you have never been boring!”

“Thanks girl. I know.” Cynthia sat up. “But somehow what I know in my head doesn’t help my heart. I hate it, but I miss him.” Her voice cracked and she pouted, “And I feel so stupid that I miss him.”

Carla sat down on the other bed across from her. “What is it that you miss? Him, or just being in a relationship?”

Cynthia’s tears started to flow, she tried to wipe them away. “It’s just . . . I really thought he was my friend. I miss a lot of things, but I think that hurts the most. I feel like someone died because I can’t talk to my friend.” She began to cry so much that Carla scrambled to find her a box of tissue. She sat next to her, putting her arm around her and handing her the tissue. She just let her cry.

“You’ll be okay, Cyn.”

Cynthia sobbed, “I do everything I can to forget him, but it hurts so much. Will this pain ever stop?”

“It will, you know it will. We’ve both been through enough to know it will. You just need to let time heal you.”

“Sometimes I just wonder if he misses me even a little bit . . .Why do men do this? He made me feel like I was so special to him. When really I wasn’t. I called Cecilia a few days after I saw the pictures of the blonde on his website and started to ask her questions . . . you know, cause she knows him so well.”

Carla nodded. “Uh huh.”

Cynthia continued speaking through her tears, “She was hesitant at first, but then she told me he was seeing two or three other women besides me and the blond. Can you believe that? I gave him my heart. I really cared about him, and I was just another one of his hoes.”

Carla asked, “Cynthia, you never caught him with anybody? I mean, no phone calls or anything?”

“No. But I wasn’t really looking for it. I just believed he was an honest guy. In hindsight, I think he would just shut his phone off.”

“Wow. What a bastard. What else did Cecilia say?”

“Girl, I could write a book with all the stuff she told me. I just really didn’t know him at all.”

“Damn girl. I’m so sorry.”

“What really hurts is that I didn’t even push a relationship, he convinced me. Why did he do that if he just wanted to hurt me? What did I do to deserve this? I feel so stupid.”

Carla got stern. “Look, I know it hurts, but don’t beat yourself up with questions that can never be answered. We’ve been girls a long time and you aren’t stupid. You’re one of the smartest and strongest women I know. What he did was stupid! Who knows why? It’s just too bad this man didn’t realize who was loving him—too bad for him I mean. This was his loss not yours. You’re a good woman, Cynthia, and one day God will bring you a man that can appreciate that. You’ll get through this just like with Darren.”

“I know.”

“And I’m sorry, I probably didn’t give you the right advice before. You were right, you should have waited. I was just hoping that he was a good man, just like you were. I’m not any good at this love thing either. Hopefully, one day we’ll have all this shit figured out.”

Carla helped her wipe away her tears, then went over to the mirror to fix her eye liner. “Now come on, let’s go do what we came up here for. Let’s go get a drink and dance til the sun comes up Fuck him. Hopefully, somebody will beat his ass in a dark alley somewhere. Karma’s a bitch. He’ll get his.”

Cynthia chuckled while blowing her nose. “Girl, you’re crazy.” She popped up. “Alright, I’m good.”

Carla looked over. “You sure? You good?”

“Yea, soon as I get my freakum dress on, I’ll be even better.” She scurried into the bathroom.

“You have a freakum dress? I gotta see this!”

The night club was just a few blocks from the hotel so they walked. Laughing, joking, and swinging their purses, they felt like school girls. It was the middle of June in Vegas, it was nine at night, and about 100 degrees out. Groups of people pounded the pavement as if it were the middle of the day. Cynthia and Carla were waiting for the light to change at the corner when a smooth polished black Hummer stretch limousine pulled up and stopped next to them. Carla couldn't help herself.

As the driver's passenger side window was coming down, she gravitated toward the vehicle. "OOH shit girl, who's in there?"

Cynthia pulled at her arm. "Stop girl! You don't know who that is. It could be some nut looking for prostitutes or something!"

Carla yanked her arm away. "Look at that car. I'll be whatever he wants me to be." She walked over to the window and leaned in. "Hi."

Cynthia stayed at a distance, thinking: "This girl has lost her mind."

The driver spoke. "My passenger is interested in your friend."

"Interested like how? She ain't a street walker."

The driver chuckled, "Oh no! I apologize—uh, not like that. He just thought she was nice looking. Where are you ladies headed? Can we give you a ride?"

Cynthia was still standing a few feet away and whispered loudly, "Carla, no!" "Honestly, I would love to, but my friend would never get into a strange man's car. Who's your passenger anyway?" Carla tried to look in the back but the privacy window was up.

Cynthia stood at the corner worried. "Carla! Girl, come on." She approached and the privacy window began to come down. They both recognized the refined movie actor at the same time and their mouths fell open.

“Hello ladies.” He gracefully nodded his head. When he spoke, you would have thought they heard The Messiah.

Both of their right hands went up, fingers waving gently they spoke in unison, “Hel-looo.”

“May I give you a ride somewhere?”

Carla quickly began to move toward the door. “Yes!”

Cynthia stopped her, then looked into the window. “Give us a minute please.”

She pulled Carla aside. “I don’t want to get in his car.”

“Cynthia! Are you crazy? Do you know who that is?”

“Yes. I know who he is as an actor, I don’t know him as a person. I’m not getting in his car!”

Cynthia went back over to the window and spoke sweetly, “Thank you. You’re very kind. But my friend and I are having a girls’ night out and were just headed right over there. We don’t need a ride. But it was awfully kind of you to stop.”

The actor seemed taken by her boldness in rejecting him. He looked over. “You headed over there, huh?”

“Yes, we are.”

“Well Mrs. . . .?” He paused and leaned up offering his hand.

Cynthia put her hand in his. “Stewart, uh . . . Mzz. Stewart. Cynthia.”

Their hands touched and Cynthia slowly drew hers back first. The actor went on, "Cyn-thia, what a lovely name. Perfect for a lovely woman."

She thought, "He's trying to mack me." Then giggled. "Thank you."

"Well, Cynthia, I have a prior engagement, but maybe I can come back later. Would that be okay with you?"

She smiled sweetly. "Uh, sure that would be very okay with me, it was very nice to meet you."

"Likewise."

Cynthia played it really cool, all the while inside it felt like she was dreaming. The window went up and they drove off. She started to cross the street and Carla caught up and pushed her shoulder.

"Dammit! Cynthia, I can't believe you sometimes."

Cynthia remained calm. "He'll be back."

"What? What'd he say?"

She lowered her voice mimicking him, "He said, 'I have a prior engagement. Would you mind if I come back later?' " She laughed.

"You think he'll come back, or was he just saying that?"

Cynthia was confident. "He'll be back. When he touched my hand, I could tell . . . He'll be back."

When they entered the club, it was dark, spacious, and crowded, and the bass from the music bumped loudly. There was a second level and people were going up and down the stairs near the entrance. The bar was centered and the dance floor was across from the front door with a section marked VIP just beyond it. There was a radio DJ broadcasting live, and his eyes shot toward Carla as soon as they walked in.

Cynthia leaned into Carla's ear. "Girl! He's checking you out for real."

"I know, and he ain't bad lookin either."

Cynthia began to float toward the floor.

Carla grabbed her arm. "Wait. Let's get a drink first."

"Okay."

They got cozy at the bar and ordered. The DJ announced his break and made his way over, taking a seat on the stool next to Carla. He appeared to be a lot older than her, but had aged nicely. His skin was light, and his eyes were green. Carla smiled at Cynthia like a she devil, then turned toward him seductively removing her jacket.

Cynthia sipped her drink. She looked around noticing the age of the crowd and thought, "Hmm, twenties." She tapped Carla's shoulder. "Watch my drink, I'm going to the restroom."
When she returned, Carla waved from the dance floor. "Come on!"

They danced a few songs, then sat back at the bar. Carla pulled her arm. "Let's find a table."

Before they could sit, a tall and very young looking man approached Cynthia. "Uh, excuse me?"

"Wow." She thought, "He can't be more than twenty one." She said, "Hi."

He said, "My friend over there wants to dance with you, but he's too nervous to ask."

She squinted and looked over. "Oh? Is that right?"

He went on, "Yea. Would you dance with me? I want to make him jealous."

Somehow, she felt like a mom doing a favor for a kid. "I guess so."

Carla leaned over in her ear while they danced. "Robbing the cradle, are we?"

Cynthia grunted, "Be quiet!"

After one song, Cynthia said, "Thank you." and then excused herself.

She sat at the table enjoying the music. When the DJ played R. Kelly her mind drifted remembering DL. She looked at the happy couples on floor and the loneliness began to set in. Just then, she heard a deep voice behind her, "Hello. Is anyone sitting here?" She looked up from her glass as she finished the last sip of her second drink. "Uh no. Have a seat." She thought, "At least he's not twenty one."

"Hi. My name is Marvin. You are?"

"I'm Cynthia." She put her hand forward. "It's nice to meet you, Marvin."

He asked, "May I buy you another drink?"

Generally, Cynthia was a very light drinker, but tonight called for something more. As she checked out the image across from her, the strength of the Seagram's 7 started to take effect. Her vision was a bit impaired and she knew she should have said no. "Yes. Thank you. Seven and Seven."

"Alright, I'll be right back."

Marvin brought back their drinks and made himself comfortable next to her. "You don't look like the clubbing type."

"Well, not usually. But tonight called for something a little out of the ordinary for me."

Marvin's face lit up. "Oh yea?"

"Hold up. Not that out of the ordinary."

As the DJ spun T. Pain's song, "Buy U A Drank," Cynthia decided to wait on sipping that third drink. "So, Marvin, what brings you here? You don't look twenty one?"

He laughed. "No, not at all. I'm here with some Navy buddies. I'm actually forty eight."

Cynthia's head moved back. "Wow. Okay."

It turned out Marvin was a hardworking, respectable, mature man. They sat and talked for over thirty minutes. Cynthia thought, "Now he seems like a stable well-rounded guy, and I'm not the least bit interested . . .What is wrong with me?" As he talked, her mind went in and out of listening. She tried to pay attention but he talked a lot. "He's not bad looking. Not really my type, but not bad looking. Been in the Navy for twenty five years. Intelligent. Nice body." She examined him and really tried . . . "Nope, just not feel-in him."

Carla approached and said, “Hi. I’m Carla.” She saw that Cynthia seemed bored. “Come on girl. Let’s go upstairs.”
Marvin finally paused, and Cynthia said, “Oh . . .Well, okay. Upstairs it is.”

She stood up and held her hand out to Marvin. “It was nice talking to you.”

He stood up. “Well, I’m not leaving, I’ll be here when you come back down.”

Carla rolled her eyes over and looked away. Cynthia didn’t quite know what to say. “Oh . . .well, okay. I’ll see you in a bit.”

As they walked away from the table, Carla decided to give Cynthia some pointers. “Girl, you’re giving him way too much of your time. You gotta learn to cut em short. Say ‘nice to have met you,’ and leave.”

Cynthia felt bad. “He was nice. I didn’t want to be rude.”

Carla stopped in her tracks. “Rude?” She pointed back. “To him? Yet you let a millionaire drive away in a stretch limo?” She shook her head. “Girl, I swear!”

Chapter Thirty

When Cynthia and Carla entered the upstairs room, it was almost completely devoid of light and smaller than downstairs, but the energy blasted through the doors like an explosion. The DJ spun house music and the rhythm shook the floor vibrating the soul. The smell of clove cigarettes floated through the air and silhouettes of bodies were so close that you had to squeeze your way through the perspiration. At midnight, everyone was just about past drink number five and the high filled the room like helium.

Someone had bought a round of Cristal for the house and everyone took full advantage of the gesture without even caring where the generosity stemmed from. Carla had been pulled away by a tall, seductive, dredlocked stranger, while Cynthia made her way out onto the patio where there was more breathing room. She caught a waitress passing by. "Excuse me."

The young woman stopped and smiled courteously. "Yes. How may I help you?"

"Just curious. Do you know who purchased the champagne?"

"Uh, not really. Somebody in back said some actor. But I haven't seen anybody."

Cynthia smiled. "Thank you." She thought, "I wonder if he's here."

She went back inside and ventured around a little for Carla, politely dodging hungry men left and right. One five foot, red-suited, gold tooth wearing man grabbed her by the arm, then leaned up and whispered in her ear, "Baby, can I take a picture of you?"

"What?"

He said, "So I can show Santa what I want for Christmas."

She said, "Are you kidding me?"

She slipped away and right into the path of another vulture, who said, "Baby, if I had a quarter for every time I saw a woman as beautiful as you, I'd have twenty five cents."

"What the—?"

She spotted Carla in a corner intimately dancing with her male counterpart. She made her way across the floor and back out onto the smoke-filled balcony, leaned over and saw the black Hummer parked just below. She jerked back in shock. "Oh my goodness!" She dashed back inside pushing through dancers and headed for Carla. She found her and grabbed her elbow. "Carla!"

Carla turned and snapped, "I'm busy."

Cynthia leaned up and spoke into her ear. "He's here somewhere . . . The limo, it's parked outside! I'm going back downstairs to the restroom and freshen up. I'll meet you at the table."

"Oh shit, girl. Okay."

They returned to the table. About an hour had passed since they'd left it. Just like he promised, Marvin was still there. Sipping his rum and Coke, he waved to them as they approached.

Carla whispered, "Damn, girl. What did you say to him? He's still there."

"Nothing, I hardly got a word in."

Carla was frustrated. "Well, get rid of him. What if you-know-who comes in and sees you sitting with him? He might leave."

"Tss. He won't leave just cause I'm just sitting with somebody."

They paused before making it to the table. Cynthia asked, "What time is it anyway?"

Carla pulled her cell phone from her purse. "It's almost one."

Cynthia plotted, "Okay, here's the plan. You stay here, in about five minutes, just come up and say you're tired. That you're ready to go."

"Alright."

Cynthia walked toward the table smiling. "Whew."

Marvin grinned ear to ear and stood up as she approached. "Having fun, huh?"

"Yea, a ball . . . So . . ."

Carla scurried over and interrupted too soon. "Come on, let's go. I'm tired."

Cynthia leaned over and smiled politely to Marvin. "I hope you have a good night. It was nice talking to you."

Marvin stopped her. "Oh, okay. Well, here's my number. Do you mind giving me yours? I'd like to take you out sometime."

Cynthia quickly glanced over at Carla, then jotted down her number, and said, "Bye. I'll give you a call."

As they walked toward the restroom Carla began her training session again. "See? You've been out of the game too long. Did you give him your real number?"

Cynthia said, "Yes, I did. I don't know why, maybe he's nice."

"He's boring. I think you've had one too many."

They entered the restroom and freshened up in the mirror. Cynthia rubbed her lips together turning her head side to side. "Is this lipstick too dark?"

Carla said, "No. Here, just put a little gloss over it."

"Oh yea, that looks better . . . Mmm, smells like fruit punch." She tasted it from her lips. "Mmm, taste like it too. Give me that. I'll give it back later."

Carla's eyes brightened. "Oh! Okay. You're full of surprises tonight." She tugged at the bottom of Cynthia's dress. "First this short sexy red dress, now we want fruity lip gloss. Hmm."

Cynthia was beginning to feel anxious. "Come on. Let's go see if he came in."

They ventured around the club. They batted their eyes at the guard and persuaded him to allow them into the VIP section, but it was obvious there was no one really famous inside. Some faces were familiar, but nobody they were excited to see.

Carla said, "It's one thirty. Are you sure you saw the limo?"

"I saw a black Hummer limo, and some actor bought that champagne, so I just assumed it may be him. Let's go look outside. If it's not him, let's go. I'm getting tired."

"Alright, me too."

They exited the doors and saw there across the lot was the stretch limo, parked. A few bi-standers wandered up and peeked in, but kept going. Carla didn't hesitate. "Let's go over. I think that's the same one."

"Ugh! Would if it's not?"

She pulled Cynthia by the arm. "Tss, just come on."

"Alright, alright."

As they got closer to the vehicle, the driver recognized them and stepped out opening the back door. The lighting was dim and you couldn't see anyone, just the vast seating area, and a full bar stocked with expensive liquor. Carla stepped up and inside first, with the driver helping her. Then as Cynthia put her foot on the step, a gentleman's hand appeared on her right side holding hers. It was him. Her body fluttered at his touch. He helped her up and guided her toward the back.

There were three others back there, besides Carla; two men and another woman. Drink in hand, Carla quickly made herself comfortable next to the other single man. Cynthia sat down. Two other people could have fit in the space between her and the actor.

He patted the seat smiling. "Come closer."

She did.

He spoke slow and smoothly like Billy D. Williams. "Would like a drink?"

She knew she needed something. "Yes. Thank you."

He handed her a glass of champagne. “Here you are.” He smiled and said, “It was about time you guys came out.”

Cynthia sipped. “Oh, were you waiting very long?”

“Uh, maybe about an hour or so. Seemed longer though. You must have been having a good time in there.”

She shyly grinned. “It was okay. I thought you would come inside.”

He laughed. “I can’t just walk in there, you know. I mean, I don’t have enough body with me tonight. Plus, I really didn’t want to deal with any commotion.”

Cynthia questioned. “Body?”

“My bodyguards. I don’t have the freedom you have, babe.”

“Oh yea. I guess there would have been quite a scene. I wasn’t thinking. I’m sorry.”

“It’s okay. No need to apologize. I was just kind of anxious for you to come out.”

His voice was calming and she looked into his sexy hazel eyes.

“You were anxious for me?”

He leaned in a little closer. “Yes. I was.”

Cynthia responded politely but a little stern, “Surely you can pull any woman you want. Please don’t take this the wrong way, I don’t mean to sound rude. Although it’s flattering, you can be real with me. We can just talk. You don’t have to mack me.”

Carla over heard. “Tss. Cynthia!”

He corrected Carla, “No. It’s okay.” He looked at Cynthia and said, “You’re very honest. That’s good. I’ll turn the mack off and we can just chill. Is that cool? You wanna take a ride?”

Cynthia smiled and leaned back. “Yes, I’d like that. Thank you.” He took her hand and she looked down. His skin was almost an exact match to hers. She examined the expensive diamond ring that decorated his pinkie. “Very nice.”

He slid it off and put in on her finger. “Here. You can wear it.” She held her hand up. “It’s beautiful. It’s a little too big for me. But wow.” She tried to hand it back.

“No, keep it for tonight. Here put it on your middle finger . . .That’s better.”

The limo spun around the Vegas Strip for over an hour and it was almost three in the morning. They were all in the back laughing and chatting. Carla had grown quite comfortable with her new friend, who bore a striking resemblance to Chris Tucker. They learned that he’d worked as a stunt double for him on several of his films.

Cynthia asked the actor, “Do you have a home here in Vegas, or are you at a hotel?” Then she thought, “Oh shoot! Now he’s gonna think I wanna go to his room. What was I thinking? Why did I ask that?”

He answered, “I’m in a suite at The Bellagio. Wanna go check it out?”

Cynthia opened her mouth but before she could speak, Carla popped up and covered Cynthia’s lips with her hand and answered the question herself, “YES! We do.” Carla sat back down and gave Cynthia a stare that would strike and kill a demon.

The actor chuckled and looked at Cynthia. "Is that okay?" Cynthia answered, smiling, "Yes, that's fine. I'd love to see it. I have a feeling I won't live past tomorrow if I say no."

He pushed the intercom. "Dave, take us back to the suite."

Cynthia's mind began to twirl as the drinks from the night seemed to all settle in her brain at once. She looked over at Carla and motioned her mouth with no sound. "I'm drunk . . .watch . . my . . .back."

Carla gestured back, but with sound, "Meee-too."

The limo pulled inside of a tunnel and drove down a few hundred feet into a basement parking lot that everyday people would never even know existed, then parked. The others shuffled out first and the actor stepped out just behind Cynthia.

She turned and looked up at him. He was at least six foot one. She thought, "Could anyone else make a widow's peak that sexy?" Then said, "I have to be honest, I'm a bit tipsy I don't usually drink very much and I'm really feeling it. I hope you can be a gentleman, cause I wouldn't even be able to put up a fight right now." He took her hand and guided her toward the elevator. "Tss. Don't worry babe. I wouldn't disrespect you like that."

She had a feeling he wouldn't. They rode the elevator all the way to the top.

They exited Floor 36. He opened the door and they all entered. "Wow!"

Cynthia seemed to sober up at the sight. She looked around. The suite had to be over 4000 square feet and it was magnificent. It was about three or four in the morning, yet there were about twenty or thirty people still up partying and shooting pool. He showed Cynthia and Carla around and introduced them.

There were recognizable faces all over. Carla disappeared with the Chris Tucker sub, and the actor took Cynthia into the kitchen.

"You want some coffee? Maybe it'll help you."

"How thoughtful, thank you."

They sat at the table in the kitchen and talked. Cynthia's mind wandered, "He's so sweet, so down to earth. But would I be interested if he weren't rich and famous? Ugh . . . I don't know."

He poured Cynthia a little more coffee, then guided her over to a cozy nook in the corner of the living area. She followed irresistibly. They sat on a plush sofa that had a 50 or 60-inch flat screen television situated just in front of it. "Sweet Thang" by Rufus and Chaka Khan was playing on the sound system.

Cynthia sat. "I love this song."

"You do? You like old school?"

"Are you kidding me? That's about all I listen too."

"You know what?"

Cynthia looked over at him still snapping her fingers and listening to the music.

"What?"

"I stopped you earlier tonight because I thought you were beautiful. But talking with you these last couple of hours, I'm seeing that you're so much more than that."

She stopped and thought, "Is he sincere, or has he turned the mack back on?" She couldn't tell. The men in her past had her so messed up she decided not to believe him and came across a little cold.

"Thank you." She leaned back.

He asked, "Are you okay?"

"I am."

He scooted closer and leaned toward her. He reached over and touching her chin with his hand, he kissed her softly. She felt nothing. Her heart had grown so hard. She thought, "What am I doing here?" She smiled and he kissed her again. Still nothing. She thought, "Any women would give their life to be where I am right now. What is WRONG with me?"

Then she kissed him and it grew passionate. He moved his hand to the small of her back and then down her thigh. He attempted to slide it up her skirt. He whispered in her ear, "Come to my room with me."

But Cynthia stopped his hand. "I can't."

He asked, "What's wrong?"

"I'm sorry. I don't mean to be a tease, but I can't do this . . . It's not you . . . I mean, of course it's not you. I've just recently been through so much, and the physical part of me is like, YEA YEA! But I'm just not this kind of woman."

He said, "It's okay sweetheart. I understand. I'm probably moving too fast. I'm just really feelin you. I couldn't help it."

Once again Cynthia thought, "Is he lying? Does he say this to every woman? Of course he does. Why do men do this? Why can't they just be honest. How do I know who's lying and who isn't? Ugh! I just want to get out of here."

She told him, "I've had a wonderful time, but do you mind taking us back now?"

He asked, "I haven't offended you have I?"

"No. Not at all . . . Please don't think that. I've had the time of my life. You're a very sweet man. I'm just in a weird place in my life right now."

"What place is that?"

"I don't want to bore you, I've just been through some pretty bad relationships. It's hard for me to be with a guy right now . . . Even a rich, handsome, famous one. Pretty foolish, huh?"

He looked at her with concern. "No babe. That's not foolish. Who doesn't know heartbreak? It won't bore me. Talk to me . . . Unless you're just not comfortable."

"I don't want to go into all the details, but . . . Okay. Can I be perfectly honest?"

He chuckled. "Uh, haven't you been all night? That's what I'm diggin about you. You know who I am and there's no facade. I rarely find that anymore."

She answered, "Okay. Like you're saying all this stuff, like you think I 'm beautiful, I'm sweet, and blah blah blah. How do I know you don't say that to every woman? How do I know if you're not just saying that to get me in the bed? I've been lied to and hurt so much that . . . Okay, you know how when a person gets into a bad car accident?"

He nodded. "Uh huh."

"They're afraid to get back into a car, and if they do, they flinch in fear at everything? That's exactly how I feel right now. I'm flinching in fear. Does that make sense?"

"It makes perfect sense. Some man has got you pretty messed up. I'm sorry that's happened to you. Really, I'm sorry for him, he obviously lost a jewel. And that's me being real."

Cynthia went on, "I mean, I've never been the type to just give myself over to any man. I can't sleep with someone I don't have a commitment with, that I'm not in love with—someone I really don't even know. I have to care for him. And when I fall in love, unfortunately, I fall really hard. If I slept with you, I know I'd end up hurt later. And I can't do that to myself anymore. I hope you understand."

"I understand perfectly. But before I take you back to your hotel, can I be honest? I mean, really honest?"

She shook her head. "Yes. Please."

"I would be wrong to sleep with you. You deserve better than me." He kissed her cheek and stood up reaching out for her hand. "Come on, let's go."

When the limo arrived in front of Cynthia and Carla's hotel, the sun was rising. Cynthia leaned over and kissed the actor on the cheek. "Thank you again, I had a lot of fun . . . Oh, I almost forgot! Your ring."

Covering her hand with his, he stopped her from pulling it off.

“No. You keep it Cynthia. I don’t think I’ll ever forget you. Don’t forget me.”

Chapter Thirty One

On Monday morning, Cynthia's anxiety was still peaking. She got dressed and to the doctor's office by nine even though her appointment wasn't until ten. She sat in the lobby still afraid of what the future held for her. This visit would change her life, whatever the outcome.

Reaching into her purse she started to read the small pocket Bible she carried with her. She'd had this particular one for many years. The date a friend had given it to her was written in the front: July 1990. That was when she first started going to church seriously, when she'd made an adult decision to follow God. Before she'd met Darren.

She thought about that time in her life, and how genuinely happy that choice had made her feel. She recalled telling her spiritual mentor how hard she thought it would be to abstain until marriage. That was who had given her the Bible. She was successful though and had abstained for four years, not sleeping with Darren until their honeymoon. She'd hoped she could do it again. She thought, "If the right man never comes along, oh well. It's just not worth this pain."

Just below the date, her friend wrote:

Dear Cynthia,
I have watched you change, struggle and fight. Always keep that spirit and God will do the rest.

1 Corinthians 6:12-13 / 18-20

Psalm 40:1-3
These passages have helped me, refer to them when life has become too much. Prayerfully they will strengthen you as they have me.
Love, Krissy

Cynthia being an hour early for her appointment figured reading the passages now could only help. She turned to the first one in 1 Corinthians:

"Everything is permissible for me, but not everything is beneficial. Everything is permissible for me, but I will not be mastered by anything. Food for the stomach, and the stomach for food, but God can destroy them both. The body is not meant for sexual immorality, but for the Lord, and the Lord for the body ."

She stopped and her body shrieked. Her legs trembled. "How true." She continued reading verse eighteen:

"Flee from sexual immorality. All other sins a man commits are outside his body, but he who sins sexually sins against his own body. Do you not know that your body is a temple of the Holy Spirit, who is in you, whom you have received from God? You are not your own. You were bought at a price.
Therefore honor God with your body."

The scriptures pierced her. Her lips quivered and decay seemed to creep into her bones. She knew these things from years ago. "How did I slip away?"

She read the next passage in Psalms:

"I waited patiently for the Lord; he turned and heard my cry. He lifted me out of the slimy pit, out of the mud and mire; he set my feet on a rock, and gave me a firm place to stand. He put a new song in my mouth, a hymn of praise to our God. Many will see and fear and put their trust in God."

She bowed her head in silent prayer, then heard her name called out. She stood and followed the nurse to the room. She sat and waited. The doctor entered, "Hello Ms. Stewart. How are you today?"

"Fine. A little nervous."

"Okay, well . . . There's good news and bad news. Which should I deliver first?"

"Uh, I guess the bad. In English please. I'm not real good at medical terms."

"Okay. I'd like to take some x-rays and have you undergo further testing. It seems you may have ovarian cysts, or perhaps Endometriosis. One of these could possibly be why your menstruation has been abnormal."

"That's it! Cyst? No diseases?"

"Well . . . no STDs anyway. Endometriosis, though treatable, is a disease."

Cynthia questioned, "But I'm not infertile. Doesn't that make you infertile?"

"Not always. It affects many different women so many different ways. A lot of times it develops during childbearing years making a woman infertile."

Cynthia teared up. "Oh doctor, you just don't know how relieved I am."

"Well, although I'm glad it's not what you thought, let's not become too relaxed. If you are suffering from either, there are some high risk concerns. If you do have cysts, for instance, we hope they are not malignant."

"Malignant?"

"In simple terms, cancerous."

"I could have Cancer?"

"Perhaps. But in most cases, even with the cyst, they are benign, or non- cancerous. Now that we may have detected the problem, I really do think you'll be fine, Cynthia. Let me give you some literature, and of course, you can find plenty of information on the Internet. In the mean time, we'll get you scheduled for your testing and x-rays, then go from there on any procedures we'll need to take. I'll prescribe something that should ease those cramps, should they come back."

Cynthia hugged the doctor. "Thank you so much, Dr. Beverly."

"You're very welcome. In the future, if you feel your doctor isn't paying attention, seek another one, okay? This could have become much more serious."

"Okay. Thank you again."

Chapter Thirty Two

By August, Cynthia's tears over DL were subsiding, although every now and then, if she thought hard enough about him, she would still cry. She knew she had to heal mentally and, more so now, physically. It turned out she did have cysts but they were not cancerous. With minimal treatment and medication, along with a healthy lifestyle, the doctor explained that they would disappear practically on their own. Dr. Beverly explained that she'd rather try the natural way first before resorting to any surgical procedure. Cynthia agreed and knew if she was not careful she would be causing more damage to her body.

That experience was a wake up call for her. She didn't take what God was revealing to her lightly. She needed to respect and cherish her body. Even though she hadn't suffered from something worse, she couldn't forget the torment when she thought she had, and never wanted to end up there again.

She allowed herself all the time she needed to grow in her happiness. Keeping her father's advice in her heart, she was determined not to rush into another relationship. She lived her life taking care of her children, working, dating new men. Usually around the second or third date was when the wall went up around her heart like a window of bulletproof glass on an armored truck. The dates were like a series of situation comedy episodes. She thought, "I know if I write this stuff down, I could pitch it to a network for a hit show. This is comedy."

There was one guy she met on a visit to Los Angeles. He played basketball for a semi-pro league. He was six foot four and handsome, and told her he was only twenty seven. Too young land was just not a place she was willing to visit. Plus, if she had been willing to look beyond the nearly ten year age difference, he walked kind of like a duck, and that was just something she couldn't get past. A friend told her all basketball players walked like that. While she was out with him, she'd spent the whole night hoping no one she knew ran into them and saw him waddling.

Another date worked for CNN. They exchanged phone numbers and talked for a few months on and off. He asked her out and she drove up to Vegas to meet him. They were getting along great. He was forty years old, six foot six, great shape, dark skin, and appeared distinguished. Their conversation seemed to flow.

They ate dinner at Chili's restaurant and when the bill came he asked, "So are we going dutch?"

Cynthia just looked up at him, shocked. "Uh, you asked me out and I just drove all the way up here."

He said, "Well, I'm just asking."

Trying to remain cool, Cynthia pointed out her meal on the check.

"Look, my dinner was $7.99."

He responded, "You got a drink too, and you didn't even finish your food."

That was so over the top she thought maybe he was kidding. "How about I pay for the movie?"

He responded, "That's cool."

He paid the twenty five dollar bill, leaving a one dollar tip on the table. She thought, “Now I gotta suffer through a movie with this dude.” She staggered behind and dropped a five dollar bill on the table as they left. They arrived at the theater and she paid twenty eight dollars for the two of them bringing the total to about the same cost as dinner.

She looked up at him and said, “Are we even now?”

He chuckled, “Yea, we are.”

Cynthia thought it was a good movie so her bother subsided a little. As they left the theater walking back to the car, he moved in close to her side, putting his arm around her lower back, then tried to grab her booty.

“Uh, don’t think so babe.” She moved his hand away.

Totally clueless, he tried to call her for weeks afterwards. He left three messages asking when she’d like to go out again. Cynthia just listened and deleted them. “He has got to be kidding.”

One Tuesday morning as she got ready for work, she thought, “I should ask the water guy out. We’ve been grinning at each other for months . . .What was his name?”

She opened her medicine cabinet and pulled out the Chanel cologne DL had given her for Christmas. She hadn’t worn it since. She spritzed a little here and a little there. She breathed in the fragrance. “Oh . . . I shouldn’t have done that, now I’ll be thinking about him all day again.”

While she was working, one of her employees, Lilly, an older woman in her sixties but still very vibrant, approached her desk smiling. “The water truck is outside.”

Cynthia's face brightened. "It is?"

"I think you should talk to him. You only live once." Lilly leaned in closer. "Mmm . . .What's that fragrance you're wearing? It smells beautiful."

"Thank you. It was a gift. It's Chanel."

"Wow, that's pricey stuff. Someone must really love you. My husband won't even spend that kind of money on me."

"Huh. I don't know about that. But thanks."

They went over and peeked out of the window, but it wasn't Cedric getting out.

Lilly stepped back. "Who the hell is that?"

Out stepped a nerdy-looking man with skin like paste, no muscles, red hair and freckles. Cynthia went back to her desk. He passed by her pushing the water jugs on a dolly, obviously because he couldn't carry them.

She asked, "Where's the guy who normally brings our water?" He stopped and adjusted the bottles, his speech was stuttered: "Oh, C-C-Cedric. He quit. He h-h-had to m-move back to V-V-V-Virginia all of the s-s-s-udden. Some f-f-family si-si-situation." He looked over at Cynthia, his acne desperately needing medication. He stuck his hand out for a shake and grinned. Spit sprayed from his mouth as he continued, "I'm P-P-P-Peter. You're st-st-stuck with me f-f-for a while."

Cynthia shook his hand; it was clammy. She mustered up a phony smile, "Oh great. Nice to meet you." Wiping her hand on the side of her slacks, she watched as he exited the office and scrunched up her face. She thought, "Is that the same uniform?"

Cynthia went home on her lunch break and retrieved the Chanel from her cabinet, then went back to work. She stopped at Lilly's desk, "Are you busy?"

"No, what'd you need?"

"I brought something for you." She handed her the Chanel still in the original box. "I've only used it two times, today and when he first gave it to me. It's still pretty new. You can have it."

Lilly's mouth fell open as she reached for it. "No! I can't accept this." She took it. "You know . . . The work policy about gifts? You, or we, could get in trouble."

"Shsh . . . I'm the boss, remember? Please take it. I insist. I'll never wear it. The guy who gave it to me . . .Well . . . Never mind . . . Please, just take it, okay?"

"Thank you, Cynthia."

"No, thank you."

Another guy lived in town near her. He worked for Coke for ten years and a mutual friend had set them up. His skin was as smooth as coffee. He wasn't very tall, but had somewhat of a muscular build. Everyone called him Ski for a nickname—although he could not. (Ski, that is.) He said his grandmother had given him that name as a child because he was born bald and it just stuck. The name and the baldness. They went out to watch a band play, then to dinner and Cynthia actually had a nice time. They went out a second time and she cooked him dinner. A few weeks later she ran into Chanice in the store, the friend who introduced them.

"Hey, Chanice. How are you?"

Chanice was trying to restrain her two year old little boy. "Whew! Tired. How's the bank?"

"Same o, same o."

"So . . . I never got to talk to you—TYLER! STOP! NO! . . . How did that date with Ski go?"

"It was okay, but there was no magic. I called him a couple of times, but he never called back so I figured he wasn't interested. Plus, I don't know what I'm doing right now anyway, so I didn't really give it much energy."

"Well, you wanna know what I heard?—TYLERRRRR! Dammit! Anyway, do you?"

"See? I gotta get out of this little town. We only went out twice. What could you have heard?"

"He thought you were a prude."

Cynthia laughed. "Ha! Really?" We went out two times, was I supposed to jump his bones?"

She chuckled under her breath remembering DL expressing that same thought. "Oh well."

"Girl. forget him. You're too good for him anyway. I heard that he's a womanizer."

"Trust me, with everything I have going on, I'm not the least bit worried about what Ski thinks about me."

A little leery about online dating since meeting DL, she still climbed out on the limb and met G. Alfred Hammond on a site called Soul Planet. He was an author who had been successful in writing and had published several self-help books. Over the course of a month, they had talked three or four times and he was honest about the fact that he was married from the start. So Cynthia resolved that they could be friends, and maybe she would learn a thing or two about getting published. But his constant compliments of how beautiful he thought she was started to strike her as inappropriate for a wedded man. Finally, she went on to amazon.com and ordered his latest book, "Instructions for Us."

The book arrived the day before she took a field trip with her son's school to the Grand Canyon. During the two and a half hour bus ride, she read the book and was moved by G. Alfred's ideas and thoughts about the deterioration of the black family. But she was caught off guard by one of the chapters suggesting that the best way to save the black race from extinction was to convert it into a polygamist society, or to encourage "plural marriage."

"Ha ha!" Cynthia laughed aloud on the bus, then restrained herself and thought, "That's why he's so complimentary. He's looking for another wife. Boy Cynthia, you sure know how to pick em."

Chapter Thirty Three

Over the passing months, Cynthia and Cecilia kept in touch off and on. Occasionally, Cynthia would go up to Vegas for church or to shop. One weekend she was planning to go up, she called Cecilia so she could stop by and visit. Cecilia had a new boyfriend and they were engaged to be married.

She told Cynthia, "My finance's cousin saw your picture, he wants to meet you. When you come up, you can spend the night at my place."

"Thanks, that'll work. But I don't know about meeting anymore men. I'm going to church on Sunday morning, and I'm already supposed to be going out with this guy Marvin that lives up there on Saturday night. He's a lot older than me though."

Cecilia asked, "How old?"

"He's forty eight."

"Damn girl, that is a lot older than you. Is he good looking?"

"He's alright. He's been in the Navy for about twenty five years, he's in good shape. I've only met him once, in a dark club. So I was hoping we could meet in a public place. You should come with me."

Cecilia suggested, "Some friends of mine have a band. They're playing in a new lounge up on the north side this weekend. Maybe we can go check them out and he can meet us there?"

"Yea, that sounds good."

"Cool. What time will you be out here on Saturday?"

"About noon."

Marvin had called Cynthia almost every day since they met that night, but she kept the call backs to a minimum. He seemed a bit clingy. She got the impression that, he being so much older, was moving fast for a reason, and he seemed some what of a know-it-all when they talked. But she thought, "Maybe I'm being harsh." She called him on Friday to confirm their plans. He answered before the first ring was complete.

Cynthia's eyes rolled up. "Why am I doing this?" she thought. He answered and she said, "Hi Marvin. It's Cynthia."

"Hey lady. How are you?"

"Oh good. Thanks . . . About tomorrow. I wanted to give you directions to the lounge, or maybe just the address and you could use Map-qu—"

He cut her off mid sentence with an arrogant tone "OH NO! No, baby!" He chuckled. "I have a GPS system in my car. I got it. I'll be there."

"Okay, the address is 13254 North Saharan Boulevard."

"Alright, got it."

"Okay, well, I'm gonna get some sleep. I'll see you there around nine tomorrow."

"Sounds good. Can't wait."

Saturday afternoon Cynthia arrived at Cecilia's. They spent the day down on the Strip at the Hilton Hotel lounging by the pool and sipping Margaritas. They went out to lunch and got back to Cecilia's place about five o'clock.

Cynthia pulled out her cell and saw that Marvin had called five times. Since they had just talked the night before she thought that was odd. Or maybe it was just that she was bothered.

She and Cecilia relaxed a little in front of the TV. Although Cynthia wanted to ask her about DL, she didn't want to compromise what was becoming a seemingly good friendship with Cecilia. As they flipped channels laughing and joking, Cecilia said, "He's miserable, you know."

Cynthia responded, "Huh? Who?"

"DL."

Cynthia's heart knotted when she heard his name aloud and there was a lump in her throat. Still, she wasn't able to speak about him without becoming emotional. "Let's not talk about him . . . I can't talk about him."

"Alright. But I want you to know, he's miserable."

"I wish I could say that makes me feel better. But oddly it doesn't. The whole thing still confuses me. I really cared about him, and I'll never understand why he did that to me."

"He's just a dog, Cynthia. Most of em are. Look at me; I'm forty two and just now I feel like a met a decent man. But I still pray everyday that at some point I don't wake up and find that he's really a dog too."

Cynthia sighed. "Did he ever mention me, C? Did he ever say why he did that?"

"I heard him say he really cared about you. But him and his brother are like kids. They're just no good. Plus, Holly put him in a BMW as soon as they hooked up."

"What? I'm so dumb. I didn't even know he was like that."

"Yep, she's got money and he's spending it."

"Wow. Don't tell me anymore. That just hurts."

"I'm sorry. I didn't mean to hurt you."

Cynthia leaned back. "No, it's not your fault. I just have to be more careful. I know God is grooming a prince out there for me somewhere. Somewhere there's a good man that's been hurt and cheated on and we can love and appreciate each other. He'll be spiritual, hardworking, educated, and as fine as LL with the body too."

Cecilia got up. "Well, good luck with that one."

"Okay, I can compromise on the 'fine as LL' part, but just not butt ugly. Is that too much to ask?"

She headed toward the bathroom. "Just make sure you let me meet him when you do. Come on, let's get ready to go."

When they arrived at the lounge, Cynthia was sure Marvin would be waiting near the front door, since his eagerness was so apparent, but he wasn't. After about thirty minutes had passed, she looked at her cell and realized it was turned off. "Oops." She turned it on. Marvin had called several times. Lost. She had told Cecilia earlier how he'd tried to brag about his GPS system, and put the phone to her ear to listen to his messages saying he was lost. They laughed aloud.

Cecilia said, "We shouldn't laugh. You're becoming evil in your bitterness."

Cynthia called him back. "Hey Marvin, what's up? Sorry I didn't answer, I didn't realize my phone was off. Are you still lost?" She shrugged her shoulders and giggled at Cecilia.

He answered, "Yea. I guess that must be a new address you gave me. My GPS is not picking it up."

"Oh, okay. Let me put my friend on, she's more familiar with the area. She'll give you directions."

Cecilia took the phone. Moments later Marvin entered the lounge and Cynthia went over toward the door to greet him. It had been a little more than a month since they'd met, and at that time Cynthia was on her second or third drink. She thought, "Did he have that Richard Pryor mustache before? Maybe he just grew it?" She just looked past it and thought, "Don't be mean, he could be fun."

She said, "Hi Marvin, come on over we're sitting over here."

"Okay, it's nice to see you again." He leaned in for a kiss and she gave him her cheek.

They joined the others at the table and Cynthia began to check out his clothes. "Typical guy club clothes" she thought. He was wearing a black button-down dress shirt that was tucked in just so, and tan slacks. No special designer, but neat. She looked down and noticed his shoes, black and shiny round tips. "Are those his Navy uniform shoes?"

He asked, "Would you like a drink?"

"Yes, thank you."

He smiled proudly, "Seven and Seven right?"

"Yes, that's right. Thank you." Marvin brought their drinks back and they began to talk. She couldn't get pass the mustache and thought, "It's so thick. It's like a mini hamster is laying across his lip."

He talked . . . and talked . . . and talked. She was so bored she couldn't believe it. The band was in sync and started to play some nice tunes.

Trying to break the monotony, Cynthia asked, "Do you dance?"

"Yea, I do. Wanna dance?" He popped up and took her hand. They went out to the floor and he started to criticize the band.

Cynthia responded, "I think they're pretty good."

Then he started to criticize her dancing, "I need to teach you how to step."

She said, "You know what? I'm tired. I think I am gonna head out soon."

He paused, he didn't even notice his rudeness. "Oh, okay. Well, can I convince you to have just one more drink with me?"

His eagerness was hard to get away from and she was being way too polite.

"Alright, I guess I could have one more." She thought she heard one of Carla's lectures in her ear. "She would kill me right now," she thought.

They ordered and Cynthia sat and listened another hour while he talked . . . and talked . . . and talked. He had been chomping on bar pretzels and the crumbs were now dancing around in his mustache.

Cynthia interrupted softly wiping her top lip. "You have a few crumbs."

He wiped away at his face with a napkin completely missing every crumb. He moved his head forward and pulled his top lip down, asking, "Did I get it?" His breath was bad.

Cynthia had a blank stare and her eyes blinked twice, "Yea." She leaned over to Cecilia on her other side and whispered, "Please save me."

Cecilia stood up a few moments later. "You ready girlfriend? It's after midnight. I'm tired."

Cynthia popped up, announcing, "Yea, me too." She extended her hand to Marvin for a shake. "I'm glad we got to hang out. I'll give you a call."

He got up. "Oh, okay. Well, I guess I'll talk to you soon. Let me walk you to the door."

When they got near the exit, Marvin moved toward Cynthia for a kiss and she turned, hugging him sideways. "You have a good-night." She couldn't have left faster if there was a fire. When they got to the car, Cecilia exploded in laughter.

Cynthia sat there irritated. "Don't laugh at me, girl, don't laugh at me."

Cecilia couldn't help it and kept laughing.

“Girl! That guy had all the personality of a lobster, and what was up with that thick ass mustache? It stood out like a fat man on the beach in a Speedo.”

Chapter Thirty Four

The next morning Cynthia got ready for church and Cecilia was stirring around the kitchen cooking breakfast. Cynthia walked in dressed and was about to head out.

"Good morning. Mmm . . . Smells good."

Cecilia answered, "Thanks. You leaving for church soon?"

Cynthia sat down, opened a compact mirror, and applied her lipstick. "In a few. Why?"

"David told me his cousin will be up here in a minute. You know the one that wants to meet you? He wants to go to church with you."

Cynthia looked up and sighed. "I don't feel like meeting any more men. I just want to go to church where I should be. Just me and The Lord."

Just as she finished speaking there was a knock at the door. Cecilia looked over. "That's him. You want me to tell him you left?"

"No . . . Don't lie. He can come with me. What harm can happen just going to church?"

He walked in and Cecilia introduced him. "Jay, this is my friend Cynthia." Jay was a little rough around the edges. Cynthia thought, "Now, I know I like a guy to be a little street, but this is like, if we get pulled over by the police we may be going to jail street."

He was about six foot and his last shave and haircut had to be well over a month ago. His shirt was casual dress with some sort of cartoon character on the chest pocket, maybe Daffy or Donald Duck. His jeans were faded black and baggy with a brand name advertised down the side. He extended his hand, "Nice to meet you. You can call me Jay-nice."

Cynthia looked beyond his shoulder at Cecilia and gave an evil eye. "Do you mind if I just call you Jay?"

He smiled. "That's cool, baby. Call me whatever you like." He looked at her as if he could see right through her blouse. Cynthia's eyes shot down at her chest to make sure everything was buttoned up tight, and said a quick prayer in her mind, "Lord, I'm taking him to church. Please watch over me." Then she said, "Well, I guess we should shove off."

As they drove the twenty-minute route to the church, it seemed to take longer as Jay explained that he was a singer and brought along one of his demos for Cynthia to listen to.

"You mind if I play my song for you?"

"Uh . . . Sure, okay."

The song that played was called "SEX-N-U." Awkwardly, Cynthia listened, hoping he would sense her unease, as it was Sunday morning and they were on there way to worship God. It seemed he did.

Kindly, he apologized, "I'm not thinkin, baby. Maybe dis ain't a good time to listen to dis."

"It's okay. Thanks for noticing. You have a nice voice though."

They went to church and Jay thanked her for taking him along. He insisted on taking her to a movie in return.

Cynthia declined. “Oh, you don’t have to do that. I really should be heading back down to Arizona soon.”

“No, I insist. I ain’t been to church in a long time and I really do appreciate you takin me. Come on, anything you want to see?”

She gave in, too tired to argue. “I have wanted to see that new Jamie Fox movie.” He flipped out his cell. “Cool, let’s go check-it-ouuut. Let me see when it’s playin.”

About half way through the movie, Jay tapped Cynthia’s shoulder, leaned in and started to whisper in her ear, “Baby? You drink Patron?”

Cynthia thought she misunderstood, “Huh?”

He whispered a little louder, “Do you drink Patron?” He reached into his inside jacket pocket and pulled out a small metal flask and wiggled it. “Patron?”

She looked up into the air in disbelief for a moment then answered, “Uh, no. I can’t say that I do.”

Jay grabbed her soda, removed the lid, and held his hand against the top as to not lose the ice, then poured the soda onto the floor. He replaced Cynthia’s non-alcoholic beverage with Patron Tequila. Straight. She flipped out her cell to look at the time: 2 p.m.

“Who drinks tequila from a flask at two o’clock on a Sunday afternoon?” she thought.

Chapter Thirty Five

After a few months of useless dating, Cynthia began to grow weary of it all. Up late one night, she tossed and turned unable to sleep. At two in the morning she called Carla.

"Hello. What's up babe? You okay?"

"Yea. I just couldn't sleep. I need to talk."

"Alright. Let me go use the bathroom hold on a minute . . . Okay, I'm back. What's the matter?"

"I don't know, Carla. I'm just so tired. I've been up thinking about all these strange men I've met. I mean, I think I'm an okay woman. I know I'm not perfect, but what is it about me that I attract so many clowns? What am I missing?"

Carla replied, "I know what you mean. I feel the same way. I wish I could help you, but all I can say is maybe don't focus on it too much. You have a lot of talent. Try doing something you love. That's one of the reasons I bought my bike—it identifies me, without a man. I love it. Not that being with a man is wrong, but you spent a lot of years focusing on Darren. Now it's your turn. You say you like to write, so start writing more. Focus on you and the kids. The right guy will come along when you least expect it."

Cynthia replied, "That's kinda what my parents told me. I guess when I married Darren, I was so ready to be a wife and a mother for the rest of my life. I was so happy to not be out there dating. I like being with one man. I feel like life just snatched it all away."

"Are you starting to miss Darren?"

"No. I mean, I'm not mad anymore . . . I don't think I'm bitter. But I just wonder why things turned out the way they did. But I don't miss him. It's actually been very nice not to be with him. I come home and there's just peace . . . I don't mind being single, but I don't want to be alone forever."

Carla said, "You won't. You'll meet the right person, Cynthia. Be patient."

"I know. I guess I've been getting worried too because these bills are getting out of hand. Darren and I had a bunch of debt already and when we got divorced, he was given responsibility for half, but he hasn't paid any. I already paid off two loans by myself and . . ."

Carla said, "Is he giving you any money?"

"Girl, no. Anyway, I guess after I moved out he was seeing a doctor but had no insurance. I got a subpoena last week. I'm being sued for almost ten thousand dollars for his medical bills, all dated after I left him . . ."

"What? Why?"

Cynthia explained, "Even though I didn't live with him, I hadn't filed the divorce yet, so legally they can come after me. I told him about it and he just said he'd call them. But he never did. Now they're going to garnish me six hundred dollars a month. I can't afford that."

"Sue him. Shit."

"I am. But without a lawyer, that's a process in and of itself. Plus, emotionally, I'm so drained. I'm avoiding collection calls constantly. Oh, and you know how I applied for that job at Bank of America?"

"Oh yea. I meant to ask you about that."

"Well, he let his Maxima get repossessed—my name was on it. The loan was through them. They were going to pay me fifteen thousand more a year than I'm making now. But when they did my credit check, and that was on there, it ruined it."

"Awe babe, I'm sorry. But you know what? You were good to Darren, and God knows that, just keep pushin. God's gonna bless you, I know it."

Cynthia was discouraged. "I'm trying to tell myself that every day. But sometimes it's hard to believe it when things are going so badly all at once. I've made so many poor choices, I don't think I ever want to fall in love again. I mean, what kind of man was Darren to just let me struggle paying bills that are his and not even care? I never did anything ill toward him. I think he's pissed off that I left him, and this is how he's repaying me."

Carla responded, "Well, even if that's true, he's not greater than God. Don't let him get to you. Just keep praying and fighting."

"I will."

"Has DL called you?"

"Girl, no. I guess to him I never even existed."

"Babe, I'm sorry. I shouldn't have brought him up."

"Naw, it's cool. It's not like I'm not thinking about him anyway. But I've made peace with it. I had to face it; he's a player and I got played like a deck of cards at a Vegas poker table. I guess I've wished he would at least call me and say he's sorry, but I'm not holding my breath."

"Well, you wanna pray before we get off the phone?"

"Yea, I think so. You go first."

"Alright . . ."

Taking Carla's input, Cynthia began to focus more intensely on her talent. She decided to register for some online writing courses hoping she could sharpen her technique and maybe publish a short story or two. She wrote every day, at least three hours. Sometimes, when the kids were at Darren's, that was all she did, barely stopping to eat. She started to write self-help, mostly about overcoming abuse. Her first article was titled "I Became My Own Obstacle." She also signed up to volunteer at a local women's shelter to try and give to others instead of being consumed by her own problems.

A couple of times she had dropped DL an email, once to say he was still in her prayers, then another towards the end of the year telling him about her poetry. She had posted a few of her poems on her My Space page. She'd received so many encouraging notes about them, she wrote him saying, "I thought you may want to read them since you inspired a lot of it." He never replied, and finally she let go.

"Caressing the Wind"

A wounded song sparrow taking flight,
lifting from an early morning breeze

A butterfly but unable to fly,
struggling to float free

I lift myself and flutter through,
the forest and all the trees

Yearning for something meaningful,
in the skies beyond the sea

Touched by an angel now and then,
his kiss mending my wings

Only to fade away like a breath,
in a sub zero winter freeze

A spirit
a silhouette
my soul longs for a true friend

The clouds protecting my solitude,
I can't be hurt again

A hollow call inside I sing,
my whisper carries the morning air

The rain washing my feathers,
my heart in fate's hands

Healing in the warmth of the sun,
searching a safe place to land

Alone and afraid, I drift on,
my wings caressing the wind.

Chapter Thirty Six

The new year started in two days, and Cynthia couldn't believe how fast it had come back around. She called Mona and asked, "What are we doing for New Year's Eve?"

Mona answered with sarcasm, "Naw! You wanna hang out with us? I thought you had three guys to choose from?"

Cynthia answered, "Girl, I changed my mind. All the bozos I keep going out with, I figured I'd have a much better time with my sisters."

"Well, Vegas as usual. Denise and Sandra will be up here around three or four, so I guess we'll head up about seven."

"Cool. I'm in."

"I'm glad. It wouldn't have been the same without you."

"Thanks, Mona."

They had a wonderful time in Vegas and when they got home it was after three in the morning. Cynthia collapsed in her bed. Her body was exhausted but her mind blew around in circles like a feather caught in a breeze.

She prayed. She was still unable to stop feeling the man she shared her new year with a year ago. She cried a little. "God, I'm so tired of my heart straying on the wrong course." She got up from bed and got down on the floor on her knees, in the dark, alone, and she talked to God. She poured out her soul and prayed specifically about forgiveness, change, her finances, her dreams, her goals, her sorrow, her children, her loved ones, and her ex-husband. And still, she prayed for DL.

"God, please help me to relinquish this bitterness, this pain, and anger. I wish him the best but, Lord, please, please remove him from my system. Help me to wait and choose men with more wisdom. I can't go through this anymore. I don't think I'll make it ..."

About midway through the new year, after several attempts of submitting writing excerpts, she was finally able to find an agent. A few weeks later, after checking her email daily, she received what she was waiting for. She grabbed the phone. "Carla, girl, guess what? I'm so excited!"

"What?"

"I got an offer from a publisher today, to put one of my articles in a nationwide magazine."

"Oh wow, girl. Congrats."

"It's just a small slot. But it's a start."

"Well, I'm happy for you. Don't forget about me when you blow up."

"You know you're my girl. Thanks so much for encouraging me to write again."

Cynthia was overjoyed. After being published and paid for her work, more than once, she began to receive offers for public speaking engagements at women's shelters, group homes, and a few seminars, helping families to overcome abuse. The more offers she accepted, the more offers came in. The more she spoke, and the more people she helped, the happier she felt. Something about it all was healing. Within two years, she was earning enough money from writing and speaking that she was able to pay off her debt, leave her job at the bank, and go back to school for her degree in therapy.

The years rolled on, and her children grew older. Lil Darren was in his third year of college and Summer was about to go. Cynthia had finally made plans to leave Kingstown. She and Darren talked briefly at Summer's graduation, after years of near silence.

He approached her. "Hey Cynthia. You look nice."

"Thank you."

"I never really got to tell you congrats on your success."

"No problem. Thanks." She headed towards her car. "Well, I'll see you."

"Where's Summer? Isn't she riding with you?"

Cynthia said "No. She's riding with her friends to the restaurant, aren't you going to the dinner?"

"Oh yea, that's right. No, I can't. I've got to get back to work."

"Oh. Okay, well, I'll see you."

"Cynthia, wait. The kids tell me you're moving."

"Yep. Back to Cali. My work here is done."

He asked, "I get off about seven. Can we talk later?"

Cynthia was hesitant.

He saw the look on her face. “Just a short talk, that’s it.”

Cynthia pointed over to a bench near a tree. “Well, if it’s short we could go sit over there. It’s away from people.”

They walked over, and he began to apologize, “Listen, Cynthia, I just want to say that I’m sorry for who I was.”

Cynthia wanted to cry but had become very good over the years at stopping herself and she didn’t. She spoke clearly, “You know it really hurt when you said that the violence in our marriage was mutual.”

“I know it wasn’t, Cynthia. I was so ignorant.”

She continued, “I just feel that you’ve never understood the magnitude of your abuse, the way you treated me, and for destroying our family. And even though I forgave you a long time ago, and things have worked out, that’s always remained like a bruise on my heart.”

He replied, “There’s no words that could justify why I was who I was then. I am so sorry. But please don’t think I haven’t felt the consequences. My life has felt like I have lived it in a grave every day. I would give my soul to change, or take back the things I did then. I’ve always been sorry. I knew that you forgave me, but I have never forgiven myself.” He leaned over and kissed her forehead. “I wish you all the best.”

“Thank you.”

Forty six years old now, Cynthia moved back to Pasadena, California, where she had grown up. Over the last six years, she had written three self-help books, one of which was a best seller. God had blessed her, and she was enjoying a successful life doing what she had always dreamed of.

She bought a quaint, restored old home that was located in the plush green hills overlooking the Rose Bowl. It had a small two bedroom back house on the property which she moved her parents into. Now well into their seventies, she wanted to keep them close by. Her sister Mona had married and moved back east to be near her husband's family.

As Cynthia unpacked, she found a big storage box of photos and started to go through them reminiscing about the kids. They had grown up so fast. Then she came across an old picture of she and DL. They were cheek to cheek, with smiles as big and as bright as the sun. She ran her finger slowly over his face as if still feeling his spirit. It was taken the night they were at the MGM watching Roger. "Mona almost got into a fight . . . ." A smile came over her and she laughed aloud. The memories of the year they shared, nearly over a decade ago, came back to her like it was only yesterday.

She thought about DL, and wondered if she ever crossed his mind. Had she impacted his life at all, the way he had hers? Or was she just a nameless, faceless thought from his past? She remembered the time they shared in love and wondered if someday she might ever feel that way for another man. And if she would ever even be able to open herself up to love again. Knowing the risks, she remained unsure.

Cynthia went over near the window of her bedroom and peered out for a few moments. It was fall, and the large oak tree in the yard was losing its colorful leaves as a mild wind breezed through it. Partly cloudy, a storm was on the horizon and the rumbles of thunder broke through the silence. Her mind began to unfold memories, one by one. She pondered her years in Kingstown, her marriage, family, and children. Her mind drifted back to the time she'd spent with DL, and she realized she could finally remember him without feeling sadness.

She grasped the handles at the bottom of the old window and pulled it up. Feeling the fresh air gently blow through the screen was like a whisper from a muse. She grabbed a note pad, pen, and a picnic blanket that was laying folded in the corner, then stepped outside and made herself comfortable under the tree. She clipped the picture she'd found of she and DL to the top of the paper, and there she began to write of the of the only love story she had ever known

"Early evening in Las Vegas, Nevada, and it was still hot . . ."

As she wrote she heard footsteps cracking the leaves along the walkway, then a knock on her front door. "Maybe that's Mom." She went through the backyard and back inside to answer the front door. There was a casually dressed man standing there holding two new packaged phone books. His skin was the color of beach sand, smooth and clean, and his head was bald. His eyes were light brown, almost like gold, and his pectoral muscles screamed through his snug sleeveless t-shirt.

Cynthia stood bewildered. "Hello." She sized him up, thinking, "Bout five eleven, maybe late forties, still works out."

His voice was deep and strong. His speech was very enunciated, like a radio personality, although he used a lot of Uh's and Um's: "Uh, hi. I'm your neighbor. I live across the street. Um, I saw the moving truck and thought I would come over and welcome you to the neighborhood." Handing her the phone books, he said, "Uh, these were extra. I thought maybe you could use them."

Cynthia took them and smiled. "Thank you."

He held his hand out for a shake. "I'm Warren. Um, Steven Warren. And you are?"

"Hello, Mr. Warren. I'm Cynthia. Cynthia Stewart." She put the books down on a small table near the door, shook his hand and asked, "Do you always greet your new neighbors while they're still moving in?"

He grinned in embarrassment scratching the side of his head. "Uh, no . . . I have to confess, usually I don't greet them at all. But I kind of saw you in the yard this morning and, um, well, thought I would introduce myself . . . And please, call me Steve."

She smiled sweetly. "Oh, okay. Steve. Well, it's nice to meet you, and thank you very much."

"You're very welcome . . .Uh. Well, is your husband here? I'd love to meet him too."

Cynthia answered, knowing his intention, "Uh, he'll be here in a couple of hours."

Steve's face fell. "Oh, okay. I guess I'll see you later." He turned to leave.

Cynthia giggled. "No wait . . . I'm kidding. I'm not married. I guess I just wanted to see you sweat a little."

He chuckled. "You have a sense of humor, that's good . . ." He pointed in the direction of his home. "Uh . . . I live in that house there, thirty-thirteen. Uh . . . Just me, um . . . Alone."

"Alone?"

"Uh . . . Just in case you were wondering." He smiled and started to back up tripping over a small stone in the walkway. "I guess I'll see you later then. Please, uh, if you need anything, let me know."

She motioned to close the door with a devilish grin. "Okay, Steven Warren. Thank you, I will."

Just then, Cynthia's mom was entering through the side kitchen door dusting her feet on a mat. She could see through the room to the front door.

"Who was that, Cyn?"

Cynthia went into the kitchen and started a pot of coffee. "One of our neighbors. He just came over to introduce himself."

Her mom stared out of the window watching him walk back over toward his house. "Hmmm, nice looking man. He just came right up and knocked on the door, huh?"

"Yep."

Printed in the United States
210515BV00001B/28-78/P

9 780981 919522